# Ragna the Dragonslayer

## A Time of Dragons I

by

## Cynthia Vespia

RAYNA THE DRAGONSLAYER

A Time of Dragons Volume I

Copyright © 2022 Cynthia Vespia

All rights reserved.

ISBN: 978-1-7376927-2-0



Cover Image: ID 199326309 © Refluo | Dreamstime.com
Back Cover Image: ElixorDesigns on Etsy
Map Design by: AEKCreates on Etsy
Additional Cover Edits: Original Cyn Content

*She was a warrior forged from flame,
a slayer of mighty dragons.*

**R**ayna thought she'd slain the last of the dragons on Atharia. Now, a wealthy client has tasked her with royal commands to seek and destroy another dragon...the very same beast which burned Rayna's home years before. But as she gets closer to the kill, Rayna learns the truth about her target that will change her entire life's purpose.

***Rayna the Dragonslayer*** is the first in an exciting dragon fantasy adventure series *A Time of Dragons*. It's a symphony of sword and sorcery, high fantasy, and a heroic quest that is like *The Mandalorian* merging with *Game of Thrones*. Fans of *Mistborn* or *The First Law Trilogy* will fall in love with *Rayna the Dragonslayer*.

# CHAPTERS

# A Time of Dragons Series

Rise of the Dragonslayer (*prequel*)
Rayna the Dragonslayer - book 1
Rayna the Dragon Warrior - book 2 (*coming soon!*)
Rayna the Dragon Defender - book 3 (*coming soon!*)

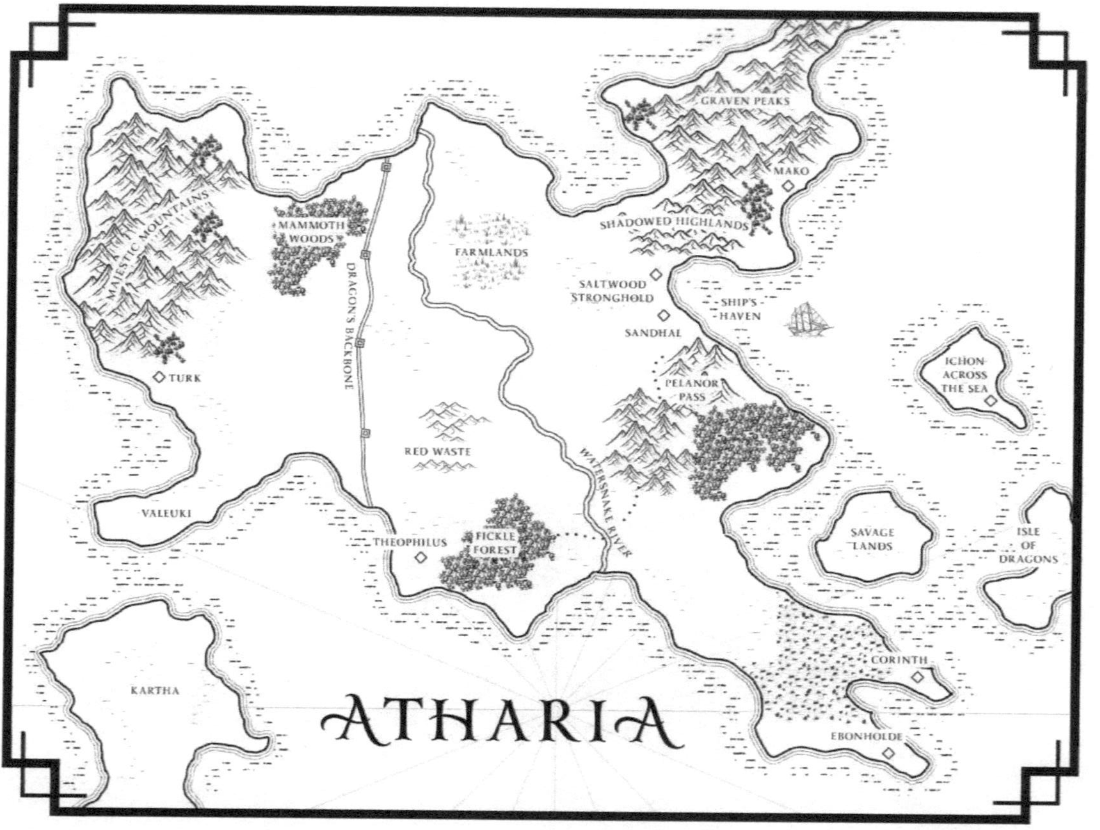
ATHARIA
DRAGONSLAYER
RAYNA
MAJESTIC MOUNTAINS
GRAVEN PEAKS
MAMMOTH WOODS
MAKO
SHADOWED HIGHLANDS
FARMLANDS
SALTWOOD STRONGHOLD
SHIP'S HAVEN
DRAGON'S BACKBONE
SANDHAL
TURK
PELANOR PASS
ICHON ACROSS THE SEA
RED WASTE
WATERSNAKE RIVER
VALEUKI
THEOPHILUS
FICKLE FOREST
SAVAGE LANDS
ISLE OF DRAGONS
KARTHA
CORINTH
EBONHOLDE

# Prologue

Endless night held the mountain peaks in its grip, causing shadows to fall over every inch of land. The dark sky proved more relentless up north than further south towards the ocean shores.

There, the warmth of the sun caressed the sands, and those that walked them. The north knew only the bitter cold. Perhaps that's how the Graven Peaks earned their name. Bleak lands touched only by shadow and death often earned names to match.

Whatever the reason, the soldiers cared not. Concern only lay with the thick of the night and frigid winds, making an already treacherous climb far more challenging.

Inching along the ravine in single formation, one man lost his footing in the dark. He stumbled from the ledge and fell down into a pit of darkness, taking his scream with him. The depth of the pit was so great the rest of the soldiers could not hear his body hit below.

Fearing their own tumble into the great void, they pressed their backs against the wall of the mountain. With shuffle-step, they moved in unison at a much slower pace.

Around the next curve of the mountain they found surer footing. The remaining five men dropped to their knees and kissed the solid ground, happy to have lived through the climb. But the true danger of their mission still lay ahead.

The leader, a stout man with a twisted mustache that reached his belly, motioned them to their feet. Swords in hand, they silently marched again through the thick snow. The deeper they moved towards the mouth of the mountain, the darker it became. Not even the moonlight shone down to guide their path.

These warriors were part of the king's elite army. They held enough skill to mark their own path without a compass or map. Still, a bit of torchlight would help the eyes adjust to the heavy night. But they didn't dare spark up torches knowing what lay ahead.

The firelight came anyway, though not by their hands. As the party moved deeper into the mouth of the cave, they saw only a spark at first. Then, as the great jaws grew wider, the fire flooded over them in a torrent.

Each man was ablaze in seconds. Armor melted to skin and hair burned from body. The elite soldiers tumbled from the mouth of the cave one after the other. Their screams echoed on the night sky and throughout the chasm below until the last of them fell dead.

With its sleep interrupted, the great beast crawled out from the cave. Arching upwards, it took to the sky on large, leathery wings. Routing a circular pattern around the area, it sought any other fools encroaching on its territory. The darkness didn't hamper its sight. It welcomed the night as a prime feeding hour.

Satisfied that no others mounted an attack, it returned to the fallen soldiers. One-by-one it plucked the charred remains of the men from the ground and swallowed them whole. Belly full and content, the creature returned to its slumber.

With a swipe of its massive tail, the soldiers' weapons were shattered and swatted away into the snow. Not a trace of the men remained. No one would ever know a party of elite soldiers came this way, daring to face a dragon.

# I
# Seeking the Slayer

A sudden, fierce wind raked coarse sand across Captain Falkon's cheek as he made his way through the Red Waste. He traveled with an escort of ten warriors far into the sprawling desert where it had been said no man had ever returned. Here they saw the remnants of a once great city now sand ridden and half-buried.

Cracked spires and fallen towers lay in ruin as they sat exposed to the unyielding desert air. These remnants of history, now corroded by time, marked the men's passage through the Red Waste.

They galloped at length with the wind-gathered sand seeming to chase them. Sometimes it met the bellies of their horses in a swarm of a sandstorm. Still, they pressed on even as the dry sand clung to their sweat covered faces.

The collection of swordsmen at Captain Falkon's flank groaned as the storm increased. Each one shielded their eyes and pulled up their mouth guards so as not to taste the bitter red sand.

They were sea-faring men used to the gentle caress of an ocean breeze. Out on the open water, exploration abounded in every direction no matter which way the ship steered. Here the sand stretched on for miles with the ruined city laying like a marked grave along the way.

Captain Falkon longed to have the shifting planks of a ship's deck beneath his feet as it routed through the pounding of high seas with full sails billowing above. Duty called him back to Atharia, and recent orders brought him to the red death they traveled through now.

Above him, the sky stood silent. No birds took flight overhead, not even the great bird-of-prey from which he gained his name. Nothing dared breech the sky now that dragons had returned to the land.

An aching spread over Falkon's skin as the shimmering sun kept pace with their journey. He longed to strip from his armor and slick his thirst with a mug of cold, dark beer.

The desert stretched on for ages in each direction. Tales of lost men going mad in the great Red Waste haunted Falkon. If not for his dedication to the study of maps, they could've taken a wrong turn and wound up in the desolation of Corinth at the edge of the world.

The men's morale grew low, but Falkon insisted they press on. Stopping under a strong desert sun threatened a deep slumber they would not soon wake from. How many bones of men were buried deep beneath the sand, lost to the sunken city? Falkon did not want to learn the answer to that question.

None of the men at his back would refute the manner of his orders except for one. Valerios, his right hand and special counsel, often held Falkon's ear. Breaking formation at the back, he galloped up alongside his captain. Matching pace with Falkon's steed, Valerios updated him with a health report.

"The men are waning under this accursed sun."

"As am I," Falkon replied, running a cloth across his dampened brow.

"Any further and I fear dehydration will set in."

Valerios was a scholarly man. He spent as much time studying alchemy and herbs as he did honing his mastery of weapons. Falkon took his advisement under consideration but dismissed it.

"They're men, not boys, and I've built them to survive worse than this."

"I suppose if you can last in this Red Waste, then we have nothing to worry about," Valerios replied with a smile.

The two of them had a good laugh at Falkon's expense. He allowed a certain amount of levity with Valerios.

They had been friends since they were boys getting muddy out by the ports and dreaming of adventures. Having a laugh with Valerios now and then kept Falkon from growing weary under the weight of duty.

"Still, I wonder if a brief rest might rally their spirits."

Falkon examined Valerios' face to deem his intent. Beads of sweat filled his dark beard and his usual tan features pinked up under the scorching sun.

It wasn't the soldiers who waned under the heat; Valerios wasn't faring well himself. Still, Falkon reminded him of the severity of their mission no longer as his friend, but as his Captain.

"King Favian himself tasked me with this undertaking. It holds such importance that time is of the essence. There shall be no rest until we reach the town of Theopilous. Now fall back in line. I shouldn't hear about the damned heat again." He waved Valerios back. "Tell the men to drink their own piss if they're that thirsty."

Valerios gave a slight nod of his head and then rejoined the rest of the pack. It didn't matter that King Favian was his father; he was the ruler of Sandhal and soon all of Atharia. That meant Falkon would carry out his orders without question. It was an honor to be leading the charge on such an important issue.

If Falkon were to ask anything of his father, it would be why they needed to trek so far from Sandhal to find one lone woman. Give him the ten good men at his back and they would make quick work of any threat to the kingdom. What could a woman warrior do that he, as captain of the guards, could not?

Perhaps Falkon would see how this woman fared behind closed doors. After he sated his hunger and thirst, she could satisfy his other cravings. Although, sell swords of the female persuasion were usually too homely to bother with. Maybe he could throw a rucksack over her head and enjoy her that way.

Thoughts of gratification gave Falkon new vigor. He pressed his horse into a hard gallop, forcing the men behind him to do the same. The burst of speed brought a stream of hot air over him like a slap to the face. Falkon grimaced but continued on.

At his back, he heard a rumble. The horses jeered, and the men sounded out in surprise. Falkon slowed his horse and angled it around to see the disturbance.

One soldier had fallen from his horse; a victim of the blazing sun. The others surrounded him, trying to encourage his rise.

"Leave him," Falkon called. "But take his horse."

The soldiers seemed surprised, but did as they were told. Falkon returned to his gallop, content with his decision. If a man couldn't ride, they didn't need him. No sense wasting time trying to get him to remount and nursing him back to health. Soon, the soldier's pleas for mercy were nothing but a distant memory.

Powering on made all the difference. Only a short time later, Falkon saw refuge in the distance. The harsh sands gave way to scrub grasslands and a direct path into Theopilous.

They never actually left the Red Waste, but rather the city seemed to spring up around them. Falkon trotted his horse onto the leveled stone streets with great relief. When he at last turned to look back, only a hazy view of structures told the story of a once great civilization now swallowed beneath the sinking sands.

The city of Theoplious had been built on the remnants of that old world. As Falkon and his men rode deeper inside the city, they found large columns of obsidian structuring the walls. It encircled the perimeter, casting down dark shadows which brought relief from the intense heat. Falkon would've thought the city itself a mirage if not for the unmistakable smells of spiced meats on the air.

Theopilous was well known for their trade markets. Merchants from all corners braved the journey to barter their wares. The town also housed all manner of thieves and murderers, some still with a bounty on their heads.

Regardless of its reputation, Theopilous remained a welcome sight after such an arduous journey. Falkon looked back over his shoulder and called out to his soldiers.

"Look men, we've reached our destination!"

They cheered his words and raised their swords high. A long journey to be sure, but the satisfaction from seeing it through made Falkon smile. Now all he had to do was to find this woman and bring her back with him. If she wouldn't go willingly, they would take her. There would be no discussion about it.

King Favian demanded an audience with the so-called dragonslayer and the king's orders would be carried out no matter what.

As the lot of them rode into town, the villagers let them pass. Those bustling around outdoors at their shops scattered from the streets as the king's guard came through. Some watched in awe as the royal colors of green and gold plumed out from the banners. Others spat on the ground as they rode by.

His father was not well liked in many parts of the land. The more Falkon traveled among the people, the more he learned of the sense of betrayal they felt after his father took the throne. King Favian laughed off their complaints, but Falkon felt all of them like a tick under his skin. When he became ruler, he would be revered by all or he would have their heads.

Theopilous was a melting pot of clans and characters. As the only thriving town before the long ride through the desert sands, it was a popular resting place for weary travelers. A man could get good food, drink, and entertainment all in one night.

Some enjoyed the spoils of the town so much they never continued their journey and wound up settling there. Still, for as prosperous as Theopilous was, Falkon couldn't wait to return to his own feather bed safe inside Saltwood Stronghold.

He instructed Valerios to take a few of the men to feed and water the horses. The remaining lot would be at Falkon's back while he talked to this dragonslayer.

They headed to the tavern first. Any respectable tavern owner would have good information, along with excellent beer. Inside the place bustled with activity. Lively music came from a two-man band in the back. One sang while the other strummed a lute. Dancing girls moved in rhythm to the tune, letting their long hair and the skirt of their dresses toss about. The smell of fresh baked bread wafted on the air, making Falkon's stomach call out.

As soon as they entered the tavern, his men's spirits had been raised. He rewarded them for the long journey and sate his hunger as well. They set up at a table near the back so Falkon could keep his eyes on the entire room. A round of beer and sweet breads were brought over shortly after. He enjoyed a few sips of the beer before seeking information.

The owner tossed out orders to his tavern wenches as they hurried out with platters of food. Falkon wedged himself between a crowd of men drinking at the bar top and called out to the owner. The man had a gruff face with a shaven head, but when he spoke, his voice sounded melodic.

"How can I oblige a kingsguard today? More beer?"

"They call me Falkon, and I'm captain of the Saltwood Soldiers, my good man," Falkon corrected him as he handed over his mug for a top off. After a quick sip, he got back to business.

"I'm seeking a woman."

The tavern owner laughed. "Brothel is next door. They have a full menu of choices."

"This one is a warrior," Falkon replied. "Hair like golden wheat. Built like an ox. Carries a large broadsword...so I'm told."

One man seated at the bar interjected himself into the conversation. The smell of cheap mead wafted off his breath, forcing Falkon to turn his face away.

"Aye, you seek the dragonslayer?"

"I don't know you, friend," Falkon told him.

"No, but I know of her."

With a stomach that jiggled as he moved, the man hopped upon the bar. Booze on his breath, he spun a tale like a traveling bard seeking a coin for his cap.

"Legend has it she's half-dragon. Breathes fire and everything!"

Hearing the start of a story, another man jumped in, stealing the attention away from his drunk comrade.

"I heard she was born of a dragon."

And then another got in on the fun.

"Aye, her mother fucked a dragon is the way it goes."

The laughs carried back and forth. Each man tried to one-up the other in vulgar statements. A voice at the back of the room spoke up over the rest. It was an appealing mix of smooth wine and crushed glass.

"'Twas my father, not my mother. And he wasn't fucked by a dragon, he was cursed by one."

Falkon turned around towards the speaker and saw a beauty unmatched by any woman he'd ever come across. Golden hair was tied back in fierce braids that caressed her shoulders. Her arms were like a blacksmith, lean and strong, with smooth, muscular legs to match. She stacked them together, worn-out boots resting on the edge of the table.

There was a roughness about her, but it did not detract from her appearance. Her simple leather garments enhanced the curves of her femininity. Sun-kissed skin proved she spent her time traveling, though her coloring suggested she wandered farther than just the deep recesses of Atharia itself.

A pipe sat between her full lips. On each puff, she let a ringlet of thick smoke encircle her head. Falkon approached with caution as the others went back to their drinks and jovial conversation.

"So, you breathe fire after all," he said in jest.

The woman smiled, tamped out the pipe, and set it aside. Shifting her legs off the table, she kicked out a chair, offering him a seat.

Falkon eagerly accepted and then regretted his haste. Only now, as he came closer, did he see her face fully. The lone candle at the table illuminated her strong cheekbones and a small metal piercing weaved through her bottom lip.

She held youth and vigor but also an underlying hardness of battle, usually worn by soldiers alone. But it was her eyes that concerned him the most. The left was a calm shade of blue that a man could get lost in, while the right was obscured by a leather patch.

Falkon saw such coverings before when he trolled the seas. Pirates wore them to hide disfigurement. It made him wonder what else she could be hiding. He steadied himself, trying hard not to show his discomfort, though he already knew he failed.

"You're the dragonslayer then?"

She nodded. "Call me Rayna."

"I'm Falkon Fourspire, captain of the Saltwood Soldiers."

Whether Rayna heard of him or not she didn't react to his title. Her heavy stare made Falkon uncomfortable. He took a swig from his mug then pointed to his own eye so as not to move too familiarly towards her.

"Part of the curse?" he asked.

Rayna leaned back and put her feet back up. This time she rested them across Falkon's lap. He didn't know what to make of this woman. She was brazen, to be sure, but something about her was more intoxicating than the finest wine in the kingdom.

"Buy me a drink and I'll tell you my tale," she said. "Otherwise, I have no use for you."

With that, her feet moved from his lap and gave him a firm nudge to get up. As Falkon stood, he continued to stare down at Rayna. She took it as a threat and moved her hand to the hilt of a massive sword he hadn't noticed before.

It rested against the wall at her side, unsheathed. The blade alone looked to be thirty inches long and the heft of it would give a grown man trouble, let alone a young woman. But Rayna forged her body for war. Something told Falkon she could handle the sword with ease. He didn't want to test his theory, at least not tonight.

She noticed his eyes fall on the sword and pulled it into her lap. Sure enough, the weight of it gave her no trouble at all. She patted the blade as though it were a child and spoke its name with the same adoration.

"It's called Bhrytbyrn."

"You named your sword?"

"A gift from my father. He named it."

Falkon studied her as she ran a cloth over the blade. Now she seemed as enamored with her Bhrytbyrn as she would be a lover. This Rayna grew more curious as the night drew on.

"I'll see about that drink now," he told her.

Falkon pushed through the crowd and made his way back to the bar. The innkeeper, Talos, awaited him there with a pitcher of mead and a platter of assorted cheeses.

"What's this?"

"Trust me, friend. She's going to want a generous amount of ale, and the cheese is her favorite. Made with goat's milk, fresh churned this morning."

Intrigued, Falkon reached over and plucked a sampling of cheese from the platter. It melted over his tongue in a robust mix of flavors that delighted his refined palate.

"A woman who enjoys fine delicacies. What else can you tell me about her?"

"She's a warrior forged from flame," Talos told him. "Legend is she lived through the burning of her family home. Walked out with nary a scratch on her."

"What happened to her eye?"

"Curse of the dragon."

"Indeed."

Falkon gave a soft chuckle to himself and then paid his fare. Many legends surrounded Rayna. There were only two reasons a warrior had so many stories about them. Either they invented the tales themselves to up their prices as a mercenary, or some parts of the tales were in fact true. When weaved together, the tapestry of deeds done stood more impressively than a made-up song or story.

So far, Rayna appeared to be more than a mere myth. Falkon wouldn't be surprised if she had survived a great fire as a child. She even smelled of smoke, her face smudged with ash. The woman had been kissed by a dragon.

# 2
# Warrior Forged

Rayna studied the captain as he stepped away to fetch the refreshments. She'd been studying him since he entered the tavern. A shiny coin standing out amid drunks and heathens.

The group of them didn't even try to blend in. Theirs was a royal arrival, and they wanted everyone to know it. Nevermind that most of Theopilous housed murderers and cutthroats. Those minor details never made it to the ears of most travelers.

To the uninformed, Theopilous was an oasis in the desert. A refuge from the harsh lands where one could enjoy all the spoils they desired. Often those travelers left Theopilous much poorer than they had come. Some never left at all. And some were never heard from again.

At first meeting this Falkon appeared too young to be captain of the kingsguard. But once Rayna engaged him in conversation, she could almost smell the hierarchy dripping from his skin. His title had been handed to him by the king for no other reason than relations. Then again, she knew better than to discredit a man simply for his age. And his rank mattered not either. What he did with that position is the only thing that counted.

The rest of the kingsguard sat far enough away to make Captain Falkon seem less threatening in his quest for information. But they remained close enough to assist their captain should he find himself in distress. It wouldn't matter how close they sat if Rayna opted to cut his throat. Her greatsword would slaughter the lot of them and be cleaned of their blood before their severed heads touched the floor.

She didn't seek trouble, but it found her often enough. The only time Rayna went looking for trouble is when it paid well. Even though King Favian was hated in this part of the realm, his gold was still welcomed.

With the king sending his only son to fetch her, Rayna expected a hefty payday for whatever deed he wanted done. Then she would finally have enough coin to get her off this rock permanently and into grander parts of the world.

Captain Falkon edged his way back through the crowd, holding a pitcher of mead and what smelled like soft cheese. Rayna reached up and snatched the pitcher from his hands, losing some of the beverage to the floor in her haste.

"Are you trying to spoil me?" she asked as she filled her mug.

"Talos said you drink this piss. You must have a death wish, young lady."

"Aye, I think I do."

"He also mentioned the cheese as your favorite."

The captain seemed so pleased with himself as he set down the platter that Rayna decided to toy with him.

"You've been hornswoggled, Captain," she said. "Talos has been trying to move that stinking cheese for days now. I think some of it may have even spoiled."

"You mean you don't partake?"

She shook her head. "Never. The drink I'll enjoy, though."

As she brought the mug to her lips, she couldn't help but crack a smile behind the rim. Only when Captain Falkon started back towards the bar did she let him in on the joke.

"I'm fooling with you, man."

She reached across and snatched a harder wedge of cheese in her fingers. Confused, Falkon returned to his chair and poured himself another drink.

"Don't they teach you highborns what humor is?" she asked, stripping the skin off the cheese. "Must be a dreary life if you can't find a laugh in things."

"I'm not highborn," he told her. "And some things

aren't meant to be laughed about."

He took a sip of the mead and then pushed it aside in disgust. Across the room, Rayna's good eye caught the rest of Falkon's men enter the tavern and take seats with the others. A slender man with a thick, dark beard watched her every move, though she made few.

"You mean like the reason you rode all this way to seek out my services?"

"Aye," he nodded. "We'll get to that. But I believe you owe me a story first."

Rayna stripped the hard skin off another wedge of cheese, then retrieved her pipe. If she were going to tell this story again, she needed a smoke first.

"Still trying to discern why I cover my eye, Captain Falkon?" she asked, wary of his stare. "Because you can't seem to look away."

"I'm only mesmerized by your beauty, my lady."

"I'm not a lady."

She trickled strands of tobacco down into her pipe, letting the air carry the wisps into the bowl. With the mounds sufficiently flowing over the rim, she packed them down with her thumb. Repeating the process, she began to tell her tale.

"My father, Rionar, was a thief. Not by trade, you understand, but necessity. Poor men can't feed their families and he had a young wife with child to look after."

Satisfied with the tamped tobacco, she used the candle from the table and circled its flame around the top. Captain Falkon leaned back in his chair as the smoke filtered into the air. The smell didn't agree with him, but he wouldn't begrudge Rayna her habit.

His father, the king, no doubt told him to keep her happy. Give the dragonslayer whatever she wants so she will ride back with them. She knew the tactic all too well and took full advantage of it.

Off to the side of the tavern, the bearded man continued to watch her as she smoked. His leather armor masked a lean, capable body beneath, much more capable than the captain. She would take advantage of him later.

For now, she would honor Captain Falkon with the remainder of her story. Then they would come to terms on the quest he sought her for.

"One unfortunate evening my father happened upon a dragon's nest, though he didn't know it at the time. All he noticed were the mounds of jewels and gold horded together in piles."

She took a moment to indulge in her smoke. It was one of the few things that soothed her weary spirit. Cold drinks, fresh tobacco, and fucking. Those indulgences were usually meant for men to delight in. But why should pleasure only be reserved for some?

Rayna's history with dragons left her with an

awareness few others would accept. Life was fleeting. Better to enjoy all the spoils of the world while one still had a beating heart.

"My father moved swift as a rabbit. It made him a very good thief. Though this night his ability would make him a target of revenge," she continued. "Dragons are very particular about their gold. I've never discovered the reasoning, though it was enough to anger this one to act. The creature came after my father and damned him. He even demonized his seed to extinguish the entire bloodline."

Through her travels, Rayna came upon many curious souls eager to learn about her story. To keep the tale from tasting stale in her own mouth, she learned the ways of the bard to heighten the drama of it all. At this point in the story, she always took a dramatic pause to reveal what lay beneath her eyepatch.

She read the guard captain as a squeamish man. Should she show him her stigma, he may well call for his cavalry to attack. They would cast her as a demon like many before them had.

Then, she would have to kill the lot of them and flee Theopilous for good. She didn't feel like spilling blood in Talos' tavern, so she simply tapped her eyepatch and hinted at what lay beneath.

"The curse of the dragon didn't quite take."

"And the fire? The one they say you walked out of

unscathed?"

Rayna extinguished her pipe and traded it for more mead. She grew weary of the legends surrounding her name. It brought too much trouble from misguided souls wanting to best the dragonslayer in open combat.

"I wasn't born of fire, as they say. The dragon grew tired of toying with our family and one night set the house ablaze under its breath," she explained. "I was meant to die, but my sainted mother Kathryn spirited me away to give me a fighting chance at life. I've been fighting ever since. Everything I am, and everything I do, is because of that accursed dragon. I've spent the last years of my life seeking and slaying them all."

"A fine tale," Falkon said, leaning back in his chair. "If I'm to believe you, it would explain the urgency of my king's orders."

"You don't believe me?" She laughed. "Did I stutter as I spoke?"

"You spoke like a traveling bard, spinning a yarn for a copper. I just have a hard time believing a lone woman could fell a dragon on her own, let alone dozens. Even a woman as formidable as you appear to be."

Rayna laughed again and kicked her feet back up onto the table.

"Then why have you come all this way, Captain Falkon? You've wasted my time and yours."

"I'm here under my king's orders. They aren't for me to

question with my own theories."

"So, you don't think for yourself, then?"

She could tell her question made him uncomfortable, angry even. Rayna knew more about Falkon Fourspire than he did of her. His rank as captain of the kingsguard was meant to mask a man as meager as a cobbler's apprentice.

Under the armor and the rank, Falkon was as soft as a pig's belly. Rayna doubted if his own sword ever tasted of blood. The man with the dark beard and even darker eyes staring at her from across the room seemed the capable one.

"I am captain of the kingsguard," he huffed. "Men follow me, not the other way around."

"Yet you're here under royal command. So, let's have it then. Why did the king send you?"

"He wishes to obtain your services as a slayer."

"To slay what? I do not murder men."

"You know what."

She studied his face under the glow of the candlelight. His features were more suited to a throne room than at the head of an army. Clean shaven and pretty, he lacked a killer's merciless stare so needed in battle. But beneath his soft brown eyes, Rayna read the truth. He held no skill in wooing her with lies. Still, his request couldn't be accurate.

"That's not possible," she said. "There haven't been

dragons on Atharia for years. I should know. I killed them all."

Now it was Falkon's turn to laugh.

"Apparently, you missed one."

Rayna thought for a moment. Her skin bristled at Captain Falkon's words.

"I've been away from these shores for a time," she said. "Perhaps one came crawling out of the darkness on its belly."

The thought of another scaled, winged beast polluting the skies of her homeland made Rayna tense up. Her battles with the dragons carried through most of her adult life. She should've known better than to celebrate their demise too soon. Especially when the one who cursed her family eluded her vengeance.

She sought that foul beast for years only to give up the chance when the trail went cold. If the dark one had returned, there would be no keeping her from it. But, she needed more than just the word of a dutiful son before offering her sword.

"This king, he's seen the dragon himself?"

"He is called King Favian the First."

Falkon spoke with pride, announcing his father in such a regal way. Rayna couldn't help but dispel his haughtiness with her own introspection.

"Does that make you the second?"

He didn't seem to catch her words as an insult. Instead,

he raised his chin a little prouder as he staked his royal claim.

"Yes, second in line to the throne of Sandhal and soon all of Atharia."

She laughed. "You royals, always throwing the crown around like it's your cock. I have no use for either."

Falkon's face soured. "You prefer the touch of women, then?"

"Women, men, both at once. You have too many rules, royal. It keeps you from enjoying the spices of life."

"I told you, I'm no royal. At least not yet."

"Well, you're not a warrior either," she explained. "Warriors are not bound by duty. We do as we please."

"For one not bound to duty, you carved quite a name as a dragonslayer. Surely, there was an easier path to take. Yet you remained compelled to eradicate an entire species. Seems like you were bound by duty then."

Rayna could see now that Falkon rested more on cunning than his prowess with the sword. Perhaps he would make a good ruler after all. But his attempts to sway her to their cause were wasted. She knew what she would do the moment he spoke of the dragon's return to Atharia. Still, she needed to correct him of his coercing.

"I hunted the dragons for riches and revenge, nothing more." She downed the remainder of the mead and stood. "So yes, I'll take up the quest until those accursed things are expelled from the land. But I should speak with this King Favian before then. Agreed?"

Rayna extended her hand. Falkon stood and clutched her arm in his own. An oath made and accepted. She would travel back with them to Saltwood Stronghold and gather the details of the dragon sighting. Then Rayna would go hunting one more time.

# 3

# Valerios the Valiant

Darkness fell over Theopilous, but that didn't mean the city slept. In fact, it grew rowdier as the night edged closer to the midnight hour.

The men enjoyed their concubines and crude behavior while Valerios sat alone by the stables. A halo of smoke rose from his clay pipe as he watched the shenanigans from a distance. A lively party to be sure, but Valerios preferred to indulge in his intoxicants away from the others.

The ashwa leaf from the eastern isles of Ischon soothed his nerves. On this night, he needed an abundance of it to keep his hands from shaking.

What terrible twist of fate had brought him into the journey of the damned? If not for his allegiance to Falkon, he would have ridden out under the cover of darkness by now. Let the Red Waste swallow him if the gods deemed it so. Better to expire in the sands than under the hot breath of a dragon.

Deep beneath the meat of his skin, he felt his bones grow cold, and it made him shudder. They were fools to even think about broaching the dragon's lair. Even with the famed slayer at their side, riding into the belly of the beast was a risk too great to take.

For some time, Valerios wondered about King Favian's state-of-mind. He seemed distant and quick to temper. Valerios could never achieve an audience alone with the king to truly seek answers. But little by little, he gathered facts from those that served his highness and pieced together his own theory. King Favian was being swayed by madness or manipulation.

As he pondered on his predicament, an icy blade pressed to his throat. With the clay pipe held tight between his teeth, he forced a response.

"I'm unarmed."

He held up his hands, showcasing no weapons. A softness of breath touched his ear in a whisper.

"Is that Sythian you're smoking?"

"Ischon," he corrected.

The blade drew back and his would-be assailant revealed herself. Rayna, the dragonslayer, settled down on a bale of hay next to him. A single torch cast its light across her face, causing her one blue eye to sparkle. The other remained covered by a dark leather patch.

Valerios found it peculiar. He hadn't seen it before. From his vantage point in the tavern, he only saw Rayna and Falkon engaged in deep conversation, not a secret between them.

All the ladies loved Falkon, whether highborn or a killer, such as the one that sat next to Valerios now. Falkon held a softness to his looks with eyes the color of the sea and a mane of sand colored locks swept back in a fashionable top knot. If he ever dropped the armor and took up his intended role as prince, he would have even more maidens chasing him.

It was just as well. Valerios preferred his books to bedroom liaisons. Stimulating his mind gave him more pleasure than a thousand whores. Though the dragonslayer intrigued him. He could learn a great many things from tales of her travels.

"I've yet to explore Ischon," she said, as though reading his mind. "Kartha is the furthest I've been from Atharia."

"Ischon is a beautiful land," Valerios replied. "You would enjoy its offerings."

Rayna extended her hand to him. "May I start with their ashwa?"

He took the pipe from his lips, wiped the tip on his shirt, and handed it across to her. She raised her eyebrows in surprise as she pressed the pipe to her lips.

"A gentleman. You don't see that much in military

forces."

Valerios leaned over and lit the ashwa for her. "No, I suppose not."

She took in the herb with slow, measured puffs and then offered her own insight into him.

"But you weren't bread of military stock."

He shook his head and smiled. "You have a good eye."

"At least one," she joked.

With the subject opened on her end, Valerios took the opportunity to pursue his own line of questioning.

"Is the other so hideously disfigured that you choose to cover it?"

She smiled and handed the pipe back over for him to finish the smoke.

"Your Captain Falkon seemed shaken by my stigma. I thought it best to keep covered for now."

Such was the difference between the men. The things which drove Falkon to retreat enticed Valerios. He wanted to learn more of the origins of all things, but especially those with a unique story.

So, in this moment, he dared reach his hand towards the dragonslayer. Knowing he took a significant risk intruding on her personal space, Valerios stopped inches from her face. Then he asked permission to go further.

"May I?"

She studied him for a moment, no doubt trying to ascertain his intentions. When she nodded approval, he felt his entire torso jump in excitement. A treasure lay beneath the crude leather patch and he was about to uncover it first-hand.

Valerios shifted on his hay bale to move closer to Rayna. Slowly, he set his hand to her cheek. The warmth that radiated from her skin surprised him. Somehow, he expected a cold-blooded killer to have a temperature to match.

He moved his fingers to the patch and peeled it back slowly to let his excitement linger. Beneath the covering, he saw something shining back at him as though a brilliant jewel sat within the hollow of her eye.

Halfway to exposing the great secret she hid, Rayna grasped Valerios' hand and halted him. Surprised, and more than a little disappointed, he tried to press forward. As her grip tightened, he realized his mistake and pulled his hand away.

"Forgive me," he said, dropping his gaze to the ground.

"Why do you apologize?" she asked. "I gave you my permission. It's just that I would prefer not exposing my shame out here."

Her words were encouraging, but also puzzled him. What such mark could shame a great beauty as Rayna? The more curious he got, the more his thirst for the answer grew. So, when she offered to bare herself to him in the privacy of her chambers, he didn't even realize the true implications of her words.

# 4

# Debts Owed

Rayna traveled back to Theopilous often. It was close to her old haunts in Corinth but still far enough away. The resident lot of thieves, murderers, and outcasts gave Theopilous extra appeal. It allowed her to blend in without gaining consistent unwanted attention. People here left her alone.

The innkeeper always held a room for her when the seasons called for her arrival. It held a hay stuffed bed on the floor and a simple cleansing bucket with a damp cloth. It wasn't much but Rayna paid well enough to keep a place to call her own.

She rarely invited others to share her space but as she led the bearded man inside her heart felt at ease on her decision. It was a great deal more fun being in the presence of Falkon's second than it had been sharing conversation with the captain. She knew little of this man except for his genuine excitement of exploring the unknown. Rayna found a kindred spirit in a man whose name she had yet to learn.

He stood in the center of the room fidgeting in discomfort until she lit a torch on the wall. As his eyes caught hers once more, she saw him try to refrain from staring at the patch. She would reward him for his courtesy but not until she got what she wanted first.

"Apologies for the scarcity of the room," she said. "I've only recently returned from abroad."

"Kartha wasn't it?"

She nodded then continued to shift the direction of the conversation where she wanted to take it.

"What's your name?"

"Valerios."

"Just Valerios? No surname?"

"I couldn't afford one."

His answer gave her a laugh and piqued her interest further.

"Lowborn without military training. How is it you've marked your spot in the kingsguard?"

"Falkon is my oldest friend. He honors me with my position in his ranks. We grew up together. I owe him a debt and I will gladly serve at his side to repay it."

Valerios rested his hand on the hilt of his sword. Rayna had little doubt he knew how to handle himself. She also knew he wouldn't strike her without being threatened first. She removed her own sword and leaned it against the wall but kept a serrated hunting knife hidden at her back. Valerios followed her lead and set his own sword aside. Once he was unarmed, she stepped closer to him.

"What debt do you owe him?"

He tried to match her game of wits. "What do you hide beneath your patch?"

"You first."

"He saved my life," Valerios admitted. "As a child I was much smaller than the other boys and also much poorer. It made me an easy target. One day several of the boys held my face down in the mud. I couldn't breathe and thought I might meet my end there at the docks until Falkon made them stop."

Rayna was surprised. "I didn't think he had it in him."

"He's a capable fighter, but he lives under the shadow of a brother that fell in battle.

"The battle for the throne at Sandhal?"

Valerios nodded then stepped away.

"I've already told you too much. I think it's best I retire to my own room for the evening."

As he moved for the door, she caught his hand and drew him closer.

"I haven't finished with you yet."

Valerios took a step backwards. "I'm sure you could find more capable men than I to suit your needs."

"Do you think I'm a whore?" She crooked her head

awaiting his reply.

"Apologies, dragonslayer."

She corrected him. "Rayna."

"Rayna," he began again. "I didn't mean to offend you."

She folded her arms across her chest. Valerios looked her over no doubt marveling at the muscularity she honed from years of training. But she couldn't read if he were intimidated by her strength or enamored with it.

"I don't offend easily," she told him. "But that's not why I asked you into my chamber. So, don't flatter yourself."

Valerios' smile lifted his beard to reveal an impressive set of teeth not yet damaged by an overindulgence of ashwa leaf. She liked his features and his lean, muscular build well enough but she only sought information. Valerios' smile told her he knew.

"What answers did Captain Falkon not give that you think I will resolve?" he asked.

A small satchel rested at the foot of her bed. She pulled from it a wooden tankard and a flagon. Prying open the flagon with her teeth she gave it a heavy pour into the tankard then offered it to Valerios.

"It's just wine," she said. "I only indulge in it sparingly but you seem like the type of fellow who prefers it to heavy ale."

He took the tankard from her hands and gave her a

salute of sorts.

"Thank you, but you needn't get me drunk to get me to talk. I'll tell you what you want to know."

"It's not a bribe, simply a friendly gesture. We're meant to ride out together in the morning, we should be friendly," she told him. "But if you don't want it, don't waste it. That stuff doesn't come cheap."

Rayna held out her hand and motioned for the tankard. Valerios hesitated then took a long sip. She gave him a satisfied smile then took a swig directly from the flagon. To her surprise, he extended the tankard and requested a refill. Rayna obliged him and they drank again.

Heavy silence filled the room as they each measured the other. Given more time Rayna would love to have a proper test of mettle with Valerios. For now, she needed proper answers. She felt something unsettling about this quest they sought her for but she couldn't stab it down.

"Have you seen this dragon that's deemed such destruction?" she asked.

"I haven't."

"Then how do you know it exists?"

"The king sent out a party of soldiers in search of it a fortnight before," Valerios explained. "None returned."

"Any number of mishaps could've fallen those men."

"Not these. They were the elite guard. King Favian wouldn't have sent them out for confirmation alone. He was certain they would find it."

"Did he expect them to kill it?"

"I don't know. I don't keep the king's counsel, only Captain Falkon's."

"What is Falkon hiding from me?"

He struggled with his response debating if it were worth crossing his captain to appease their sought-after guest. Finally, he answered in a truth Captain Falkon regrettably did not share.

"King Favian saw the dragon in a vision."

As she digested the meaning of his words, a coldness swept through her. She did not like Valerios' answer. Her travels took her all over Atharia and never had she met another who held the same sight that she held.

"Impossible," she replied, a fist balled at her side.

"I swear it is true."

Rayna tossed her flagon to the ground. She sat on the edge of the bed and watched as the dark wine leaked out across the wooden slats of the floor like fresh blood. A gentleman through and through, Valerios bent down to clean the mess for her.

"Leave it," she told him. "And leave me."

"But I thought...."

She looked up at him affirming her orders with a creased brow and clenched teeth.

"I have a tremendous headache in my eye and we have a long ride out to Saltwood Stronghold in the morning."

Valerios set the tankard and flagon by her feet,

collected his sword, and gave her a small bow before leaving. As the door shut behind him Rayna cursed under her breath. Something strange was afoot. Dragons plagued her dreams for years, that is how she tracked them. Now another gained the sight. How could that be if not the same curse?

Only one thing she knew for certain, if the dragon sighting was real, she needed to kill it. Laying back on her bed she kicked off her boots and rested her hands beneath her head. She wouldn't sleep this night.

Thoughts of slaying another dragon would keep her occupied well into the next morning. They would continue to plague her days until she dealt a death blow to the entire accursed lineage.

# 5
# Fickle Fables

Come the dawn Falkon had his men gather supplies and ready the horses for their journey back home. He wasn't looking forward to riding back through the Red Waste, but few other roads would return them swiftly to Sandhal. The rest of the roads were far more treacherous than biting hot sand.

As the men stocked the gear for travel, Falkon helped himself to a breakfast platter at Talos' tavern. The day crowd was much more docile than the drunks cursing and carousing the night prior. Falkon preferred the peace and quiet to enjoy his morning meal of fire-roasted potatoes, mutton, and fresh breads with honey.

"Tell me Talos, how do you preserve such fine foods so close to a desert?" he asked between bites.

"An agricultural mystery," Talos replied with a sly grin.

Valerios offered an alternative answer as he sat down with Falkon. His own plate was filled with a colorful variety of fruits, no meat in sight. Falkon often wondered how Valerios stayed so strong when he ate like a chamber maiden.

"The desert, or Red Waste as we call it, stretches over a mile out north," Valerios continued. "Yet, to the south you'll find green grass and flowing streams. It's a marvel I tell you."

Falkon looked over at Talos. "Is that the way of it then? A marvel?"

Talos shrugged. "If he says so. I'd always heard Theopilous was the vision of a traveling warlock who dreamed it up as shelter from the desert storms."

"As I said, a marvel!"

Valerios raised his glass in the air as though he'd won a victory. Then he slapped Talos on the back and requested more fruit.

"You're in jovial spirits," Falkon said as he tore a thick piece of bread in half.

"Why shouldn't I be? We return home today."

Falkon drizzled fresh honey over his bread and ate it down in two bites. He wiped the back of his hand over his sticky lips and took a drink of sweet wine before getting to the matter that troubled him.

"So, your good mood has nothing to do with Rayna then?"

The puzzled look on Valerios' face displeased Falkon, but he allowed him to speak his side of things.

"I'm happy she's returning with us and the mission was a success," Valerios replied. "That is all."

"Some of the men saw you leaving her private chamber late last night."

Falkon let him digest the heaviness of his accusation while he waited for the serving girl to clear the table. Once she stepped away, he asked Valerios outright.

"Did you lay with her?"

Valerios chewed on a slice of apple while deciding his best response to the accusation. It didn't matter what he said. Falkon knew it was the truth. He just wanted to give his old friend an opportunity to own it as such. Lies did not suit their relationship.

"I met with her for conversation, nothing more happened."

His rebuttal was weak. So, Falkon continued to press him on the matter. He'd seen his father break a man with just a few sentences. Falkon wanted to learn that skill for himself.

"She's a beautiful woman," he said. "I wouldn't begrudge you if there were more."

"She is that," Valerios replied. "But you know I don't partake in such affairs."

Falkon pushed his plate of food away. Suddenly, the sight of it turned his stomach. Valerios and his consistent blathering of a moral code made him poor company sometimes. Falkon preferred using his position of power to get everything he desired. Time and again, Valerios wasted opportunities.

"What did she want?"Falkon asked in a huff.

"Answers that you did not give her."

"Lousy bitch." He spat his words, causing crumbs to spill across his chest. "What did you tell her?"

"The truth," Valerios admitted. "I felt it best to be upfront rather than risk her not returning with us."

Falkon leaned back in his chair and laughed.

"You're a fool, Valerios. Or is it that you smoke too much of that Ischon weed? If she refuted our proposal, we would've dragged her back by her filthy blonde hair. I don't know what father wants with her, but I deliver, regardless."

This time Valerios pushed his plate away. He leaned across the table on his elbows and dared to point his finger at Falkon.

"You are the fool if you don't see something is plaguing your father's mind."

"What would you have me do, consult a seer? Like you?"

Realizing he crossed a line, Valerios softened.

"I'm just saying it might be worth looking into before we end up like the elite soldiers."

"I would hardly call those fools elite. They probably

ran into a pack of cutthroats who murdered them for sport."

"The dragonslayer, there's something special about her."

"Aye, she's a nice piece of ass," Falkon laughed. "I'm going to have her ride up front with me so the men have something to look at on the road back."

Valerios shifted his eyes and shook his head as though displeased. It made Falkon rethink including him on future quests.

"You disapprove of my words?"

"It's not for me to question."

"Not everyone is chaste like you, Valerios. Now I know you didn't fuck her!" Falkon gave a full laugh followed by a satisfied belch. "I'll hear no more about how special this slayer is unless you've seen her naked. Better still, I'll find out for myself."

They gathered their things and left the tavern. Returning to the stables, Falkon was pleased to see his orders fulfilled. The horses were saddled with enough supplies to keep the men sustained through the Red Waste but remain fleet of foot. As Falkon looked them over, he noted one rider missing.

"Where is the dragonslayer?" he shouted.

The men gave no answer, so he looked to Valerios for one.

"You didn't kill her in the night, did you?"

Valerios shook his head and then pointed to the rear of them.

"Here she comes now, captain."

Rayna galloped up on her own horse, a magnificent mare with a coat the color of cinnamon. For the coming fight, the warrior woman armed herself well. Her scant leathers and soft furs had been replaced with black and gold armor fitted to her form.

As she drew closer, Falkon noted aspects of her ensemble had been harvested from those she'd slain. Dragon scales reinforced her vambraces, greaves, and chestplate. The craftsmanship showed a skilled hand not even Sandhal's blacksmith's could match.

The dragonslayer's jovial demeanor had become battle-hardened. A smudge of what looked like ash ran across her cheeks and down her chin. Her giant sword rested in a harness across the saddle, close enough for Rayna to draw it at the first sign of trouble. As she approached, Falkon gave her a once over then forced a smile.

"Impressive armor, my lady."

"Call me Rayna. Or dragonslayer if you prefer," she told him. "But again, I'm no lady."

Of course, she was no lady. She looked like common street trash, save for the magnificent sword and polished armor. Falkon wouldn't make the mistake of honoring her with respect again.

"Rayna then," he corrected. "I gather you're well

hydrated for the journey."

"I have enough wine in me to keep your company, if that's what you mean."

Some soldiers chuckled until Falkon ordered them silent. He would not be made a fool of by this girl, or anyone else. They hadn't even left town, and she was already testing his patience.

"We have a long ride through the Red Waste. It's not for the weak or the timid. Some of my men almost didn't make it through the first time. Perhaps you should swap the wine for flagons of water."

"Perhaps you should've taken a different route here," she argued.

"It's a narrow pass from Saltwood Stronghold down to Theopilous," he reminded her. "We either travel the Red Waste or lose more than a day's ride circling around the Dragon's Backbone."

"Or we can cut just through Lynwood Forest."

Rayna seemed so sure of herself that Falkon couldn't help but laugh. "That forest is filled with deadly creatures. They live among the trees and attack when you least expect it. That's why it's been called the *Fickle* Forest."

Now Rayna gave a laugh. "Childhood fables, Captain Falkon. I assure you, there are no monsters in the forest. But if it makes you feel better, I'll guide you and your men through to safe passage. This way, we save time and avoid blistering our skin under the scalding sun."

Her disrespect of his order and his title was already wearing on Falkon. If not for his father's wishes, he would have silenced her with a backhand right then.

Instead, he gave her the lead as she requested. Better to have her out in front when the tree-folk came for them. They would grab her first while the rest of them rode to safety. Then he could tell his father he tried, but the mighty dragonslayer fell to the Fickle Forest.

# 6
# Fire & Steel

They marched out of Theopilous with Rayna at the lead. She could feel Captain Falkon's stare on her back. Whether he coveted her ass or wanted to cut off her head, she couldn't tell.

The captain didn't like her, that much she knew. Truth be told, she gave him plenty of reasons to be prickly. At their first meeting, she dared to keep him dancing, an insult to be sure. Most royals expected their boots to be licked the moment they announced themselves.

Captain Falkon's opinion of her didn't matter. The distrust went both ways and Rayna's sights were set on King Favian. After liberating the truth from Valerios, she was eager to know more about the dreams of dragons he claimed to have.

She led the men west to a steep ravine where they needed to tread their horses lightly. Having taken the path many times before, Rayna pushed hers faster than the others dared. Captain Falkon struggled with his the most and needed Valerios' help to guide the steed down to level ground. Once the horse was surefooted again, Falkon's frustrations with embarrassment took over.

"Are you trying to lead us to our death, woman?"

Rayna gave a soft chuckle. "That's hardly a deadly fall, Captain Falkon. You might muddy your fine clothes, though."

She continued to give him reasons not to like her. She didn't care. They may sit in Saltwood Stronghold and rule the people there, but Rayna never answered to kings and queens. She bested dragons. What could a monarchy do to impress her?

However, Valerios seemed to share in her humor, stifling his own laugh at Captain Falkon's expense. She gave him a subtle nod that he returned with his own. Something about this man intrigued her. Should they have time before her dance with a dragon, she would like to learn more about him.

Pushing the horses forward, they soon came to a thick column of trees standing in their path. The forest spread deep enough to where the eyes couldn't discern exactly what lay ahead.

Rayna had run afoul of creatures in the Fickle Forest before. They weren't the mythical beasts Falkon had carried on about, but they were dangerous enough. She knew the path through well enough to avoid any serious attacks. But before they breached the threshold, she needed the men to mind her lead.

"Stay at my flank, single file. No matter what happens, don't veer from the path."

"You heard her. Stay in formation," Captain Falkon echoed.

Rayna advanced slowly, pushing branches aside to clear her view. The morning air was still, which troubled her. All manner of pest should be hissing and whining as they entered the forest, but none spoke up. She motioned the men to stay further at her flank as she pressed forward.

Delving deeper into the forest, she found a wide cut path rounding the bend. It held all the markings she remembered from past travels. The flat of the leaves, the smell of the pine, and a precise line of sunlight laying across her mare's snout were all familiar to her. Still, something felt off.

Waving her hand, she insisted the party close ranks. As they did, Captain Falkon came up alongside her, no doubt casting judgement over her lead. While he spoke, she kept her ears and eyes focused on their surroundings.

"Is there trouble?"

"We're being followed," she whispered.

"I warned you of the creatures tucked within these woods."

Falkon gritted his teeth to bite back his anger as he spoke. Rayna resisted the urge to backhand him in the face to keep him quiet. Instead, she clarified the manner of danger approaching.

"Monsters don't tail us, Captain Falkon. Men do. A pack of them. Silent but deadly. I suggest we proceed with extra caution."

"I fear no man," he scoffed.

Ignoring her protests, Captain Falkon drew his sword and rounded his horse. Swinging his blade in the air, he shouted towards the trees with a bravado he could not back up with action.

"Show yourselves, treacherous dogs, and taste my fine steel!"

His men, loyal to their captain's commands, also drew their weapons. All but Valerios followed Captain Falkon's foolish decree. Valerios was an exceptional man with a sound head on his shoulders. He wanted to keep his head, so he remained as still as Rayna and watched the woods for movement. But the captain and his guardsmen caused such a ruckus that discerning an advancing party now proved difficult.

Rayna tried to silence them, but to no avail. They were so caught up in the pageantry of being royal soldiers that they ignored their surroundings. Then it happened. One man stepped his horse off the path and sprung a trap.

A snare pulled both the man and his horse high into

the air. More snares followed, thrown from the bushes and down from the trees. The men were so pinched together within the confines of the forest that they couldn't maneuver out of the way in time.

A net caught Captain Falkon as well, knocking him from his horse. Even Valerios fell prey to the attack as heavy ropes looped over his torso and dragged him down. Rayna reared back, watching the events unfold. She had a choice to make now. Either leave the men to their fate or save their skins and increase her asking price. She was never one to run from battle, though this one presented a fierce challenge.

Drawing her sword, she waited before advancing. Soon their enemy made an appearance from the forest. As she expected, a small army of men came out of the trees. They were clad in greens and browns to match the forest floor. A good disguise. No wonder she couldn't catch proper sight of them as they mingled within their surroundings.

The lot of them kept tight to the ropes holding down the Saltwood army. One man broke from the back and stepped towards Rayna. He wore similar colors, though the cut of his clothes marked more authority than the others. A wrap of cloth around their mouths and noses shielded each man's appearance. The leader's wrapped over the top of his head and neck as well.

Rayna pointed the tip of her sword towards him as he

approached. Her gesture caused him to stop advancing though others now surrounded her flank. She cursed the openness of the woods, leaving her back exposed. Undaunted, she held ground.

"Are you their leader?" she asked.

"Are you theirs?"

The man gestured over his shoulder at the soldiers all subdued at the hands of a filthy little gang. Another embarrassment for Captain Falkon, but Rayna would take ownership of it.

"In a way," she replied.

"I encourage you to drop your sword," the man told her, his voice muffled by the mask. "One lone woman against the lot of us doesn't fare well."

"That woman has fell dragons," Valerios cried out. "Your lot will be no match for her."

Rayna wished he hadn't unveiled her secret just yet. She intended to draw in the band of ruffians and find out their intentions before showing her hand. Now when the leader asked, she didn't hold back the truth.

"You're the dragonslayer?"

"That I am."

The man gave a laugh. "I remember when you were just a whelp," he said.

As he pushed back his coverings, Rayna recognized a familiar face. A dark shag of hair fell just past his ears, framing a powerful jaw. Seeing his piercing blue eyes unobstructed brought back memories from her younger days. Recognizing him as more friend than foe, Rayna tucked her sword away and hopped down from her horse.

"It's been too long, Jagger," she said, giving his hair a tussle. "You were just a lad when I saw you last."

"You weren't that much older, Rayna."

"Old enough to know better than to get caught up with the likes of you."

"Instead, you're traveling with this lot?" He scrunched his face in disappointment and motioned over his shoulder.

"Long story," Rayna told him. "But I'm going to have to insist you set them free now. We have a long journey ahead."

Jagger walked in a circle past the men pinned down in their ropes. Finding his way to one of the bannermen, he lifted the colors from the ground. He pinched the banner between his fingers before tossing it back into the dirt. The soldiers grunted in anger and were promptly poked with blunt sticks to keep them in order.

"These are royal cunts," Jagger said, turning back to Rayna. "What're you doing with royals?"

"Business… which is none of yours."

"You of all people should know I can't just turn royals loose without a finder's fee."

This time, Rayna circled the men in their snares. As she

passed Valerios, she patted the hilt of her sword and gave him a wink with her good eye. He shifted his bodyweight into a kneeling position and prepared to act.

"Is that why you've entrenched yourself inside Fickle Forest?" Rayna asked Jagger. "You force a toll on unsuspecting travelers? That's low, even for you."

"You've been away a long while, Rayna," he replied. "Times have been tough since that sea dog took the throne. We do what is needed to get by."

"I don't begrudge you of that," she said. "But while I'm certain King Favian would pay a righteous fee for his son, we just don't have the time to waste."

All the while she spoke, Rayna noted Jagger's men closing in on her. She kept speaking until their circle grew tight enough for her to act. Wasting no movement, she held her sword aloft and cast her eye upon it.

No longer covered by the leather patch, the iris shone bright as an amethyst stone under the cascading sunlight. A slit of a dark pupil focused on the thick part of the blade, igniting it into flame. The men jumped back as Rayna's sword came alive with fire. Jagger himself held position.

"I should've remembered the eye," he said.

"Considering how much it disgusted you, I'm surprised it slipped your mind."

"As I recall, it disgusted you more."

"We can reminisce later," she told him. "Right now, I

must insist on my team's release."

She swung the flaming sword overhead, keeping the bandits at bay. On her next arc, she brought it down across the bonds that held Valerios. As expected, he sprang to his feet and drew his own sword to take up the fight with her.

Captain Falkon's cries for freedom went ignored. Rayna couldn't risk him getting in the way as she tried to settle this predicament with as little bloodshed as possible.

"Jagger, I don't want to hurt you," she told him. "Stop this foolishness and we'll come to terms."

Jagger stared into her eyes for a long while. She was surprised he kept her gaze. A quick glance to the flaming sword, then back to Rayna, and he called off his men. They held their batons and blades at the ready but kept them pointed towards the ground. To signify her own show of peace, Rayna tamped out her blade in the dirt to douse the fire. But she kept the broadsword tight in her grip.

"Of all the parties to stumble through our woods, it had to be yours," Jagger quipped.

"Sorry to disappoint," she told him.

"Not at all. This is the most fun I've had in a long while."

"We'll have to do it again sometime."

Jagger nodded agreement, then nervously bit his lip

before asking a favor.

"Can you help an old brother out?"

Rayna didn't hesitate. "After everything we've been through, I wouldn't dare leave you empty-handed."

She went to fetch her saddlebag, pressing Valerios to stand down as she passed him. From the horse's saddle, she took her satchel of coins and gave the full weight of it to Jagger.

"That should be enough to pay our way clear and cover the toll of the next unfortunate soul that passes through here."

Jagger felt the heft of the coins in his hands, then tucked them away. Rayna kept watch on his every move and those of his men. She hadn't seen Jagger in a long while, but mistrust still ran deep.

"You must be getting an excellent bounty for you to give up that much gold," Jagger said. "Need a few more hands?"

"Not this time," she replied.

"Still hunting dragons?"

She gave him a nod, and a look of concern crossed his face.

"May the gods help us all."

"They sent me, so your help is here."

Rayna gave a terrible little curtsy, drawing a laugh from the bunch. Jagger dared step forward and embrace her. She returned his affections, albeit briefly, then pushed him back.

"Take care of yourself, Rayna," he told her. "Best let us leave before you free your men. This one looks ready to make a mistake."

Jagger pointed down at Captain Falkon, who looked like a mad dog seething in his cage. Rayna agreed to let Jagger and his men slip safely into the trees before they lifted the traps. As they hurried back out through the bushes, Jagger gave one last look back and dazzled Rayna with a smile before disappearing into the forest.

# 7
# Curse of the Dragon

The moment Captain Falkon was free from his binds things grew ugly. He collected his sword and attempted to press it against Rayna's throat. She moved back but held her composure and did not strike. Valerios watched the mess take place and admired her restraint.

At first sight, he assumed her a violent savage, always primed for attack. Learning more about her over the past two days, he realized how he misjudged her. As it turned out, her beautiful visage also held more than he initially thought.

The reveal of her dragoneye and the powers it possessed were a marvel. He needed to know more about the story behind such a rare gift. That wouldn't happen if Captain Falkon continued to flaunt his authority. Rayna's calmness wouldn't hold up for much longer.

"I should've known you to be in allegiance with a band of thieves," Falkon shouted, his sword still pointed towards Rayna's throat. "Tricky woman led us right into their grip. I could have your head for that."

"You could try," she replied.

Valerios needed to play peacemaker, and he needed to do it quickly. Stepping in between his captain and the dragonslayer, he leaned on words he hoped they both would listen to.

"We all made it out unscathed. No need to spill bloodshed now."

Rayna looked at him, her dragoneye still shining like a gemstone and drawing him in. Realizing it remained exposed, she slipped on the leather patch and concealed it once more. Turning her attentions back to Falkon, she opted to stand down but not without reminding him of the price she paid for their heads.

"If you recall, it was my bag of coins they walked away with, not yours. Had I been in allegiance with them, we would've killed you all where you stand."

"That's supposed to bring us comfort?" Falkon asked, sword still at the ready. "You clearly knew their leader."

"I know Jagger from my younger days. They're not thieves, they're mercenaries. And may I remind you, Captain Falkon, that you sought me out, not the other way around. If you prefer, we can table our business and

I'll be on my way."

Now she grew angry. Valerios feared her dragoneye would make another appearance and it wouldn't be pleasant for any of them. He focused his efforts on Falkon and tried to make him call a truce.

"She speaks the truth, Falkon. You said yourself that King Favian requests her presence and you intend to follow through on his orders. It's best we let cooler heads prevail and continue back towards Saltwood Stronghold before night falls."

Falkon kept a heavy stare upon Rayna for an uncomfortably long beat of time. Then his eyes clicked over to Valerios as though he woke from a trance and finally absorbed his words.

"Very well. We'll continue on and sort all this out with my father. But now that we're through the thick of the woods, I'll take the lead. She can ride in back with you. If she breaks rank, kill her."

The tension remained thick between them, but at least they were on the move. They slipped through the rest of the woods with nary an incident or an altercation. Once back out onto open land, Captain Falkon made a point of pushing the horses into a hard gallop.

He often rode hard when he was angry. His temperament being what it was brought many a rough ride in which Valerios had trouble keeping up. The dragonslayer seemed to take it in stride. She moved her mare gracefully, as though she'd been born to it. Valerios tried to match the pace with her but fell behind. Noticing his struggle, Rayna slowed enough to let him catch up.

"I would hate for your captain to think I'm trying to break from the pack and make my escape," she said with a smile.

"He can be a bear at times," Valerios advised.

Rayna made her own assessment. "He's arrogant. It leads to mistakes and inevitably conflict."

"I hope any conflict raised with you has been tempered."

She looked over at him as they rode. The wind tussled her blonde hair about like a lover. Her lean, muscular frame was taught as she moved her mare at a fine gallop. Valerios found it pleasing to watch her ride. Ashamed, he turned his gaze forward as they brought up the rear of the brigade.

"He is wise to keep you as his counsel," Rayna told him. "Without your words to guide him, Captain Falkon would've lost his head long ago."

"Perhaps, but he made a fair point back there. You knew those men. That much was clear." He took in her stare once more. "Would it be asking too much to have you clarify the details of your history together?"

"Do you really want to do this now?"

"I think it would put Captain Falkon at ease if he knew a pack of mercenaries wasn't at our back. Besides, it's a long ride home. I find a pleasant tale always passes the time."

"I never said it was a pleasant tale."

Rayna slowed her horse, so she did not have to shout across the sound of heavy hooves. Valerios matched pace and kept his horse alongside hers. From his vantage point, the patch covered eye is the one that addressed him. He longed to get another look at the dragoneye lurking beneath the covering, but he would bide his time. For now, he remained silent and let Rayna tell her story.

"Jagger and his men aren't following us and I don't side with them. But there was a time when I did," she began. "After my family was lost to a great fire, I wound up with distant relatives in a small village. That didn't last long. I was too spirited for them and they sent me off to the academy, where I would learn to be a proper young lady."

She raised her eyebrows in jest, as though mocking the system that dare try to break her spirit. It made Valerios smile.

Rayna held a confidence in herself. She knew whom she was and wouldn't conform to suit someone else's needs. That confidence is why she and Captain Falkon butted heads straight away. He was used to those who submitted to his command. The men that surrounded Falkon were followers, even Valerios himself, to a degree. Rayna the dragonslayer was a leader in her own right and one who didn't take well to orders.

"So, what happened?"

"You mean other than me becoming a fine little lady?" she joked, then her tone grew serious. "I never made it to the academy. At that point, I already learned how my parents died and I was determined to seek revenge on the beast that killed them."

"That's when you became the dragonslayer?"

She grimaced. "I don't like that title, but yes, that's when I started down that path. So, when the wagon taking me to the City of Lost Souls halted to refill their water flagons, I slipped away into the woods."

"How old were you?"

"A girl of fifteen."

"That's still quite young to be wandering the woods by yourself."

"I learned how to take care of myself," Rayna explained. "It wasn't long after that when I fell in with Jagger's crew, The Foresaken Force. He was just a boy then himself. But his father Darius was a well-known mercenary."

"Darius the Dreaded? I have heard of him."

"To me, he became a second father. I learned much of the skill I carry from my days with those so-called mercenaries."

As her story unfolded, and the mystery around the dragonslayer gave way, Valerios wanted to learn more about the woman regardless of her mysterious eye. Before that could happen, Captain Falkon called him to the front. With a small nod to Rayna, he rode forward at his captain's command.

Coming up alongside Falkon, he waited for his next order. Instead, silence fell between them. Only the sound of horse hooves pounding the ground filled the space. Dust and sand fell far behind as they entered Pelanor Pass. Lush green grass spread out over dramatic pastures thanks to the three falls that ran from nearby rugged mountains. They were inching closer to Sandhal, the city just outside Saltwood Stronghold. Soon they would be home.

Minding the distance that still lay ahead of them, Captain Falkon brought the horses to a trot. It was then that he spoke with Valerios. His tone remained calm, though his words felt accusatory.

"What were you and the dragonslayer speaking on?"

"I asked her about the pack who jumped us in the Fickle Forest."

"And?"

"She knew them a lifetime ago, but she's insistent that they are not on our heels."

Valerios gave Falkon just enough information to keep him fed without offering the intimate details of Rayna's past. She provided him alone with that tale, and he did not want to betray her trust.

Falkon fell silent again. His usual boisterous manner gave way to something darker, and it unnerved Valerios. He knew Falkon to be a flamboyant man, always quick to conversation and a lively story. Only recently did his temperament turn sour and aggressive.

Valerios wondered if both father and son suffered the same affliction. After a pull from his water flagon, Falkon addressed him again.

"You saw her eye, didn't you, Valerios?"

"Only briefly," he lied.

"I saw it. Such a strange power to behold," Falkon said quietly. "She is cursed by the dragon. That much is true. Father was right to seek her."

He took another drink of water, then regarded Rayna, who still rode at the back of the pack. Finally, Captain Falkon levied his command to Valerios.

"Study her as only you can," he said. "I want to know how she calls fire to blade. I want to know everything there is about this dragonslayer. Then, when we no longer have use for her, I want you to kill her."

# 8
# Soldier Son

As they rode upon Sandhal, the townsfolk gathered to give Falkon the royal greeting he deserved. Passing through the gates, they welcomed him with cheers and jubilation. It made Falkon sit taller in his saddle, knowing his people adored him in such a way. Then, among the celebratory shouting, he heard words that gnashed his teeth in anger.

"Hail the dragonslayer!"

The people gathered in Sandhal Square with more pouring from their homes to see a one-eyed woman. A scoundrel with a sneer and shoddy boots. How could a mere miscreant demand such adulation that it would rival the return of the captain of the guards and the rightful prince of Atharia?

"Quite a display," Valerios said.

He too, had fallen under this slayer's spell. If she could

dazzle a fine mind the likes of Valerios, there was no telling how she might corrupt the king. Falkon would not allow the deviant to bedevil the royals with her demon eye. He pushed his horse through the thick of the crowd and headed up the path towards Saltwood. Valerios started at his back and Falkon shouted at him to remain.

"Stay with the woman!"

It was important that he have words with his father in private before the dragonslayer made her presence known. He dismounted at the gates and hurried the rest of the way on foot. As the towers of Cragstone Keep came into sight, Falkon paused in his trek to revel in his return home.

No drunken tavern brawlers or forest thieves dwelled here. Grass and stone were under his foot rather than red hot sand. The air smelled crisp as a gentle breeze and brought the scent of the sea with it. Even though back in the town they welcomed Rayna like a champion rider, the Saltwood Stronghold would herald Captain Falkon's return alone.

He hoped to change into a clean tunic, but time wasn't on his side. So, he walked to the throne room, still wearing his armor and muddy riding boots. As he entered, Falkon found his father sitting upon the throne, nursing his neck. King Favian had complained of headaches a lot lately, as though the weight of the crown upon his head was too much to bear.

When he saw Falkon approaching, he straightened in his seat and glared at him. His father's gray eyes marked every flaw he saw in Falkon with one simple stare. It made Falkon's palms sweat and his chest grew heavy. A part of him wanted to turn on heel and hurry back out to the courtyard. He would saddle his horse again and ride straight for the shores, taking the next ship out across the Cira Sea, never to return.

Instead, he took a deep breath and continued a slow march forward. He held important information for the king. Now was not the time for father and son squabbles. He bent the knee in a show of respect and waited for the order to rise. Instead, with his son still kneeling before him, Favian opted to chastise his appearance.

"You're a filthy mess. Have you no respect for the throne room?"

"Forgive me, my king. But I have pressing news that could not wait."

At that, Favian slipped from his throne and struggled down the dais. His father was an older man, but not one who should appear so feeble. Still, he struggled with every step and when he tapped Falkon on the shoulder to rise, his hand shook with effort.

"The dragonslayer? You found her?"

"Yes, your grace. But I don't believe we can trust this woman. She is uncouth and heralds a strange demonic eye. I implore you to reconsider aligning with such a witch."

His father laughed and poured a goblet full of wine. He didn't offer Falkon any, and he dared not help himself. His father ran a strict court. If he didn't offer, you did not indulge. Falkon wondered how his lack of hospitality would fare with Rayna. She seemed used to taking whatever she wanted.

"Did I request your counsel, boy?" Favian asked him.

"No, but given what I experienced on the road, I thought it best that…."

"I didn't seek your counsel and yet you're still speaking as though I need your advice."

Falkon closed his mouth and gazed upon the floor. His hands shook at his sides in frustration. If the old man would just listen to him for once in his life, perhaps the reign of King Favian wouldn't be so tarnished. Then the people might actually respect the king and his son rather than curse their names.

Favian drank back his wine and circled Falkon. His fine robes trailed across the floor like a peacock's plumes. He still tried to maintain the cockiness he held in his younger days, though his appearance betrayed him. The lines of age touched his face and gray hair replaced his once golden mane. Still, Favian saw himself as a god among men. Even his own son couldn't compare to his greatness. Especially not his own son.

"Very well, Falkon. What is so urgent that you track mud across my floors and insult me with the stench of riding?"

Falkon lifted his head and held a firm gaze. He knew if he wanted his father to take him seriously; he had to address him with confidence.

"The woman, Rayna, she led us into Fickle Forest where a pack of mercenaries attacked us. These mercenaries were known to her. The leader knew her name and she his."

Favian made his way back over to his throne and slumped down into it. He glared at Falkon again, as though examining both his words and the man himself. Finally, he gave his response with equal arrogance to how he walked the floor.

"Of course, she's linked with mercenaries. That's why I called for her," he explained. "I need someone with enough ruthless aggression to track and kill this beast before it becomes a problem."

"Forgive me, father, but won't pestering the dragon cause it to come down from the mountains? Surely the presence of the guards already angered it. Why not let sleeping dragons lay?"

"You really are a fool, aren't you, boy?" Favian mocked. "If you ever expect to wear this crown when I'm gone, then you should learn the art of warfare. Better to attack the enemy when they're least expecting it. How do you think I won this throne and conquered Sandhal?"

"Apologies once more, father but how is the dragon our enemy?"

Favian's hand trembled as he brought his goblet of wine to his lips. His gaze fell over Falkon's shoulder and into the recesses of his mind, where a single image repeated itself as a dark, foreboding warning.

"I have seen it. The beast will come on wings of black death. Its deadly fire shall churn the waters of the Cira Sea and leave Saltwood in a pile of ashes."

The description made Falkon shudder, but no more so than his father's blank stare as he recalled his vision. Many times, Valerios mentioned King Favian's mental stress as a warning of something deeper. Madness, he said. But Falkon would not hear of such things.

His father was a strong man, both in body and brain. Even though his advancing years decorated him with age, he still held his faculties. Falkon was sure of it. And if his father was certain of the impending doom this dragon would bring, Falkon wanted to be the one to kill it for him.

"Then let me go," he said. "I'll lead an army into the Shadowed Highlands and slay the dragon myself."

Falkon readied himself with fevered energy and awaited his father's blessing. Instead, laughter shook the throne room. Favian laughed so hard he spilled the remainder of his wine on his fine silk robes. His head flung back, almost knocking his crown to the floor, and his eyes grew wild.

"You?" he mocked. "Are you that eager to follow your brother to the grave?"

Falkon straightened up, still trying to hold himself high despite the warmth of tears filling his eyes.

"I am not my brother."

Favian's tone grew serious. "I know. Everytime I see you I'm reminded of that fact. Now bring me the dragonslayer."

His quest to stay strong in the face of his father's cruelty failed once again. Shoulders slumped, and with the rush of excitement dissipated, Falkon began his slow trek out of the throne room to seek the slayer once more.

# 9
# Salty Dog

A parade of patrons regaled her as Rayna entered the town of Sandhal. Since her growing fame as a slayer of dragons she dealt with admiration often. The pawing of unfamiliar hands upon her skin never felt any less awkward.

She smiled and waved as she imagined royals must do when they're greeting a throng of followers. But her royal escort abandoned them the moment they pushed through the gates.

Captain Falkon forced his horse through the crowd and headed up towards the castle taking most of the guardsmen with him. Rayna wondered if he trampled over any of the townspeople as he moved with such haste. His departure left her in the company of Valerios and that suited her just fine.

"They adore you," he said as they passed through the

crowd.

"I don't know why," she admitted. "I'm cut from the same cloth they are."

"No, Rayna. You are something special indeed."

"Are you trying to make me blush, sir?"

"Not at all but I'm pleased to know you still can."

His smile was effortless, and it put Rayna at ease. Still, at the back of her mind she held onto the very strange reason they brought her to Sandhal. Before she ever set foot out towards another dragon, their king needed to provide more answers. But first a drink.

Slipping from Valerios' side Rayna pushed through the crowd until she found the local tavern. She heard Valerios calling after her but ignored him. A chaperone she didn't need. He caught up with her at the door to the pub and tried to dissuade her from entering.

"Your presence is requested up at the castle."

"I'll need a drink before I speak with your king."

"I'm certain they'll have many libations to suit your liking."

"In my experience the wine is always too sweet and the beer too bland," she told him. "The local establishments carry better spirits than royal houses."

Valerios could say nothing more to pull her from what she wanted. They were meant to keep her happy, and she meant to keep the king waiting. Showing up inside his royal halls at his immediate call would signify that her interest in the cause consumed her. Even though that was true, she didn't need to let on that fact to them. So, she would drink, and she would eat, and the king would wait to have an audience with her as she spoke with his constituents first.

Rayna hadn't lied to Valerios. She preferred the commoner's touch when it came to refreshment. They took pride in their craft and brewed their ale and mead with love. The perfumed masses stuffed into the kitchens of castles mixed too much shit into their intoxicants. That approach meant to please a very aristocratic tongue. Such refinement lost all sense of satisfaction for those who truly knew their drinking.

The establishment she chose to occupy held a distinct charm to it. Unlike Talos' Tavern which was rough around the edges with worn-out seating and patrons alike, The Salted Inn held a warmth to it. In fact, what little she experienced of Sandhal so far offered the same welcoming warmth.

Somehow, Rayna expected towns lorded over by royal pricks to be as cold as they were. Perhaps she would find King Favian to be a delightful man to deal with unlike his son.

With Valerios on her heels like a mongrel dog, Rayna made her way to the bar. It stood center of the room in a circular pattern that allowed many diners to occupy the space. Usually Rayna would post up at the back of the room to keep watch on her surroundings. This time she wanted to ingratiate herself within the townsfolk and see about unearthing secrets about this King Favian. She couldn't do that with Valerios sniffing about so she chose a single empty seat at the bar. Knowing he held enough authority in town to dismiss the diners next to her, she forced her hand as the king's invited guest.

"Be a good man and report back to your king that I apologize for my delay but I shall be there within the hour."

She imparted her words to Valerios with a stone jaw and an icy stare to which he took her true meaning. Time alone to relax and reflect before a new quest called her back onto the road.

"Right away," he said with a nod.

She caught his hand before he departed. "But Valerios, don't go too far away."

His easy smile curved his beard high upon his cheeks. Rayna offered back her own to keep his favor. Once he left for the castle, she turned her attentions to the townsfolk. Now is when her famous name would garner a wealth of useful information.

First up to collect from would be the barkeep. Every barkeep she ever spoke with held more knowledge than a seer and was far more accurate as well.

"Ale, please, my good man," she called. "My throat is dry as sand and I need something cold to quench it."

The barkeep turned to greet her and, to Rayna's surprise, was a woman. She was stocky, with a full face and a tangle of red hair wrapped atop her head.

"Apologies, my good woman," Rayna corrected.

"No apology needed, dear," the woman responded. "Isn't the first time I've been mistaken for a man and won't be the last. But with the size of your arms, I'm willing to bet you get the same confusion from time to time."

Rayna laughed. "Not often, but it has happened."

"Do you take offense?"

"Sometimes I take them to bed and show them how wrong they are."

The barkeep laughed deep from her belly, to which Rayna smiled. She leaned across the bar and introduced herself, intent on keeping the woman talking.

"I'm Rayna."

The woman took her hand and held it firm while her mind sought the reason for familiarity. Then it struck her and she smiled.

"Ah, the dragonslayer."

"That's what they call me."

"They call me Conchata. What're you drinking Rayna?"

"Depends. What's this place known for?"

Passing the decision to the owner of the establishment always got them excited. Their eyes grew big as they discussed a passion for cooking or concocting new spirits. It allowed Rayna to steer the conversation by pretending to show interest in their work.

Conchata didn't hold the same enthusiasm for her dining options. She rattled off what the regulars deemed as their favorites. To her, it was just food and drink with a heavy dose of salt.

"Salted pork. Salted deer meat. Even salted rims around our cups to make the liquor go down quicker. That's sort of our theme," she explained.

"I noted the salt theme laced throughout town."

"That's King Favian's influence. When he conquered these lands, he brought with him the seafarer's ways. Even cut a path out towards the Cira Sea where his ships are docked. Not that he ever uses them. These days they just sit in port rusting to ruin."

Rayna took in the information with nary an upward glance. Then she ordered food and drink as though that had been her primary interest all along.

Conchata poured her a fermented beverage said to be made from an agave plant. An interesting prize Favian the First brought with him when he came to these shores.

It held a unique flavor that was enhanced by the salted rim of the cup, as Conchata explained before. Rayna took a few sips before deciding against it.

As she waited for her food to cook up, she scanned the room for the next person to pull information from. A lone man sat in the corner, eating a bowl of stew and staring at the wall. Taking her cup in hand, Rayna joined the man at his table and gave him something else to stare at. Her presence surprised him, and he shifted his hand to a knife at his belt. Rayna set her cup on the table and slid it to him.

"Thirsty?"

He pushed the drink away with hardly an upward glance. Then he went back to eating his stew.

"I wouldn't drink that piss if you paid me," he told her between bites.

"It's not my favorite either. How about if I order us a couple ram's horns of mead instead? They have mead here, don't they?"

The man gave a laugh. "Young lady, I'm about twice your age. Why don't you prostitute yourself with one of these younger lads and leave me to eat?"

Rayna arched her brow in surprise. Seems she wrangled a feisty one. That just meant he had better stories to tell than the rest of the lot inside the Salted Inn.

"I'm only here for conversation, nothing more," she told him.

"Have little to say to you."

"Why is that?"

"Saw you enter with the king's councilman. If you knew what their leadership was all about, you'd turn your horse around and ride on out of here."

From the center bar, Conchata called out Rayna's order. Not willing to let go of a fish she had on the line, Rayna motioned for the food to be brought to the table.

"Over here. And bring a couple mugs of mead for my new friend and I."

Conchata hefted the heavy food platter and matching mugs onto her shoulder with ease. She was a working woman, not afraid to get her hands dirty. Rayna respected that.

Too many times she came across women just waiting to find a rich husband to take care of their needs. Many suitors were eager to conquer and tame the famous slayer of dragons. They all failed.

That type of life didn't suit Rayna's palate. She preferred adventure and exploration. An entire world still existed out there, which she had yet to explore. If only the damn dirty dragons would stop calling her back to Atharia.

"Found yourself some company, did ya Cyrus?" Conchata asked as she passed out the food.

"We're having a fine chat," Rayna answered. "Cyrus here is full of stories."

"I don't doubt that given the life he's led," Conchata told her.

Cyrus gave a grunt and finished up his stew by tipping the bowl into his mouth. He wanted every last drop of his meal. Something told Rayna it would be the last time he had a good one for awhile. She waited for Conchata to leave, then passed one mug of mead across the table.

"Now, how about you tell me why you hold such disdain for your king?"

Cyrus took the mug but didn't immediately answer her. His eyes kept falling on the platter of food. Noting his interest, Rayna pulled it closer towards her and savored a piece of the meat.

She intended to make it appear so appetizing it would draw Cyrus in deeper with interest. But once she took a taste, the amount of salt covering the deer overwhelmed her. The meat wasn't tender either. Instead, it held the consistency of leather.

Trying to remain stoic as she chewed took effort, but eventually, she got the food to go down. With a forced smile, she offered Cyrus the plate. His grime covered hand reached across and dragged slices of meat into his empty stew bowl.

"I used to work for the city. Even had a seat on the royal council. That was before Favian the First," he began. "Once that insufferable son-of-a-bitch took the throne, everything changed."

Rayna watched as Cyrus mopped up the tinge of remaining stew with the deer meat. A wise way to tenderize the meat, but the hefty taste of salt still stung her throat. She continued to give his tale the proper attention, but thwarted her new thirst by drinking back half a mugful of mead.

"His kind are foreigners to our shores," Cyrus continued. "They came with great galley ships, stopping to restock their food and drink. But in the night, Favian's forces marched on the castle. They were merciless in their attack, yet the people praised them."

"Why? Was his predecessor an evil dictator?"

"King Kullen was firm but fair."

"That's what every king says when he's imposing his will over the people. Perhaps they grew tired of it."

"Perhaps. Whatever the case, they championed this Favian as he led them to believe false promises. He whispered in the ears of those who would listen and made them yearn for better days under his rule.

Prosperous days were promised. Instead, as he took the throne, he imposed more laws, more taxes on his people. He would look down from his castle, rechristened Saltwood Stronghold and laugh. Those of us who tried to reason with his decisions were cast out into the streets, not a coin to our names."

As Rayna listened to Cyrus tell his tale, she understood. It was the same with any ruler she'd ever known. They imposed their will, took whatever they desired, and left their own people to rot. In some instances, the people revolted and tore their rulers from the castles. Either way, most cities fell to ruin, and the castles crumbled not long after.

Conchata had come by to refill their mugs and caught the last of Cyrus' words. She gave him a nudge much harder than a friendly tap, which Rayna read as a cue to be silent.

"Telling stories again?" she asked. Then to Rayna: "Gotta be wary of this one, hasn't had his head on straight for years. He tends to mix up memories."

Cyrus muttered, then tucked his nose into the mug of mead. The time for talking was over. In fact, Conchata seemed to insist on it. She motioned for Rayna to step away from the table and follow her back to the bar. As they walked, Conchata gave her own account of what had happened years before.

"Poor Cyrus has gone a little gray-minded in his time," she said. "Things weren't as bleak as he might've let on."

"What's your account of matters, then?"

"Mind you, I was just a girl at the time. But my father has recounted how Favian the First conquered Sandhal to me many times."

"Like a bedtime story?"

"Like a history lesson," Conchata's voice grew stern. "Favian and his ilk brought a new rule to the land, that's for certain. But I'd venture to say it made things more prosperous from the scarcity King Kullen's time on the throne brought."

"That might well be true for some," Rayna said. "Your family has this inn featuring the fine food and drink of

Favian's realm. Others, such as Cyrus, barely have a copper to eat a meal."

"Cyrus is fine. We let him stay so long as he keeps out of trouble. Speaking of coppers, maybe it's time you pay up and be on your way."

Obviously, Rayna pushed the limits of what could be discussed in the capital city. She intended to let it alone until a group of men began harassing Cyrus over his words.

Four of them pushed and cursed the old man. He did his best to ignore them, which only seemed to increase their anger. It was when they pulled him from his booth towards the door that Rayna intervened.

The men dragged Cyrus outside the Salted Inn intending to beat him. As one of the four reared back with a club, Rayna stepped in. She caught his arm before the club smashed poor Cyrus in the head.

Only now, as she stood nose-to-nose with the man, did she realize they were the same guards she traveled with from Theopilous. It was too late for that to matter. She was already in the thick of things. Besides, no one was going to beat a helpless old man in her presence.

Twisting her body, she flipped the soldier overhead and sent him crashing into two of the others. As the fourth came towards her, it was Cyrus who took action. He extended his leg and tripped the soldier as he ran.

With all four guards nose first in the dirt, Rayna took a

minute to help Cyrus to his feet. He thanked her, and she motioned for him to leave the area. This fight was far from over, but it belonged to her now.

A crowd gathered in the street watching the action. Rayna didn't intend to cause trouble, it just seemed to follow her wherever she went. But she knew if she let this go any further, word would travel back to the king and their business arrangement squashed.

She needed to learn what King Favian knew about this dragon sighting. It could also hurt Valerios if Rayna got into a brawl when he was meant to be watching after her.

So, she went a different route to remedy the situation and opted to broker peace.

"Gentlemen, I am a guest of your king… you know this. What say we all put up our arms and go back inside for a drink? Or would you rather test your might against mine?"

Rayna tapped the broadsword hanging from her hip. Then she moved her hand to the leather eyepatch and peeled it back. The soldiers knew what she could do once her dragoneye met the sword's blade. Each of them tucked away their weapons and agreed to go back inside The Salted Inn. Rayna expelled a breath of relief and followed close behind them.

# 10⊕

# Messenger Messiah

Valerios didn't feel comfortable leaving Rayna behind, but by now he knew better than to argue with her. Besides, how much trouble could she find at the Salted Inn?

The worst she would run into there is if she tried the deer meat specialty. Valerios enjoyed little of the local cuisine since returning from his travels to Ischon across the sea. There they knew how to stimulate a palate. Since returning home, Valerios realized everything smelled like wet dog. It made him miss Ischon terribly, among other reasons.

The more immediate problem was locating Falkon. Since he disappeared from the square, Valerios worried his fit of rage might make him do something foolish. He knew how much the adoration of the people meant to Falkon. Seeing them regale Rayna as she rode in must've felt like a spur under the saddle.

Valerios left his horse tied up in the courtyard rather than riding to the stables. He hoped to find Falkon swiftly and then return to Rayna. His urge to rush back to her lay not in keeping her safe. The gods above knew of all women that one could take care of herself. His was a yearning to be near her again, to feel the energy radiating off her lean, muscular body and take in her scent.

This realization made Valerios chastise himself for such weakness. He was only meant to be there to follow orders and do his duty, nothing more. On this, he already failed. Falkon told him to stay with the woman, but here he stood without her.

Shuffling through the courtyard, he found his feet didn't want to move. They spent many days in the saddle to and from Theopilous with little rest or recovery. Truth be told, he would've preferred to stay at the Salted Inn and grab a proper drink of his own. With the quest that stood in front of them, he wondered if this would be the last time his boots touched the earth of his adopted home.

Familiar faces greeted him as he made his way up to the tower of Cragstone Keep where the soldiers' sleeping quarters were held. To most of them he gave a courtesy wave and continued on his way. But when the scholars passed, Valerios had to fight the urge to tell his brothers what he learned about Rayna.

Instead, he gripped hands with each of them and kept moving. They would no doubt learn of the dragonslayer and her mighty gifts in time.

He took the stone steps that wound around Cragstone two at a time. At the top, the entry split into sections that marked the men's sleeping quarters. Further down, he would find Falkon's private chambers and hopefully Falkon himself. As he moved with haste down the hall, he heard a voice call to him from below.

Recognizing the voice as that of his king, Valerios stopped in his step and looked down to greet him. King Favian stood at the bottom of the wooden steps that led deep into the castle. As he saw Valerios catch his eye, he motioned for him to come down.

Valerios looked to the door that led to Falkon's room just paces away. He almost made it safely inside, but now the king's command could not be ignored. Turning on heel, he made his way down the large staircase. At the bottom, he gave a bow to his king. Favian waved his hand and motioned for Valerios to rise. Then he chastised him for actions he deemed disrespectful.

"You're in such a rush to see my son, yet you have no time to greet your king?"

"Apologies, your Grace. I sought Captain Falkon for an urgent matter, though I should have an audience with you as well."

"You should always come to me first, Valerios."

"Of course. My apologies."

"Stop apologizing and tell me of this matter you mean to discuss. Does it involve the dragonslayer?""

King Favian waved his hand and motioned for Valerios to follow him as he lumbered back towards the throne room. His worn and withered body no longer had the strong shoulders to carry his heavy robes. As such, they dragged over the stone floor, fraying the ends to slivers.

Valerios found himself unable to speak as he watched the once mighty king muddle his way into his massive throne. He looked small and frail within the enormity of the gilded throne. Once a symbol of his power, it now seemed more like his prison.

Favian's gray eyes stared down at Valerios, awaiting his report. Within his gaze Valerios still could not discern if madness settled there. One thing that could not be missed with his advancing age is the lack of patience he now had.

Valerios often wondered if he would share the same urgency of things when his sand thinned at the top of the hourglass. For now, he preferred to savor in all things life offered. One couldn't take treasures to the next life, but perhaps memories would hold true.

"Speak!" King Favian demanded.

"Yes, I bring word of the dragonslayer," Valerios began. "She sends apologies for her delay, but shall arrive within the hour."

Suddenly, as though several years had sloughed off his back, King Favian hopped from the throne. He moved surprisingly fast and clutched Valerios' arms with a grip that pinched the skin. Now just inches away from King Favian's face, Valerios could see something strange and sinister danced behind his eyes. As he spoke, flecks of indigo laced throughout his gray orbs like lightning. A true excitement filled his words.

"You've seen her? Spoken to her?"

Valerios could only nod in response as the king's excitement grew.

"Where is she? Why is she not here now?"

"She stopped at the Salted Inn. The people seemed quite taken with her and she wanted to be gracious with her time."

Valerios tried to explain Rayna's absence in a way that made her sound diplomatic. In truth, he didn't understand her interest in carousing with the locals when more important matters presented themselves.

"The people? Why should their opinion on things matter?" King Favian asked in disgust.

Valerios shrugged. "Is that not the manner of ruling?"

To this, King Favian spat on the ground.

"I thought you were the smart one, but it appears you have more to learn than even my gentle son."

During his time of scholarly study, Valerios learned

many ways in which kings ruled their countries. Some commanded with wisdom and others with crushing strength. There were lessons in all approaches.

King Favian's rule centered on himself and strengthening his house for years to come. Even as his own body gave out, he continued to focus on building his empire.

"Go find the dragonslayer and bring her back here."

At King Favian's command, Valerios bowed and made his exit. He could hear the king behind in a fit of coughing. The sound echoed off the walls of the empty throne room like a death rattle.

# 11
# Little Treats

Falkon could hear his father's phlegm-filled coughs echoing the grand halls below his chambers. He hoped one day his father would be taken by those coughs. Then Falkon could rule the kingdom in a manner which he saw fit.

Or, more likely, he would abandon his crown and return to the waters where he truly felt at peace. Why suffer the same grim fate his father endured just to call himself king? Those noble pursuits were meant for someone bred to rule, like his brother Fenton.

Thoughts of his older brother drew him to the drink. Falkon already began indulging in his private stash after the unsettling interaction with his father. Now he sat shirtless upon his bed, wallowing in whiskey like a town drunk.

He meant to dress in more appropriate attire and then

present Rayna to his father like the prize he thought her to be. But once the demons of regret began plaguing his mind, nothing except increased drinking would quiet them.

Once or twice he tried to stand and kick off his muddy boots, but his balance betrayed him. He stumbled back upon the bed and abandon the thought of dressing in favor of more drinking. Soon, he no longer cared about the dragon woman, his father, or anything, really. Only the crisp drink upon his lips mattered.

As his mind grew fuzzy, Falkon thought he saw a shape standing in the corner. Perhaps a phantom, perhaps a dream, or maybe nothing at all. He called out to the dark shadow, hoping in his soul his brother's voice would respond from it. Looking again, Falkon saw nothing but the empty corner of his room. The shape, however, didn't dissipate entirely.

At his back, Falkon felt the weight of another crease his bed. Soon hands touched his skin and massaged his shoulders. He leaned back as the pleasure of it aroused him. The hands ran over his bare chest, caressed his belly and then his cock. Recognizing the touch now, he relaxed deeper into it. Each stroke pulled from him the weight of disappointment and despair.

"I've missed you, my darling," he whispered.

"And I you."

As she spoke, the rest of her body became form beneath

him. His beautiful Xara came to him at last. She cradled his head in her lap, stroking his hair with one hand and his shaft with the other. Falkon reached back and squeezed her soft bottom as she played with him.

"You were gone much longer than you told me you would be," she said, her voice a whisper in the air. "Did you bring her back? The warrior woman?"

Falkon looked up at her to gauge her disappointment. He hated disappointing her. She was the only thing in this world that meant anything to him now. The curls of her black hair tickled his nose as she leaned over him, still awaiting his answer.

"Yes, I found the dragonslayer and brought her back."

"Is she mighty?"

"Indeed."

"Is she pretty?"

"I suppose she is."

A frown covered Xara's thin lips. "Do you like her better than me?"

The subtle hurt in her sweet voice stung his heart like a thousand arrows. He shifted over and drew her into an embrace.

"My darling, Xara, you know I only covet you and no other."

Xara giggled and in an instant, she disappeared from his grasp, causing Falkon to fall nose first into the bed. When he looked up, he saw her standing by the window.

The sunlight at her back bathed her in glowing light, yet no shadow spread across the floor. Falkon never questioned such things. He didn't care where she came from, or what magic she possessed in her body, only that her body remained his.

He hopped from the bed and rushed to claim her. As he wrapped his arms around her, she disappeared again, only to reappear on the bed. Her naked body beckoned him with full breasts and long, smooth legs. Slipping out of his breeches, he crawled on top of her.

"I've waited so long to feel you again."

"I'm all yours, darling. Always. So long as you continue to heed my wishes."

In his rush to press himself inside of Xara he did not fully discern what she said to him. He dismissed it as the ramblings of a woman in love. That's what they were to each other, lovers. Falkon knew that from the first moment she appeared to him. Since that time, all he wanted was to taste her, feel her, and let her body envelope him in ecstasy.

# 12
# Fevered Dreams

The blood on King Favian's hand was a fresh addition to his growing black lung.

Unimpressed, he wiped it away on the flow of his robe and tried again to draw a full breath.

So heavy his chest felt. Such malaise in his body. Nothing seemed to break-up the sickness and now what dreams may come with it? His were wasted days and sleepless nights filled with dragon fire. Somehow, he knew that to quell the dreams and his malaise; he needed to seek the dark dragon. For that, he needed the dragonslayer. The voices in his head told him so. And the woman dares insult his royal wishes by getting drunk at the inn?

He had a good mind to march his men down into Sandhal Square and have them root her out. Then he would condemn the Salted Inn by royal decree. The thought of such actions brought a smile to his worn face. His happiness only lasted a moment before another coughing fit doubled him over on the throne.

His coughs brought the servant girls running in to aid him, as they often did. He waved them out of the room, this time throwing his goblet after them as well. It clattered across the floor, spilling red wine everywhere. As Favian looked upon it, he saw blood rather than wine. The image frightened him, and he shrank back into the comfort of his throne.

Shuddering under the weight of worry, he suddenly felt a soft touch at his temples. Delicate fingers ran over his forehead and cheeks, relaxing him with subtle pressure. Favian reached up and took hold of the hand in his own.

"Where have you been, Xara?" he asked, his voice quavering. "I'm falling apart in my own throne room."

"Calm yourself, good king," Xara responded. "I had another matter to tend to. Perhaps if there were more of me to go around."

At her words, another woman appeared at the foot of the throne. This one had a darker complexion than Xara but same beauty. She slithered up onto Favian's lap and set her hand to his chest.

The moment she made contact, he felt his lungs expand with air. Full, unrestricted breaths were his once more. Xara leaned over his shoulder and pressed her lips to his cheek. Her dark curly hair mingled with the white of his beard. The luminosity of her skin was a complete contrast to his weathered, sun-darkened face.

"Xiomara is now duty-bound to you, as am I," she told him. "Whatever you desire is yours, good king."

King Favian felt a tear roll down his cheek as his health returned to him.

"You are sirens sent by the Goddess of Water to honor me," he wept.

As the women continued massaging Favian, he felt more and more at ease. Xara came to him a fortnight before bringing him comfort from his unsettling dreams and the malaise that followed. Now, Xiomara held the same special touch but also the same inquiry.

"Where is the dragonslayer?"

King Favian's eyes opened slowly.

"She is on her way."

He knew the importance of the dragonslayer. It was foretold within his dreams that she would come. When he related his visions to Xara, she confirmed it. She could foresee what Rayna would mean to the kingdom and called upon her special gifts to seek her location.

It was then that Favian dispatched his men to Theopilous, his own son at the lead. Theirs was a quest that needed completion, no matter the cost.

"The days grow shorter, good king," Xara told him. "The dragon will come on the night sky. You must cut off his wings before the kingdom burns."

With his strength returned to him, King Favian felt

renewed vigor. He stood from the throne and raised his fist in the air, remembering the feeling of steel within his grip. His line of victories was not easily counted, and he intended to add one more to his name.

"Yes, the dragon shall fall!"

As he turned on heel to propose victory again, he saw the servant girl staring at him from the hall.

"Were you calling for me, your Grace?" she asked.

"No, fool girl, I'm talking to them."

As Favian turned to point out Xara and Xiomara, they were no longer there. His throne stood empty, not another soul visible in the room.

"Talking to who?"

Peculiar how two women could vanish from sight without a trace of their presence. He rubbed his eyes and looked again, only to find the same empty throne.

The women weren't there. Rather than press the issue, he simply disregarded the servant girl's question and instead passed down commands.

"Make certain the sleeping quarters for our intended guest are well stocked with womanly needs. And have a bath drawn for her too."

The girl nodded and went to carry out her orders. Things were on the move, just as Xara had foretold. Now all King Favian needed was to get the dragonslayer to the castle.

# 13
# Rebel Heart

The longer Rayna waited the more eyes fell on her. After the dust up with the soldiers, the town seemed to turn on her with a shared disgust. She didn't know how long she could keep the peace.

To ease the growing tensions, Rayna ordered a round of the Salted Inn's finest mead for all who dined there. Conchata and her staff were happy to indulge the request though Rayna knew she was growing impatient with the dragonslayer as well.

The more Rayna ordered, the higher her tab became which any tavern owner or innkeeper would meticulously keep track of. But Rayna realized awhile back she no longer had any coins to pay her fare.

Her lot went to Jagger to save the heads of Captain Falkon and his foolish men, some of whom drank with her now. Rayna would need to wait for Valerios to fetch her and make good on her promise of payment.

She hated having to wait for help. Her ability to take care of herself started when she was a very young girl. Any trouble she found herself in she could resolve on her own. But when it came to mastering coin it wasn't her strongest asset.

More often than not, her name garnered her gifts from food to drink to bedding. In Sandhal, they regaled her arrival but were quick to turn against her.

Half of them thought she came to liberate them from the tyrant King Favian. The other half thought she posed a threat to their good king. It seemed the people in Sandhal were a mixed-up lot.

Sitting at the bar with another drink in hand she watched the crowd with her uncovered eye. After plying them with round after round of mead they started to grow more jovial than before. Scowls were lifted and replaced with song. A lively tune started at one table and spread to the next and so on. Soon, the entire inn was singing in merriment. That is when Valerios finally returned.

A look of bewilderment crossed his face as he stepped inside and saw the display. Some of the townsfolk insisted he join them in song to which he politely declined.

Pushing through the swaying bodies he located Rayna

at the bar. She smiled at his approach and decided to have a little fun with him. He was too handsome to be so serious all the time.

"I think you should sing with them," she told him. "It would win you favor."

"No, believe me it wouldn't," he replied. "My singing voice is rougher than the sands of the Red Waste."

"C'mon, let me hear it and I'll be the judge."

"How much have you had to drink?" he asked, ignoring her request.

"Just the one."

She tipped her drink towards him to show it still full to the brim. He raised his eyebrows in surprise.

"I prefer to keep my wits sharp in unknown surroundings," she told him. Then she let her voice fall into a whisper. "Besides, I was wrong. The local food and drink here are not appeasing."

"There's a veritable feast awaiting you back at Saltwood Stronghold and your presence is requested." He held his arm out for her. "Shall we go?"

"Yes, we can go now. But first you need to pay my good lady Conchata her fee."

"What's this?" he asked.

"It seems I gave the last of my coin to Jagger in the Fickle Forest incident," she explained. "So, I told Conchata as his royal highness' guest that the king would be good enough to cover my expenses here. She didn't believe me at first but when I mentioned your name she softened. It seems they call you Valerios the Valiant around here."

Speaking on his honor caused Valerios to acquiesce. He took a small pouch from his belt and pulled out a handful of coppers.

"How much is owed?"

Rayna swiped the coins from his hand and set them atop the bar.

"That'll do."

Valerios reached out to retrieve them until he noticed Conchata make her way over. She saw the payment in excess on the bar top and smiled wide.

"Thank you, good sir."

Valerios looked to Rayna then back to Conchata and offered up his own smile.

"My pleasure. Thank you for taking such good care of our esteemed guest."

"She's a handful that one," Conchata admitted. "But bring her back by anytime. Rayna, I've truly enjoyed meeting you."

"I as well."

Rayna reached across the bar and clutched hands with her. A tender heart rested beneath the calloused hands and it endeared her to Rayna. As she exited the inn with Valerios, he felt compelled to ask what went on while he was away.

"What type of trouble did you get into?"

"Why do you assume I'm a woman of trouble?"

"A woman such as you wouldn't have it any other way."

"Well, you should've seen your face when I had you depart with your coins," she laughed. "You royals are too tied up in riches and reward. Experiences should be your goal in life not gathering up more profit and baubles than the next man."

He shook his head. "You forget, I'm not a royal. I came from simple beginnings and I still prefer to keep it that way."

"Perhaps I misjudged you then."

"And I admit to misjudging you as well."

Their horses were brought round by the stable hand. Mounting up, Valerios took the lead towards Saltwood Stronghold. Rayna learned just enough information during her time inside the Salted Inn that she was now ready to meet King Favian.

Should he have trickery in store for her she would be ready for him. But if the dragon they spoke of was real, then her song remained the same as it always was. Every last dragon needed to be eradicated.

# 14
# Royal Greeting

Her travels kept Rayna mostly on the outskirts of towns in the fields and forests as she tracked her prey. The longest she stayed with royals was a fortnight when she carried out an ill-advised affair with a member of the court in Kartha. That house was small in size and in name, centered just past the coast of Valeuki.

What she saw as they crested the hill towards Saltwood Stronghold was grand in design. Eight rounded towers stood watch over everything below them like guardians of the realm. Small walking bridges connected each tower to low walls which traveled to the main house. Crenelations meant for archers and artillery were scattered across those walls. The untrained observer would never see them at first look as the eye went to the stylish windows instead.

The king knew his defenses well. That was made even more evident by the hot oil pots which hung over a great gate with massive metal doors. The Stronghold was well guarded but as with anything that seemed indestructible one only need learn its secrets. Rayna knew for certain a man the likes of King Favian would've insisted on secret passages lined throughout the castle grounds. An idea taken from his predecessor King Kullen no doubt.

Once through the mighty gate they dismounted, and Valerios walked her through the gardens. Even as Saltwood Stronghold started to show wear in its face, the gardens remained well kept. Fresh flowers bloomed in an array of colors making an otherwise plain field appear magical. She bent and took in the sweetness of their fragrance.

"Quite a difference from the aroma that filled Theopilous," Valerios said in jest.

"Ah, those are the smells of life," Rayna corrected him. "But this is quite a spectacle."

"I take it you're not impressed."

"I don't impress easily," she told him. "So, if your king expects me to fawn over him, he is mistaken."

"I don't think he expects that."

"Let's go find out, shall we?"

As Valerios led her towards the main hall, they were stopped by Captain Falkon. He lumbered down the stairs with a twisted look upon his face. As he drew closer, Rayna realized the captain was drunk.

His clothes were disheveled, and his hair in disarray but he seemed unusually joyful. Perhaps he was a jolly drunk. It gave Rayna amusement but Valerios grew tense at his approach.

"Nevermind, Valerios, I'll walk our guest to father," Falkon stammered.

"I don't think that's a good idea," Valerios told him.

"Nobody cares what you think. Did you ask him of his thoughts, dragonslayer?"

As Falkon addressed her, she could see his agitation flaring. If he walked her to the king, it would create a mess of things that she didn't have time for. So, as Valerios struggled to keep Falkon from falling over, Rayna took matters into her own hands.

With a quick step forward, she wrapped her forearm around Falkon's neck compressing the vital nerves that lay there. In an instant he fell unconscious into Valerios waiting arms.

"What did you just do?" he asked in shock.

"I restricted the blood flow to the brain momentarily. The drop in pressure rendered Captain Falkon incapacitated," Rayna explained.

"That could be considered an attack on the captain of the guards… the king's own son!"

"Well, isn't it lucky that nobody saw what happened?"

She eyed Valerios waiting to see how far his sense of

following the rules went. Beneath her dark patch she could feel the dragoneye twisting as it awaited its release. Since her travels abroad, Rayna had become more consistent with wearing her patch even at the behest of her eye. But even with one eye covered she could see Valerios having a difficult time deciding his next move. So, she decided it for him.

"Take Captain Falkon back to his chambers and let him sleep it off," she said. "It wouldn't do to have him sputtering around the castle in his shape. When he wakes, he should think this mishap all a dream."

"What about the king? You are to have an audience with him," Valerios argued.

"I'm a grown woman. I can find my own way to the king."

At her words, she caught Valerios look over her body. To this she stored a secret smile but outwardly she remained stoic and insistent.

"I should like to have a private audience with King Favian anyway. Now go do as I ask. I'll tell the king I evaded you purposely so you won't be punished for not escorting me in."

Valerios hefted Captain Falkon's dead weight in his arms and started on the move. He left Rayna with words she found peculiar but she did not dismiss them.

"Be careful," he told her.

The warning gave her pause and once she stood alone

in the corridor she took a moment to adjust her weapons. They may ask her to relinquish her sword as a courtesy. If so, she still wanted to remain prepared for battle. She moved the hidden dagger at her back to the front of her leather skirt. The hilt rested against her firm belly while the blade sat uncomfortably against her womanhood. Better to endure a minor discomfort than have a guard find the blade.

She walked with a slow, measured tread through a short passage and into the great hall. It was a beast of a room three times as long as it was wide. Elaborate decorations framed the walls and windows high overhead.

Deeper within the hall, Rayna found a fireplace large enough to step inside. The embers were cold and looked to have been that way for quite some time. An overmantle with stone carvings showcased King Favian's coat of arms, dual flying fish. Not a frightening sigil but he seemed to have an infatuation with keeping his seafaring ways in memory.

Rayna stopped to study the fireplace noting the breadth and depth of it. Surely, this was an entryway into a passage that wound up beneath the castle. A hidden means of escape should the Stronghold fall to siege.

At the other end of the hall she heard a low voice call out to her. She continued her trek to find a dais where a top table sat. Behind it the king waited to receive her.

His appearance threw her. Under the bejeweled robe and lavish crown, he looked haggard by age and maybe even disease. This wasn't the same Favian the First she heard stories about. Those tales heralded him as a mighty conqueror with hair the color of coal and a thick beard to match. In those days he stood well over six feet with a barrel chest. Massive arms swung a double-axe as though it weighed little more than a stick.

Perhaps the tales of Favian the First were as embellished as Rayna's own. She knew stories of her battles with the dragons had grown into legends. Most of what they said about her wasn't true. They knew little fact about her dealings with the dragons or how she almost didn't make it out alive on the first attempt. She still wore the scar across her hip to remember that day well into her graying years.

Seeing King Favian slumped in his chair, she wondered what scars he carried on body and mind which left him in such a wounded state. She stopped paces away from the dais and gave him a simple nod. There would be no bowing and certainly no curtsy. This was not her king. She followed no man's rule.

Curiously, she saw no guards posted nearby. No chambermaids waited on him either. King Favian sat alone in the great hall with nothing but his memories of war to bide his time.

To Rayna's surprise, Favian stood with ease. His worn-out appearance did not seem to hamper his movement as she thought it might. Now she wondered if the lack of guardsmen meant he didn't need them for defense. Perhaps King Favian only looked feeble but still held the wit and skill needed to remain a threat.

He peered over at her from his perch. Looking down upon his guests from up high must give him a sense of power. Rayna didn't like heights. Any time spent climbing sent her head into a spin and her chest constricted with an irrational fear. She preferred to keep her boots close to the ground.

"You're the one they say slayed a thousand dragons."

Rayna smirked. "No wonder I'm so tired."

The king frowned in dismay. He seemed as humorless as his son. Rayna didn't want the meeting to crumble into headbutting so she gave a more suitable response.

"At last count it was no more than five."

"Still, a memorable feat especially for a young woman. Even one as clearly able-bodied as you."

"Thank you."

The king struggled down the small steps on the dais and came to face Rayna. As he grew closer, she took in a hint of a scent she'd only encountered one other time. It was ancient and made her shudder in remembrance of the wearer.

He was a magic user invested in the dark arts. His

misuse of it swallowed him whole in a blue flame and turned him to ash before Rayna's very eyes. King Favian carried this same scent, though more subtle in nature. He noticed her discomfort and mistook it as a look of fear.

"No need to be frightened, dear girl."

She turned to face him then and let him know his presence did not impress her. Only now did he notice the dark patch upon her eye and it caused him alarm.

His lips quivered as though he spoke to an invisible source. Rayna felt a chill run over her as she watched his strange movements. The coldness grew so deep within the marrow of her bones she wished to spark up the massive fireplace and lay beside it for warmth.

Both king and his requested guest circled each other like animals assessing the interest of the other party. King Favian stopped studying her and gave a nod of approval.

"You are a fine specimen indeed, swordmistress Rayna. Do you know why I called you here to Saltwood Stronghold?"

"Captain Falkon informed me that you have a dragon in your kingdom and you wish me to kill it," Rayna replied. "But there's a problem with that King Favian."

"You have a problem with killing dragons?"

"Of course not. I have a problem with their being any dragons left to kill. The last one fell to my blade well over a year ago. So, before I offer my services to you, I want to know how you've come by your information. Where did you see this dragon?"

To her chagrin he didn't honor her with an answer. Instead, the king clapped his hands together and called forth food and drink. Rayna stiffened as the servants and staff began filling the room. She had hoped this king wouldn't fill their meeting with fanfare and spectacle.

To her, the sighting of a dragon in the skies or on the cliffs should be treated with urgency. King Favian seemed to think it meant having a party. That notion came back around to Rayna's bloated legend. His toast told her as much.

"A salute to you, Rayna. Champion slayer of beasts."

He handed her a goblet of wine that smelled more pungent than the flowers lining the gardens. She set it aside and tried to compel the king to give her the information she sought.

"No need to salute me," she told him. "I haven't taken up your quest yet."

"I have no doubt that you will. That is why you are here. It's been foreseen."

"By whom?" she asked, the discomfort returning to her.

The king motioned for her to sit at one of the long dining tables to which she hesitantly obliged. Then he offered a plate of food which she ignored.

Something within the castle walls did not sit well with her. It felt as though another presence watched over them as they spoke. She wondered if spirits of the dead wandered the halls. Perhaps certain members of King Kullen's rule did not realize their house had fallen.

King Favian received another full goblet of wine before relating to Rayna the details she longed to hear.

"I have not slept well for many days, my dear," he began. "Every night I fear closing my eyes for I know what awaits me."

His story wasn't meant for theatrics. He didn't script it on parchment or retain it to memory to tell in the taverns for a copper. King Favian's story came from a place of fear.

The pictures he saw in his mind during the night frightened him so that they etched themselves in his memory. His hair turned shock white and his body twisted in terror as the dragon came calling for him.

"Great leather wings the size of a mariner's sails. Dark scales lining its massive frame. A row of teeth, each as large as your broadsword."

King Favian paused in his description to drink down his wine and fetch another goblet full. Rayna didn't move a muscle. She simply sat still and digested the information as it came to her.

"The flames," he began again. "Dragon's breath covering all of Sandhal… and beyond!"

Rayna felt her nails grip into the wood of the table. Her leg twitched with nervous energy and her dragoneye burned with the need to be released. But even still, she waited quietly for Favian to conclude his tale.

"I've never seen such power wielded by anything other than a catapult," he admitted, his shoulders slumping over in defeat. "It will come and it will kill us all unless you can stop it."

Her thoughts betrayed her. Peculiar the circumstances surrounding their meeting. No guards, no royal council, and yet King Favian felt secure enough to break bread with a known slayer. Rayna knew her name carried substantial weight all throughout Atharia and beyond, but how the king came to call on her remained unclear.

For Rayna such minor details no longer mattered. King Favian's depiction of the great dragon is all she needed to hear. This was no imaginary foe dreamed up as a tavern tale to scare the locals. Nor did it seem a ploy to lure the dragonslayer into his employ for an abhorrent quest.

The dragon King Favian detailed is one Rayna sought for a lifetime. A dragon made of magic; the source of all dragons since the age of man. All across Atharia she tried to uncover its trail. After more than five years with nothing to show her otherwise, she finally lamented that it did not exist and gave up her search.

Such a fool she was to step away from her calling then. Traveling, smoking and fornicating did not fill the empty void inside her. Only killing the legendary beast would fulfill that need.

Rayna disliked magic even more so than heights. If she could not understand how a thing came to be, she couldn't surmise a way to kill it. The dark dragon presented this dilemma. Her sword of fire had never failed her in battle before but the challenge was different now.

A pure flame against magical dragon's breath may not bode well. She needed an alternative strategy rather than her usual approach. For that, she would need an army. Sitting in front of her, awaiting her response, was the man capable of giving her what she needed.

"I can stop it, King Favian. But, alongside my usual fee I shall require supplies, arms, and a group of your best men to flank me. Is this favorable to you?"

"My house is at your service. Whatever you wish you need only ask. In fact, we have set-up a private chamber for your sleeping quarters supplied with the finest of items to appease your every desire."

Truth be told, Rayna would've gone after the dark dragon whether or not Favian agreed to terms. Even the hefty fee she expected to claim for this service no longer mattered to her.

Seeking and destroying the dark dragon was personal. Still, having the backing of a king would prove useful in this quest. And before the day ended, she would have one last request.

# 15
# Foolishness of Men

V alerios attempted to carry Falkon over his shoulders, but the weight of him proved too much while climbing the winding stairs. Halfway to the top, Valerios' back gave out, and he was forced to switch positions. He cupped Falkon under the arms and dragged his body the rest of the way. His heavy boots slapped off the side of each step, causing an exceptional thud in their wake.

The noise brought soldiers from their quarters to inquire as to the source. When they caught sight of their captain's unfortunate situation, Valerios barked at them to return to their quarters. He didn't want Falkon to endure more embarrassment. If he knew the disrespect his own men showed when they spoke of him, Falkon may have all their heads.

He'd already dispatched many good men for just looking at him sideways. It was getting too difficult to replace them. Even Valerios' travels to Ischon proved fruitless. The men on that isle took their vow to protect Emperor Kivu Kazo very seriously.

They remained loyal until their last breath. That type of respect is something Falkon didn't have from his own men and he would never earn it if he continued acting the way he did.

Valerios knew the hardships Falkon faced just by being his father's son. The ills many held towards Favian the First spilled across his bloodline regardless of the son's part in his rule.

Such unfair judgement made Valerios think of the curse Rayna endured throughout her life because of her father. But she bore the weight of her stigma with chest held high, even if she covered the mark of it with an ominous patch.

Falkon, on the other hand, let the judgments cast upon him cave in his chest and slump his shoulders. He needed a proper victory in battle to show he was a capable leader, and not just one of name and title. For now, he needed to sleep off his drunken stupor.

Entering Falkon's room proved to be another challenge. The weight of the door forced it to keep closing on Valerios as he fumbled with Falkon in his arms. With an audible grunt, he hefted Falkon up higher and then pushed the door open using his back.

They stumbled inside and fell to the floor with Valerios landing on top of Falkon. He scrambled to his feet and began apologizing until he realized Falkon remained unconscious. Taking in a deep breath, Valerios bent to retrieve Falkon once more. At his touch, Falkon woke and tried to take a swing at him. Valerios moved back just in time, but Falkon kept coming for him. Heavy intoxication slurred his words.

"I'll fight any man who looks at my Xara!"

Valerios knew none by that name, but Falkon remained adamant at protecting her. Eyes filled with rage and whiskey didn't see he attacked a friend. Valerios wasn't under the influence of anything. He only indulged in ashwa during the night. So, he could not bring himself to return blows he knew were thrown haphazardly by his good friend.

Still, he couldn't let Falkon's belligerence continue. If Falkon found his way to a blade, it would make matters much worse. Valerios hearkened back to Rayna's manner of quieting Falkon before in the corridor. He knew enough about the workings of the human body to impose the same move if he could get hold of Falkon. Valerios used the one thing that seemed to bring his good friend such grief in that moment.

"I covet your Xara. What will you do about it?"

Falkon gave out a howl that could only come from a man in love. Strange that Valerios knew nothing of this woman before this day. Falkon swung wildly with his fists and feet. Valerios avoided the clunky punches but a knee shot struck him in the groin. Had he not still been clad in his riding leathers, it would've dropped him.

The blunt blow offered enough of a sting to cause Valerios to react. He struck out and caught Falkon high on the temple with the flat of his forearm. The force of the impact spun Falkon around, giving Valerios the position he needed to attach Rayna's move.

Valerios wrapped his arms around Falkon's head and neck and gave a squeeze. It took less pressure than he expected. Falkon crumpled in his arms so swiftly he thought he killed his best friend.

He dragged Falkon over to the bed and lay him down, then took stock of his breathing. Hearing no signs of breath, he leaned in to reassess the situation and that is when Falkon spit up on him. Valerios could smell the meat-filled breakfast mingled within Falkon's retch. He wiped the mess from his face and stared down at his friend, passed out like a drunken fool.

"I'm no longer sorry I hit you."

His words were met with a grunt, and then Falkon started to snore. Valerios rolled him over on his side in case he vomited again. With luck, he would sleep off his drunk and the worst of it would be a terrible headache in the morning.

Valerios was ready for rest himself, but his work wasn't finished. Rayna must be in conversation with King Favian by now. He would hurry down and join them in Captain Falkon's place. First, he needed to clean the vomit from his shirt. It wouldn't do to smell of rotted meats and whiskey in the king's presence.

He stripped off his shirt and grabbed Falkon's water basin. Valerios would use it to clean with, then bring it back filled with fresh water. In the morning, Falkon would feel the dehydration set in and a replenishing drink is the first thing he would want.

As Valerios slipped from Falkon's room, he found himself face-to-face with King Favian. So unexpected was his presence that Valerios dropped the basin, shattering it upon the floor. He bent to retrieve the broken pieces, some of which struck the king's boots.

"Leave it," Favian demanded.

"Your Grace," Valerios said, straightening back up.

"I came to see why my son insults me with his lack of escort for the dragonslayer and behold, I catch you sneaking from his room."

King Favian's appearance had changed. The vigor returned to his voice, and he was not at all pleased. His assessment of the situation was mistaken, but Valerios couldn't tell him the truth either. If he knew his son's disappearance came from the drink, it would not go over well.

A lie then, though Valerios never could tell falsehoods that sounded convincing. But as King Favian noted the vomit-stained shirt in his hands, Valerios came up with a story he could spin.

"Captain Falkon grew very ill. Something plagued his stomach the moment we returned to the grounds. His strength to stand left him as well, so I was tending to him. I was on my way to fetch fresh water just now."

"We have servant girls for such things." Favian gave him a hard stare where flecks of indigo flashed through his eyes. "I should not have you inside my son's chambers again. Understand me?"

Valerios nodded. "It won't happen again."

"See that it doesn't. Besides, your presence is requested elsewhere."

Valerios awaited the king's commands, wondering how far away he would send him this time to keep him from Falkon. He knew King Favian didn't approve of their friendship. Valerios' fascination with study gave him a different way of looking at things. His approach to life was rubbing off on Falkon in ways that had him thinking for himself, rather than blindly following his father's rule.

This angered King Favian, so he drew up an alternate, more tawdry conclusion about their relationship. To him, such things would not be tolerated in his kingdom.

Valerios was bound by duty to follow his king's commands, but they were growing more aggressive. He felt certain he wasn't meant to return from his last trip to Ischon.

"Rayna has agreed to champion our cause and battle the dark dragon," Favian continued. "However, she has asked for a list of provisions and soldiers to back her in this quest. One man she asked for by name was you."

Valerios felt a mix of emotions course through him. He hoped that once they found the dragonslayer and brought her back to Saltwood Stronghold, his part in the journey would be over. After coming to know Rayna more, he respected her and felt honored she would ask for his company. But he was not a foolish man.

Hunting a dragon brought with it great dangers. The elite guards whom King Favian sent out before were all burned to ash without a trace of them remaining in this world. Even with the famed dragonslayer at the lead, he knew some lives would be lost. Only a foolish man didn't fear facing a dragon.

King Favian noticed his trepidation and edged closer to him. The purplish spark that laced through his eyes before seemed to take greater root. It gave his iris the look of an angry sea.

The king's strange behavior left Valerios with many questions relating to the quest to claim the dark dragon. True, visions coming to a man in the night could be from a place of prophecy. But another, darker force might also be the source of the images. How to discern which it may be eluded Valerios.

"You're a strange one, Valerios," King Favian said, looking over his bare chest with disgust. "But however strange your interests are, you will give the dragonslayer whatever she desires. She awaits you now in her private chambers. Appease her and I will forget I ever saw you coming from my son's room. Fail to make her happy, and I'll feed you to the dogs, starting with your manhood."

He knew King Favian's threats held merit. More than once, he saw the kennel master disposing of the bones of men. Favian ruled with an iron gauntlet rather than a gentle touch. Sadly, Falkon was leaning in that direction as well.

It made Valerios wonder how Rayna had her demands met by spilling no blood. Her status did indeed lend her unique sway. That included calling for Valerios himself. Bowing his head without another word, he started towards Rayna's private chambers to do as his king commanded.

# 16
# The Source

Her bed chamber was spacious but too obstinate for Rayna to get comfortable. Decorative tapestries in bright colors hung on the walls to keep out the evening chill. They were of the finest threads, but the patterns were too erratic to please the eye.

King Favian lauded her with fine silk clothes, plates of fruit, and even a personal jug of wine. Rayna tried a cup of it and found she enjoyed the delicate taste so much she indulged in another. She intended to drink just enough to help ease her to sleep. But the fine taste and her troubled thoughts led to overindulgence until her head swam in a sea of wine.

The bed inside the chamber promised its guest a proper rest. On any other night, she would fall asleep with ease wrapped in such fine skins. But this night, her mind raced with thoughts of the dark dragon. It seemed the presence of this new dragon in Atharia would haunt her nights the same as the king's.

With a third cup of wine in hand, she sifted through the fine silk dresses King Favian had waiting in the room for her. She found it curious why he would go to such an expense for a hired sword. If he intended for her to stay on at Saltwood Stronghold after completing her quest, he was mistaken. Staying in one place for too long made her restless.

Even with a head full of wine, she could not fall asleep, opting instead for an indulgent bath. Slipping into the water, she let the warmth of it ease her tired muscles and soothe her mind. As the water caressed her bare skin, she finally relaxed. The fragrances they dressed the bath with were an unexpected treat. Rayna found their subtle scents pleasing, and it enhanced her relaxation. Perhaps after the soak, she could attain the rest she needed.

A knock upon her door wrestled those plans of away from her. Stepping from the bath, she loosely draped a chiton around her shoulders and let the length of it flow down her body.

As she drew open the door, she found Valerios there. His long hair was pulled tight to his head and he no longer sported the thick facial hair.

"I preferred you with a bit of scruff," she told him. "You're still a handsome sight, though."

"King Favian said you requested me."

Rayna furrowed her brow. "I did, for the dragon quest. You didn't need to seek me in the middle of the night."

"It is my duty to fulfill your needs."

He sounded as though he were reciting scripture prepared by the king. She looked him over, standing straight with his hair pinned back and wearing his best dressing clothes. Rolling her good eye, she sighed and shook her head.

"You really are a foolish man."

Rayna grabbed the loose tail of his shirt and dragged him into her chambers. Once inside, Valerios undressed, and she had to give him a light slap on the hands to make him stop. He stared at her in confusion.

"But I thought...."

"I need your mind, not your body," she told him.

With his sculpted belly partially exposed, she wondered if she dismissed the notion of laying with him in too much haste. They could explore that option another night. For now, she needed to join Valerios' strong mind with her own, not their bodies.

At the moment, her mind still felt warm and dizzy from the wine. She offered him a cup, which he took down in one gulp. After pouring them each another, Rayna began the discussion.

"Your king related his dreams of dragons in great detail to me."

"So, you believe what he's seeing in these dreams is a real dragon?"

"I know it," she told him. "I've been chasing this particular dragon for what feels like an eternity. The dark dragon is the source. It is the one vessel from which all other dragons were created."

"That is an intriguing dragon to chase."

"I don't know how King Favian is seeing these visions." She paused as the question nagged at her, then shook it off. "That is a matter for another time. What I do know is that the dark dragon won't be easy to defeat."

"You've killed dragons before."

"This one is different."

She shook her head, hoping the fear of what stood in front of them wasn't etched on her face. Whether King Favian was a good man or bad didn't matter. He was doing what was needed to ensure the safety of his people.

They knew he called on Rayna to save them from the flame of the dark dragon, and that is why they rallied around her in the square. She could not fail them, nor could she fail herself. But this time, she needed help to ensure victory.

"There is magic inside the dark dragon. He breathes blue fire and bleeds pure acid."

"If it bleeds, we can kill it."

"Before you cut off the dragon's head, it is wise to

make sure it won't grow another just as deadly."

"What do you propose we do, then?"

"That's why I asked for your council," she told him. "If we combine our knowledge, we can come up with a proper plan of attack."

"I'm not the captain of the guards."

"Your Captain Falkon doesn't hold half the tactical knowledge that you do."

Valerios stood and paced the cold stone floor. He seemed to put a shell around himself whenever Rayna offered him a compliment. It was as if he dulled his shine for Falkon to allow him honor and glory he never really earned.

"There's no glory in being a hero," he said, as though reading her mind. "I prefer wisdom before weapons, but it seems the battle plan has already been drawn up."

Now Rayna stood as well. She did not like what she was hearing from Valerios lips.

"Is this the type of counsel you offer your Captain Falkon?"

"I usually keep my own counsel," he told her. "But I will follow my captain's lead without question."

"Because of your self-proclaimed debt? That type of thinking will get you killed."

"As will rushing off to fight a dragon."

His face twisted when he spoke, and Rayna finally read him enough to discern his emotions.

"You're afraid."

"When a man meets a force he cannot destroy, he eventually destroys himself instead."

"The smart ones call on a woman to take up the task."

"For all your bravado, you fear facing down this creature just as much as I do."

"Of course I fear. I'm not a fool," she told him. "But I also have a debt to repay and I will not let that fear stop me from collecting it in full. I've used my pain to doll out justice to the dragons that have plagued these lands. Now I have one more to face. Whether or not I fear facing it is irrelevant. It's just something that has to be done. If you do not want to join me, I will relieve you of the burden."

She sat upon her bed, crossing her bare legs beneath her. Valerios remained standing so as not to be too familiar in his host's room. Though his eyes wandered over her form as the chiton clung to her damp skin.

Having him hover over her made Rayna uncomfortable. She patted the corner of the bed and motioned for him to sit. He obliged her, though still kept his distance. She drank down the rest of her goblet of wine and continued her tale.

"I thought I eliminated the lot of dragons from Atharia years before. Looking upon the sword of flame with my special eye gives me a way to track and kill them. But the dark one I could never see. Why would it come to your king now?"

Valerios averted his gaze from coveting her body. He spoke a truth that Rayna instinctively knew but hoped to be wrong about.

"King Favian converses with mages and seers. They have told him a great many things he's taken to heart. It's because of their warnings that he sought your services."

A shiver of cold ran over Rayna's skin. It forced her to slide across the bed until her back rested against the wall.

"Dark magic," she muttered. "Now it makes sense why I smelled it on him before."

"You can smell magic?"

"I have an unsettling history with magic users. And yes, I smell it on you as well."

"magic itself is not inherently good nor evil. It's the practitioner who deems it as such."

Valerios spoke in a rushed manner, as though trying to defend his indulgence in the dark arts. To this, Rayna smiled, knowing she was one step ahead of him.

"Another reason why I asked for your aid in this task. Your knowledge of magic will be beneficial to my cause. So, will you join this monstrous cyclops on her journey into the Shadowed Highlands to seek a dragon?" she joked.

"I see no monster before me," he told her. "But it shall be my honor to fight at the side of the dragonslayer."

Something shifted in the energy between them. Whether by the weight of his stare upon her, or the amount of wine she indulged in, Rayna felt a desire she didn't intend for.

She moved to pour them fresh wine, and Valerios stopped her. Setting the goblets aside, he took her hands in his own. She felt the callouses of a swordsman's grip on both of his palms. Only a true talent could manage such mastery of the blade.

Staring up at him, she tried to decipher his discontent and found him impossible to read. It was a first for her not knowing a man's true intent. Unraveling the enigma of Valerios grew more appealing by the hour.

"I admit, I do carry the weight of fear," he told her.

"There's no shame in that," Rayna replied. "You'd be a fool not to with what we are to face."

"It's not death I fear, it's you."

"Me? How so?"

"I fear these feelings I'm having for you."

She smiled knowingly at him. "Because of another?"

He nodded, finally allowing his secret to come to light.

"Your captain?" Rayna asked.

Valerios chuckled. "I love Falkon like a brother, nothing more."

"Does he know that?"

Captain Falkon seemed to cling to Valerios too tightly. It was either love or a sense of ownership that didn't permit Valerios to go far from Falkon's side. Either way, it would mean death to any who tried to interfere with that relationship. But as Valerios continued speaking, it seemed someone already had.

"Across the sea on Ischon, my beautiful Kemi awaits my return to her," Valerios continued. "We are to be married."

Valerios' journey across the sea awarded him with more than just knowledge and a tasty ashwa leaf. He found a bride on the isle as well.

Rayna could read the woe on his face like a roadmap. His mind was conflicted over a great many things. Some of which he tried to explain away, as any brilliant thinkers of his time would do.

"But I feel a great deal of attraction to you as well."

The trouble with thinking too much is that it often stood in the way of what was important. Rayna believed emotion should be the driver for life's most complicated choices.

Using the heart to guide one's journey rather than the head may lead to trouble, but also to truth. Rayna placed her finger across his lips to silence any further discussion.

"I cannot counsel you in affairs of the heart, but I can tell you this: time is fleeting. The most precious moments of life should be savored and shared.

"But you don't need to say anymore, Valerios. I can see you're conflicted, so I'm going to send you away now.

Though I'm certain we would enjoy each other; we need to keep clear heads for the journey. Our thoughts should remain on the dark dragon alone."

"I appreciate your wise words on the matter."

"Ah, you're one of the good ones, Val. Let's keep you that way, aye?"

She slapped him high on the shoulder as a fellow soldier would do. Rayna spent a lot of time in the company of men who were like her brothers. She knew the traits to share and which to hold back in order to keep out of their beds. Now that boundaries were set with Valerios, they could put the focus back on the dark dragon.

"Bhrytbyrn, my flaming sword, is rooted in the dragon's curse. It's proved worthy before, but the dark dragon is of magic as well. Should my flaming sword fail me, I'll need the rest of the men to hold its attention while I take an alternative approach."

"If your Bhrytbyrn fails us, we may all perish."

"Surely there is something in the armory that can aid our fight."

"Nothing in our storage is that powerful… except maybe the pyromancer's work."

Rayna shook her head. "I won't deal in black magic."

"Pyromancy is more primitive," Valerios explained. "Most sorcerers mock the practice due to the rudimentary spells and simplicity."

"Meaning any fool can wield its tricks?"

"No, not just anyone. There is skill involved that must be passed down from a master pyromancer to his pupil."

"You've studied under this master, then?"

Valerios nodded. "I like to learn."

"Tell me more about this trick he's created."

"It's akin to the hot tar that hangs over the gates, only much deadlier. Once it makes contact, it will stick to anything, including the steel of a sword or the men's armor. Trying to snuff it out with water only feeds it. The oil will continue to rage like a monster and burn everything in its wake until only ash remains."

Rayna watched him as he spoke. His description rang true, as though he'd seen the pyromancer's work with his own eyes. Many troubled memories hid at the core of who Valerios was as a man. She respected him for holding his head high and marching on through life rather than letting it break him.

"This oil is how Favian won the throne, isn't it?"

Valerios nodded. "He burned King Kullen's entire force with just a few drops. At the time, many people believed King Favian was a dragon himself."

"Fools," Rayna laughed. "A dragon would've destroyed them all. Which is why we need to stop this one...among other reasons."

"The oil is crude and unstable," Valerios told her. "I don't know if we can carry it safely all the way to the

Shadowed Highlands."

"Tomorrow we will go to the pyromancer and discuss it. We need every advantage at our disposal."

"I'll met you there first thing in the morning."

"Good. For now, I think we need to get our rest."

She kissed him on the cheek and then motioned for the door. Valerios started to leave then turned back to her. He rested his hands upon her cheeks and pulled her to him. Their lips met like crashing waves upon the rocks. Rayna felt a rush of energy race over her body she'd not known in some time.

"We'll most likely die tomorrow," he whispered. "Better to live here… now… with each other."

"That's just the wine talking," she replied.

"It isn't."

He kissed her again, this time pulling her body to his own. Rayna gave into the kiss and let his hands explore her supple curves. When Valerios moved his hand towards her eyepatch, she tamped down her emotions and stopped him.

"Let me see," he whispered.

She shook her head against the palm of his hand.

"No one sees."

"It's ok. It's just me."

He kissed the patch then and her attempts to thwart him fell away. Slowly, he pushed back the patch from her eye and continued to reassure her.

"It's ok."

This time as the patch came off, the dragoneye remained dormant, relaxed, even as Rayna shuddered under Valerios' touch. As he saw her stigma close up, he did not falter or stumble back the way others had.

"Why do you hide such beauty?" he whispered.

Rayna hated her deformity. To have a piece of the beast that destroyed her family as part of her own body made her want to pluck it out of her skull. It taunted her in reflective surfaces with its ghostly hue and the slit of a pupil staring back at her.

"A curse, nothing more."

"How so?"

"It's a reminder of a terrible time in my life that I'd rather not languish in," she told him. "Like the scars on your hands or the ones you hold close to your heart."

"We all have painful pasts. It's how we use that pain which forges our direction in life."

He spoke as a man with a sordid past of his own that he did not wish to share now. Rayna grew weary of hers. She tired of hearing bards and minstrels tell her tale like a legend. To her, the past felt like saddlebags filled with rocks heaped upon her shoulders.

"Let's not talk about the past," she told him. "All I want is here and now."

She slipped his hair from its delicate wraps and wound the length of it through her fingers. Pulling him towards her, she shut her eyes and focused only on his taste and touch.

In one swift movement, he stripped her of the chiton and let it drop to the floor. His rough hands moved with gentleness over her naked body. He explored every curve, every scar, until he found her wetness awaiting his fingertips.

The softness of his touch made her flush. As her arousal grew, she began exploring his body. Slipping off his clothes, she found a dense musculature to him that she wasn't expecting.

The thick muscles were taught, and he was hard everywhere. His firm chest pressed against her breasts as they kissed once more. He leaned her down across the bed and followed with his own. Deepening his kiss he shifted atop her, then he pulled back.

Rayna opened her eyes and found him looking at her with such a desire it burned her very core. He kept his gaze locked on hers as he pressed himself inside her.

He was a gentle lover, not like the warriors she lay with before. She wrapped her legs around him, then shifted her weight to roll Valerios on his back. Straddling him, she took over control.

To her delight, Valerios moaned in pleasure. Rayna tossed her head back and shook out her damp hair as a wave of ecstasy overtook her. Valerios sat up and met her lips again in such a fury that he cut his own lip on her ringlet.

He paused momentarily, and Rayna gave a small chuckle. She used her tongue to slowly lick the speck of blood, then darted into his mouth where he met hers with his own.

Their bodies remained interlocked in the ultimate communion until climactic satisfaction found them both. Then slowly they melted out of their embrace. Both of them fell back upon the thick pillows slick with sweat and heaving ragged breaths.

"You really are a remarkable woman, dragonslayer," Valerios told her.

"I know."

They both had a laugh and another cup of wine before Rayna sent him on his way. It would do her no favors to have Valerios seen slipping out of her room. She needed the men she traveled with on the morrow to follow orders, not whisper about her dalliances. For now, she needed rest that still wouldn't come despite the energy she'd spent in bed with Valerios.

Her thoughts drifted back to the dark dragon. The size of it, the weight. These were things she usually knew before facing the great beast. Hunting it blind with mere visions from a possibly mad king left too much room for error.

Rayna would not sleep that night. The rest of her evening would be spent going back over every dragon battle she ever had. A skilled tactician knew how to pinpoint both their strengths and weaknesses to improve upon both.

Heralded as a great dragonslayer, those that regaled her knew not the peril she faced every time she hunted. Sitting on the edge of her bed, Rayna remembered them all. Her eye ached with anticipation of seeking and slaying another dragon.

# 17

# Sweetness & Swine

Outside his chamber door, Falkon heard Valerios' usual bravado crumble in the presence of his father. Hearing such weakness brought enough aggravation to rouse him from his drunken stupor. When he finally staggered out of his room, and caught up with Valerios, he saw him entering the bedchamber of the warrior woman for a second time.

The betrayal's were mounting. Valerios lied about his dealings with the dragonslayer. Why else would he be creeping around the castle in the dark of night? Falkon tasked Valerios to uncover information about Rayna, but he did not request her fornication habits. He could learn those on his own.

Falkon remained transfixed on the door waiting for Valerios to come out. He could hear the sounds of their love-making on into the night and it grated across his ears. When Valerios finally emerged, he looked smug and satisfied. A sheen of sweat touched his brow just under a tangled mass of dark hair.

*"He plays you for a fool."* Xara's whisper fell suddenly upon his ear.

"Valerios has been loyal to my service," Falkon argued.

*"He told your father of your woes and made you appear as a weak man."*

"I felt dizzy, I don't remember what happened."

*"Valerios purposely knocked you unconscious. He positions himself to take your place by undermining your authority. Now he woos the dragonslayer to his side as well."*

Xara lingered on his shoulders whispering words that called into question Valerios' loyalty. The more Falkon thought on matter, the more it raised his ire. What outrageous arrogance Valerios must have to perform such deeds behind the back of the man who made him.

His long-suffering silence at Falkon's right hand built into betrayal. Xara spoke truth. Valerios fed them all lies that caused them to look down upon Falkon with disrespect. Such daring would not be allowed while he still breathed.

He let Valerios step far enough away from Rayna's chambers before catching his arm. Clean-shaven and perfumed he looked as though he were a high-born ready to attend a grand feast in his honor.

*"He seeks to take what's yours,"* Xara told him.

Falkon agreed. Valerios was inserting himself in places of power to upset the balance of their relationship. Master strategist or not it was time Falkon reminded Valerios where he stood in the hierarchy.

Without Falkon's aide he would've remained a low-brow wharf rat out on the docks begging for scraps. It was Falkon who provided him purpose and now Valerios sought to undermine him. Such a betrayal pained Falkon more than a dagger to the heart.

"This is the second time you've been alone with the dragonslayer in her private chambers."

Valerios did not immediately respond to the accusation. Instead, he feigned concern for Falkon's well-being. He even gave him a friendly pat on the back.

"Good to see you on your feet, Falkon. I was worried."

"Worried I may not wake from the chokehold you put on me, or worried that I would?"

Valerios grew defensive. "You became belligerent and took a swing at me. I only meant to subdue you before you hurt yourself or others."

"And once I was no longer conscious, you took it upon yourself to speak for me. First, in front of my father and now with the dragonslayer inside her very chambers."

"It's not like that. The king gave me a direct order."

Falkon looked him over, disgusted at the sight.

"And did you honor that command? Did you bed the warrior woman even at the risk of word getting across the Cira Sea to your beloved Kemi?"

Valerios had no answer. No matter which he admitted to it would bring him shame. Either the death of duty or his declaration of love. He simply lowered his eyes and spoke in a low plea.

"Falkon, please, I beg you."

"I am captain of the kingsguard and the royal heir to the throne. You should address me as such."

"I did not mean to insult, your Grace."

"But you do insult me, Valerios. You insult me with your persistent conspiring behind my back and then feeding me lies."

*"He's undermined your every proclamation and turned your father against you,"* Xara whispered.

Falkon nodded to her in agreement. "Yes, you're right."

"To whom are you speaking?" Valerios asked in confusion.

"She isn't your concern," Falkon told him. "Walk me through what went on in Rayna's chambers. Or should I knock on the door and get the details from her lips instead?"

"She wishes to procure the pyromancer's aide to forge weapons against the dark dragon," Valerios admitted.

Falkon crooked his head. "If she needs our pyromancer,

why do we need her?"

"Rayna knows a great many things about the dragons."

"Yet she summoned you for your knowledge? Or was it just your cock that she was after?"

Falkon reached out and grabbed hold of Valerios' manhood and gave it a hard squeeze. Valerios knocked his hand away and stepped back in surprise. His voice grew louder echoing off the stone walls as he insisted on his role of the honorable do-gooder.

"You ordered me to stay at her side and learn all I could."

"What did you learn, dear Valerios? Her favorite position?"

Valerios shook his head.

"I'm starting to wonder if the tales of this dragonslayer aren't merely myth to earn her coin," Falkon said. "She traveled with thieves and assassins, disappeared to the tavern the moment we arrived, and now takes my consultant into her bed to draw secrets from him. Sounds more like a charlatan than a slayer."

*"You'll go with them on the journey,"* Xara told him.

"I suppose we'll find out just how good she is when we find this dragon. I'll head up the charge in the morning."

"Forgive me, captain, but I don't believe your father intends for you to go with us. The danger is high."

*"He tries to keep you from glory. Your father will be pleased with your assertion."*

"Don't presume to tell me of my father's wishes. He will be pleased I've taken charge."

Valerios dipped his head. "As you wish."

Falkon watched his eyes as they sought his precious Xara. A covetous man Valerios had become. First the dragonslayer and now Xara.

*"He's a snake who seeks power at your expense. Keep him close. He should not be trusted. Nothing can interrupt the quest to find the dragon."*

"You'll stay close to me for the duration," Falkon said, setting his hand upon Valerios' shoulder and giving another hard squeeze. "Just like old times, friend."

The first rule of warfare Falkon ever learned at the foot of his father was to lull the enemy. Make them think they are secure and then watch them for weakness. From there, proper strategy could be formed to secure their destruction.

# 18
# Path of Vengeance

At dawn, Rayna's naked eyes soaked up the sunrise. In the time of dragons, the skies always filled with smoke. Thick ash poured over cities like a perpetual snowfall. Whether it be morning or evening could hardly be ascertained. As Rayna dispatched each dragon, the skies began to clear.

The long-lost blue of the morning and the twinkle of stars at night returned to Atharia. Now, she watched the sun rise over the western mountains with full, rich color. From her window in the tower, she could just make out the port where Favian's massive ships remained docked. The sunlight cascaded over the Cira Sea like shimmering copper. It reminded Rayna of the first stoke of a fire.

She stepped away from the window and took up her broadsword from where it lay. Brandishing it from the sheath, she fixed her dragoneye upon it. Simple focus drew the power of flame to the blade. It twirled and danced over the tip in waves as she moved the sword through the air. Each hard slice forced more fire to erupt over the blade. Satisfied that no underlying magic in the castle blocked her charms, she relaxed the flaming sword.

With a calming stare, the flames retracted back down from whence they came. Where that place was, she never really knew. The sword came from her father when she was very young. A gift, he told her, for his blessed child.

At the time, she was in awe. Such a mighty weapon in the hands of a young child didn't happen often. For girls, holding a weapon of any kind was irregular. But her father always treated her like a princess and bestowed the best presents upon her.

Only now did Rayna realize he was compensating for the curse he brought to his family. She imagined the true origins of the sword were a tale of thievery, just like the rest of his gifts to her.

Though the broadsword was too heavy for her to heft, then she could still sense the greatness flowing through it. Her eye called to the blade the moment it was in Rayna's grip. They were like two lovers who hadn't been together in years. Their culmination created a firestorm that raged out of her control.

She panicked as the flames licked up towards the roof of her bedroom. Her mother was the one who taught her how to draw the fire back. Calm, focused intent pulled the flames down from the blade and back into hiding.

With disaster averted, her mother took the fire blade from her and an argument between her parents ensued. Rayna's mother believed a child should not have such powerful weapons, while her father insisted she keep it for protection.

Even then, he knew the curse of the dragon would be upon them. Had he been honest with them, perhaps they all could've escaped with their lives. Instead, another fire erupted inside the house, only this time, tragedy would not be averted. Those terrible events led Rayna on the path she walked now. A path of vengeance.

Having the fire spew from her blade reminded Rayna of the dragon's breath that torched her home. That memory gave her enough strength and conviction to carry out her mission of revenge. Even the threat of the dark dragon wouldn't be enough to sway her.

Any sane woman would run from the fight knowing she could be torched alive. Rayna never claimed to be of sound mind. She just knew in her heart what needed to be done. That alone guided her.

At the pyromancer's shop, she would pick up more fire. While she awaited Valerios to join her, she toured the armory. With King Favian providing a hefty bounty and catering to her requests, Rayna found it the perfect opportunity to replenish supplies.

Marching into the hills of the Shadowed Highlands

would require wool and heavier leathers than what she wore now. Down near the southern tip of Atharia, the air remained warm. Rayna preferred to stay where the sun shone over the earth. A leather corset and skirt with her dragon-scaled armor on top is all she needed there.

She even traveled farther down across the Golden Isle to the land of Kartha. Tan bodies and libations welcomed her there. Though Kartha was not without its own troubles. In time, Rayna returned to Atharia.

Theopilous became her adopted home. It was a place she could get lost in and expel the dreams of dragons from her mind. Then Captain Falkon came calling with tales of the great one. A sickness opened up in her as Falkon spoke. She felt the need to conquer another winged-beast wash over her like a fever.

Now as she picked over weapons and supplies to bring on the quest, her hands trembled. It was excitement, not fear, that shook her body. When she felt all the dragons were expunged from Atharia, she didn't know what to do with herself. Getting lost in drink and a night's pleasure only sated her for so long. Now, she held purpose again.

Scouring the armory, she realized that the wear on her own dragonarmor needed repair. Each patch of scales stretched across the thin metal plates represented a kill, Rayna remembered with fondness. But sentimentality aside, the damage was taking its toll. Having a king finance her in this fight opened many doors. Once she told the armorer that her requests were backed by King Favian's order, he began work at once.

Loaded with furs and freshly repaired armor, Rayna sought the pyromancer on her own. Though she only knew Valerios for a short time, he didn't seem like a man that went back on his word. Duties to the king or his captain must've kept him from meeting her. So, Rayna would have to charm the pyromancer herself.

His workspace remained covered in shadow even though the sun stood at its peak. He worked instead by lamplight; the flame kept low in its cradle. Rayna could scarcely see her way around the shop and had to resist the urge to expose her dragoneye to compensate.

She spotted the man himself in the shop's corner. He was slender and pale of flesh. Dark circles rimmed his eyes, and his thinning hair stood in disarray.

"You there," she called out. "Captain Falkon's right-hand man, Valerios sent me."

"Valerios the Valiant," the man muttered.

"Yes, that's what they call him."

He jerked his head up from his work abruptly. The weight of his stare caused Rayna to pause in her step.

"Not anymore," he told her. "What is it you want?"

"I seek the means to kill a dragon."

He looked her over, then scoffed. "I thought that's what they brought you here for, dragonslayer."

"It is, old man," she replied, stepping up to his workbench. "But even the greatest warrior could use an edge."

"Your edge looks mighty fine," he said, pointing to her broadsword. "They say you can make it dance with fire. I should like to see that."

"That can be arranged," Rayna said, patting the hilt. "First, I'm in need of something special for this dragon I seek to slay. Valerios told me you may have what I need."

"Ah, he sent you here for the Chaos Fire."

The name which the pyromancer invoked was meant to instill fear in those who dare do battle with Favian the First. For Rayna, it sparked her interest even more.

"Forgive me, good sir. Valerios was meant to be here to introduce us. I am Rayna. And yes, I do seek this Chaos Fire you speak of."

"I am Merrick. The Chaos Fire is not for sale."

"Then you mean to gift it to me?"

"Young woman, it is not meant for untrained hands. You'll likely blow up the entire town before you even leave my shop."

"I'm a quick study, Merrick," she assured him. "As you said yourself, I've handled weapons of fire before."

"A mere parlor trick, not like the Chaos magic."

Rayna shuddered at the mention of magic. She thought the work of the pyromancer would've dealt with matters of alchemy, not in the world of the unknown.

Merrick looked her over, then shook his head. "No, I don't have time to teach you."

"You're right, you don't have time. None here do," she argued. "Soon the dragon will come from up high and incinerate every living thing in its path. Your Chaos Fire and your rules will die alongside everything else."

He stared at her, his eyebrows twitching with concern. Then his face softened, and he stumbled out from behind the workbench.

"There's no need to get so melancholy," he said. "I will instruct you, but first, a bit of history so you can truly respect its essence."

"Of course," Rayna agreed.

Learning at the foot of assassins and other assorted warriors, Rayna came to learn the importance of understanding a weapon's history. Past triumphs and mistakes both helped a wielder become more skilled. If Rayna could uncover the history of her firesword it would surely be even more powerful than it already was.

So, she sat and listened quietly to the pyromancer's tale. Merrick handed her a cup of warm cider and motioned for her to sit. While he spoke, he busied himself by filling small jars with black powder.

"Before the practice of pyromancy, fire magic was only used by witches and sorcerers."

"I was informed that pyromancy held a different

distinction from dark magics," Rayna said, hoping Merrick would calm her concerns.

Drinking the cider warmed her, but Rayna still felt a chill creep over her skin at the mention of magic. Any entity that held ties to another realm couldn't be trusted. Dragons were said to be of magic. They came at a time when magical beings roamed free over the world. During her battles with the beasts, Rayna learned they were simply flesh and blood. And if a creature could bleed, she could kill it. The dark dragon did not abide by the same rules. Therefore slaying it would be her greatest challenge.

As Merrick continued his tale, he hearkened back to a time of dragons when the winged ones littered the skies.

"The witch Nadiuska, and her Daughters of Chaos, used sorcery to create the first flame. They challenged the ancient dragons with it, intent on harvesting their power within for themselves. They failed. But the knowledge of the flame sorcery was left on the battlefield. From that grew pyromancy."

"You speak of the days of old, when all manner of magical creature walked Atharia."

"They walked, flew, and even traversed the Cira Sea," Merrick said, his voice rising with enthusiasm. "And not just Atharia. Across all lands the magics reigned. Now, nothing but a distant memory. True magic has all but vanished from the land."

"Except for the dragons."

"Yes… and you."

"I am not magic, old man."

He glanced at her covered eye with a crook of a smile. "Indeed."

Rayna never wanted to admit that some type of sorcery ran through her veins. The curse of the dragon left her with stigmas, both physically and internally. She culled them the best way she knew how, but the stain of the curse could never be washed away.

"Dragons are a stubborn lot," Merrick continued. "But you've done well to root them out and slay them."

"You almost sound disappointed."

"Who am I to say? Just an old man who likes to play with fire."

Merrick finished up packing the powder. He leveled each one off at the top, then cleaned the jars of any loose granules. With the completion of his task, ten rounds of Chaos Fire stood ready. Rayna was left disappointed with the turnout.

"That's all?" she asked.

"Afraid so. Supplies haven't been coming in quite so often since the king fell ill."

"He seemed fine when I met with him."

Merrick gave a small laugh. "That's because you didn't know him before. There are those that serve in the towers who have seen King Favian speaking to himself.

Touched in the head if you ask me."

"Telling tales again, old man?" Captain Falkon said, pushing through the door.

Valerios entered with him. When he saw Rayna, he tried to mouth an apology to her, but was cut off as Falkon stepped in his way. He looked Rayna up and down, then foraged through her belongings.

"I see you've wasted none of the expense my father has graciously allowed you."

Rayna thought to stand and confront Falkon to let him know he held no power over her. Instead, she leaned back and finished her cider.

"There are strong wind chills in the Shadowed Highlands," she said. "You'd be wise to increase your furs as well."

"It's covered," he replied with a grin. "The men are gathering everything we need for the journey. Valerios and I came to collect our prize possession."

"The Chaos Fire?"

"No, silly girl. You. We can't expect a victory without Rayna, the mighty dragonslayer leading us into battle."

Falkon was intentionally trying to insult her. He had a healthy arrogance for a man who never really saw battle before. Perhaps she'd let him broach the dragon's lair first. One look into its terrifying face would shut him up permanently. For now, she let his insults roll off her.

"You're right. You can't expect victory without me."

Valerios gave a small chuckle, which caused Falkon to chastise him. Rayna grew tired of the royal heir. The sooner they left Sandhal, the better. She needed to concentrate on the quest, not the foul blathering of an infantile highborn.

"Right then, you need me and I needed armaments. Is the Chaos Fire ready?"

"It is," Merrick told her. "I should tell you that the manner which you intend to use it will produce a limited range from its pure state."

"I'm so glad we wasted the better part of a morning waiting on a weapon with limited effect," Falkon mocked.

Rayna waved him off. "We'll plan ahead and predict our enemy's attack. Isn't that what all good tacticians do in battle?"

Now it was her turn to mock Captain Falkon. She knew that most of the combat decisions came from Valerios. This irked Falkon, and he would no doubt retaliate in some childish fashion. Rayna would have to keep her eye on him or risk losing her head before they even reached their destination.

# 19

# Into the Dark of Night

They rode out towards the Shadowed Highlands with nary a word among them. Now that the hour drew nearer, the depths of the challenge they would face silenced even the boldest tongues.

Each of the men carried one bottle filled with Chaos Fire. Rayna took none for herself. She was certain Falkon claimed both his and the bottle meant for Valerios. For a man trying to carve out his own name away from the deeds of his father, he cut many of the same corners.

A parable Rayna once heard spoke of children inheriting the worst traits of their parents. And whether or not they tried to walk their own path, the blood always came calling.

In her worst moments, she recognized traits of her father: quick to temper with a foul mouth. But she held her mother's compassion in her too. She did not like to see others suffering, especially children. On more than one occasion, the combination of her parent's temperaments led her into a fight.

With Sandhal in the distance, Rayna thought about the men who rode with her. Each of them served their king out of duty and honor. At what cost? Many of them had families, and they rode towards a destiny that likely wouldn't see their return.

If she could've faced the dark dragon alone, she would have. Many times, she faced down a mighty dragon, certain she would die with no one to know. Having the men fight with her now was necessary. Rayna made her peace with that. She simply would not take the time to learn their personal stories. Unlike Valerios.

Rayna knew he longed to return to his betrothed Kemi. She wanted to tell him to go. Throw down his sword and sail away back to Ischon. Damn whatever debt he owed Captain Falkon! He owed another to his Kemi.

It proved near impossible to speak openly with Valerios on the ride. Falkon remained by his side throughout the journey. It was just as well. They need not rehash their night in bed together. It was a physical release, nothing more. Rayna no longer allowed herself to catch heavy feelings from her dalliances. More important matters lay ahead than pleasures of the flesh.

Rayna traveled at the front in silence. She used the time to plan her attack. The dragoneye stayed dormant. Not once had it called to let her know they approached the dark dragon. Such was the problem with hunting this particular winged beast.

In her other conquests, the pull from the eye would radiate through her. She would see clear visions of the dragon's lair and the beast's movements within. Nothing but blackness came to her now.

They tread into the Dying Valley, a place where magic once reigned supreme but since withered away. Barren trees lined the route with piles of dry, fallen leaves surrounding them. A sudden chill bore right through Rayna's thick furs. In the distance, the Graven Peaks loomed. A mass of black mountains which blocked out the sun turned the lands beneath to darkness.

"Ready yourselves," Rayna called back to the men. "We approach an area of malice."

They tightened their reins and steered the horses up into the Shadowed Highlands. Rayna never traversed so far north of Atharia. The area was foreign to her and any maps of the land held no details of what lay beyond the Dying Valley. All the party had to go on were King Favian's fevered dreams. Rayna hoped his sight beyond sight proved accurate.

"Avoid the towns," Captain Falkon called out. "Nothing but magis and mischief makers out this way. They'll only slow us down."

"How do you know? Rayna asked.

"I have my sources. It's just best to avoid them. Trust me."

Trusting Captain Falkon was the last thing she intended to do. But if there were magic dealers in the area, she held no fault in his reasoning. They were a treacherous lot only out for coin. Nevermind that selling outlawed magic to those unfamiliar with its use could be deadly. So long as they got their fare, they moved on to the next mark. Their type would slit a throat for a simple copper.

Avoiding the towns invited another problem when it came time for rest. None knew what creatures roamed the open area. They would need to keep the campfires going until morning to drive back any that happened on their path.

As they drew closer to the peaks, Rayna felt her anticipation rise. They would need to scale the Graven Peaks to reach the lair of the dark dragon.

This would be the battle she longed for since first learning of the dragon's curse upon her family. But as she determined the sheer size of the peaks, she knew her vengeance would have to wait another day.

At the foot of the peaks, they set up camp. The journey from Sandhal had been a long one. They needed rest and replenishment before tackling the climb ahead. But as they prepared the campsite, an unforeseen challenge faced them.

Whether by wind or witchcraft, no fire would burn up there. Now that they were no longer on horseback, it made them easy targets. Already they stood in the open too long without a warning of flame to hold back predators.

To his credit, Captain Falkon ordered the men to watch the perimeter. They stood in a circle guarding Rayna, Falkon and Valerios as they decided on the next move.

"We should keep moving," Falkon said.

"Your men are tired, Captain," Rayna explained. "It won't do any good to face the dragon with exhaustion weighing us down."

"What then? Surely, we can't stay exposed. The elements alone will kill us."

Falkon hugged his cloak tighter to his body. Rayna's insistence that he wear proper gear went ignored. Now he was paying for it as the air grew thin and frigid the higher they traveled.

But he was right. They couldn't just wait out the night in formation. For one thing, the darkness was endless. The sun dared not encroach on the Shadowed Highlands. Only specks of daylight would aid them come morning. Rayna did not like what she must do next, but it was inevitable if they were to survive.

"Stand back," she told them.

Falkon and Valerios stepped away but remained safe inside the circle of soldiers. With them far enough back,

Rayna drew her broadsword and began.

Brushing back the patch from her eye, she made a silent wish that her efforts would not be futile. Holding the sword aloft, she focused her dragoneye upon the blade.

It felt like an eternity waiting to see if the magic flame would cast upon her sword. The longer it took, the more she doubted. It also created a great strain upon her eye to keep it fixated on the blade for so long. But then Bhrytbyrn came alive.

Great plumes of flame cut a swath through the night sky and bathed the lot of them in light. The spark of the fire caused the men to cheer in admiration. Even Captain Falkon smiled as the warmth of the flame touched his cheeks.

Rayna pressed the tip of the sword into the campfire and was pleased to find the fire pass over. With the campfires lit, she could extinguish her blade for the night and try to relax.

They ate and drank, but kept the chatter low. Any boisterous laughter or songs would bring unwanted attention. Captain Falkon appointed his men in shifts to watch the perimeter while the others slept.

Rayna did not expect to sleep. Her nerves remained on edge knowing the dark dragon made its home just above them. She needed rest just as much, if not more, than the others. So, when Captain Falkon fell to slumber, she nudged Valerios awake.

At her touch, he went for his sword. Seeing her staring back at him, he relaxed his grip. She motioned silence and then instructed him to follow her. They slipped away from the others but remained close enough to the light of the fire.

"I need something to help me sleep," Rayna whispered.

"It might be too cold for me to perform, but I'll try my best," Valerios joked.

Rayna gave him a grin. "I'm happy to see you still keep your humor. You looked very grim riding with Captain Falkon."

"He questioned my loyalty to him. It pained my heart to hear it."

"I'm sorry for you, but I am also curious."

"Of what?"

"You owe him so much that you would forsake your love across the sea?"

"What do you mean?"

"Why are you on this rock with us instead of in Ischon with your Kemi?"

"You misunderstand, Rayna," he told her in a stern voice she'd not heard before. "I aid you in this quest to make the lands safer for my Kemi. When the dark dragon is no longer a threat, I mean to bring her here to be with me."

"I'm surprised Emperor Kazo would let his daughter leave her homeland."

Valerios shook his head. "He cares only for the welfare of his sons. His daughters are used for trade."

"Now I know why I never traveled to Ischon."

"It's beautiful land."

"With wonderful herbs to aid in sleep," she said with a smile.

Valerios nodded and passed her the ashwa leaf.

"Enjoy," he said, patting her hand.

"You will not join me?"

"Not this night."

"Very well then. Have pleasant dreams of your beloved."

Valerios gave her a smile and went back to camp. Looking up at the darkened sky, Rayna smoked and let her thoughts wander.

What would her life be like without the threat of dragons overhead? She started living that life when she thought they were all extinguished before. Traveling the land with the freedom to do as she pleased. It only indulged her for a short while. Then she returned to Atharia with an emptiness in her soul.

Hunting the dragons gave her purpose. Nothing else seemed to fill that void. She thought about seeking a cure for her stigma. What good was the dragoneye without dragons to seek?

But she let it sit as a reminder of their dirty deeds. She would never forget what the dragon's curse cost her family. The dark memories filled her and soon she drifted to sleep.

# 20

# Some Things Wicked

A piercing scream wailed across the night air and brought Valerios awake. He shifted onto his haunches and drew his sword. Next to him, Falkon stirred.

"What is it?" he asked, still half asleep.

"The fire has gone out," Valerios replied.

Falkon scrambled to his feet and collected his own sword. Without the firelight, it took Valerios time to focus his eyes in the dark.

He stayed low and scanned the area. The men remained sleeping under their furs. But the soldier meant to be on watch was missing, and so was Rayna. Falkon noticed her disappearance as well.

"The dragonslayer, where is she?"

Valerios shook his head. "I don't know. I heard a scream."

"If she's dead, we're all doomed."

Falkon roused the other men with swift kicks while Valerios sought Rayna. He worked his way back over to the path they walked earlier in the night and called out in an urgent whisper.

"Rayna!"

No answer came. He felt his heart jump as thoughts of her death swirled through his mind. Double gripping his sword, he edged closer, intent on finding her still standing or else a body on the ground. What he found instead terrified him.

A creature towered over him. It looked fresh from the grave, with its bones pressing through ashen skin. Dark eyes sat deep within their sockets, looking down at Valerios.

The thing opened its tattered lips, emanating a strong odor of decay and death. From the depths of its tattered body came a low moan that grew into a howl of rage.

With surprising quickness, it came for Valerios. Arms the length of its torso swiped at him. He moved back before taking the full impact of the blow, but still suffered a gash from the being's massive claws.

Even a glancing blow proved to hold great power. Valerios was knocked off his feet into the dirt. He stared up at the creature, certain this would be his end.

But then a great flame emerged from the neighboring trees. Rayna, firesword in hand, came racing towards the creature. She stepped in front of Valerios and stared the thing down. As it saw the flame, it retreated into the woods.

Captain Falkon and the rest of the men showed up moments later. Falkon pulled Valerios to his feet and looked over the massive claw marks left upon his breastplate.

"What in the world could cause such damage?"

Valerios still felt his body shaking. It took him time to catch his breath before he could even relate what he saw. Unable to find words to truly describe his horror, he said the first thing that came to mind.

"A monster sprung from the depths of darkness."

"They're called Shadax," Rayna told him.

"You've battled this creature?" Falkon asked.

She shook her head. "I've only heard tales about it. As with most tavern stories, it grew into a myth and nothing more. But sure as we stand here, so does the Shadax."

"What are they?"

"They are said to have once been men who fell to hunger in the cold. Now they roam dark forests, seeking sustenance. Once found, they wait until their prey sleeps and then drags them deep into the forest to feast. Somehow they've become set on the taste of human flesh. Nothing else will sate their hunger."

Rayna had not moved from her stance. Bhrytbyrn remained extended in front of her as she watched the trees for movement. Valerios dared to reach a hand upon her shoulder. She tilted her head to register his touch, but did not turn. He squeezed the furs that cloaked her to infer his gratitude.

"Thank you."

"Thank me later," she replied. "The Shadax isn't finished with us yet."

"Your magic fire went out during the night, dragonslayer," Falkon told her, almost spitting his disgust. "It left us vulnerable to attack."

"I don't pretend to understand these lands, captain," she said. "You seem to know more than I do."

Under the noise of their arguing, Valerios made out a faint cry for help. It came from the opposite side of the campsite and grew increasingly anguished.

"Quiet!" he said sharply. "I hear someone crying out."

"It must be Jhord," Falkon replied. "He wasn't at his post."

The men of the kingsguard were well-trained and loyal. None of them would've abandoned their post unless something in the trees warranted inspection.

Jhord may have stepped away to uncover the source of a noise and become a victim to the Shadax. Now he cried out in pain as he awaited it to return and finish the job.

"We have to help him!"

Valerios started towards the man's cries, and Rayna pulled him back.

"What're you doing?" he asked, shaking free of her grip.

"The Shadax's wail mimics that of a man," she explained. "It's part of the myth that they were once human and a sure way to lead others to their death."

"We can't just leave Jhord out there to die."

"He's already dead."

Her eyes were wild and insistent. She had not replaced the patch since lighting the fires, and Valerios now saw the full extent of the dragoneye.

It flared like a deep amethyst jewel. The iris lay in a slit of a pupil making Rayna appear monstrous as the shadows danced over her face. He had to step away from her. The entire night played tricks on his mind, and his adrenaline still ran high.

"Stay here if you like. I'm going after him."

Valerios was halfway into the bushes when Captain Falkon gave him an order.

"Stand down. As Rayna told you, Jhord is probably already dead. There's no sense in losing more men just to determine that. We need to get out of here before that thing returns."

"Agreed, captain," Rayna said.

Seeing the two of them come to terms was unsettling for Valerios. For most of their time together, Rayna and Falkon were at odds. The evils at the foot of the Graven Peaks made for strange camaraderies.

# 21
# Creatures of the Night

Falkon tried to make sense of the night's events while Xara whispered to him the next move to take. He did not know how she traveled so far from Cragstone Keep, but he was thankful to have her there.

She hid so the others would not see and covet her beauty. Even as stunning as Rayna was, she would surely feel the heat of jealousy should Xara show herself. For now, she allowed only Falkon to see as she showed him the way.

"Here."

He motioned towards a path in the woods Xara pointed out for him. His soldiers gathered in formation and cut through the dense trees. Even Rayna followed with Bhrytbyrn lighting the way. But Valerios hesitated. He kept looking back whence they came, as though

Jhord still called out.

*"His nobility will get him killed and you as well if you do not keep him in line,"* Xara told him.

Falkon nodded silent agreement to not bring attention from the others. He called out to Valerios then as his captain not his friend.

"I said move, Valerios. Before you get us all killed!"

As Falkon called out, he heard a rustling in the brush next to him. Rayna had disappeared into the thicket with the soldiers taking the light of Bhrytbyrn with her.

Her departure left Falkon cloaked in darkness with tall trees circling him. He shuffled his feet, trying to judge the distance from them. One tree sprang to life and came for him with malicious intent.

Long, sinewy arms reached out to clutch him. Off reaction, Falkon swung his sword up and struck the extended claws. The edge of his blade sliced the withered flesh and cut two of the claws from the hand.

The Shadax gave a guttural wail but still pressed forwards. It caught Falkon around the neck with its other claw and raised him up. The pressure on his flesh almost caused a loss of consciousness. Staring into the hideous face was as though death itself became form.

Falkon struggled to no avail. His life was only spared by the intrusion of Valerios. He charged towards the Shadax with wild abandon and hacked into its arm.

As the blow struck, the Shadax released Falkon from its

clutches. He fell hard upon the forest floor, unable to catch his breath. Above him, Valerios battled the Shadax with heavy strikes coupled with graceful movements. His skills truly were the very best in all of Atharia.

Skilled or not, the Shadax proved too powerful. Even though the majority of his sword strikes landed on the creature, it did not seem to inflict enough pain to deter it.

Rearing back, it struck Valerios in the side of the head. He tumbled to the ground and lost his sword in the shadows of the night.

Falkon scrambled to his feet, his own sword just paces away. His movement caught the Shadax's attention. It lurched towards him with its long arms. Pressing off his haunches, Falkon rolled underneath its grasp and caught the hilt of his sword.

With an angled swing, he slashed the beast in its crooked leg. He took a chunk out of its gray flesh, but no blood came from the blow. Only dust and crumpled skin broke away from the creature in its step.

Falkon remained on the ground, his sword extended in front of him. The Shadax looked down on him with hollow eyes. Its hideous mouth drew open as it leaned down towards him.

He could smell the stench of death and rot coming from its maw. A low moan sounded from its belly and Falkon now knew his predicament. The Shadax grew hungry, and he was meant to be its next feast.

Tears stung his eyes and his sword hand trembled, making it difficult to hold aloft. As the Shadax grew closer, Falkon cried out to his beloved.

"Xara, I beg your favor!"

In the midst of beseeching her, aid came swiftly. Rayna led the way, pressing back the Shadax with the light of Bhrytbyrn. The creature balked at the sight of the fire and tried to maintain distance from it. But Rayna proved the swifter of the two.

She bounded past Falkon and dove at the Shadax. Her body flew through the air like a human arrow and plunged into the torso of the Shadax.

Bhrytbyrn ripped into its tattered skin, sending Rayna straight through the backside. As the firesword lit into the dust and decay, the Shadax instantly came ablaze. Its long limbs thrashed, causing the flame to spread swifter.

Soon, the entire being was engulfed in a wall of fire. Realizing its peril, the Shadax wailed so loudly it hurt the ears. But Rayna wasn't finished with it yet. She flipped her sword over and used it to plunge into the chest of the Shadax. Using her great strength, Rayna dragged the blade of the Bhrytbyrn through the blackened bones, shattering every rib.

The Shadax fell to its knees in front of her, still burning like a massive torch. Rayna swung her blade again, this time severing the thing's head from its body. It fell into little flaming bits at her feet.

Rayna tamped out her sword and hurried over to check Valerios first. Still shaken, Falkon stood and looked down at the remains of the Shadax. He poked at the flaming bits with the tip of his sword.

Its remnants looked like simple coal burning down. But the memory of its hideous face, ready to swallow him whole, would haunt Falkon for the rest of his days.

# 22
# Straight Fire

ayna's heart still raced. Moving through the Shadax the way she did left her with a chill on her bones she couldn't shake. It stained her furs with dust and grime, but also the taint of a spell. The Shadowed Highlands were cursed with the darkest of magics.

Rubbing the filth from her face, she hurried to Valerios. She hoped he hadn't sustained a severe wound. They needed to rouse him quickly and keep moving.

Rayna didn't want to frighten the others, but she knew the Shadax hunted in packs. Another would be along soon. They needed to put distance between them before that happened.

Bruising covered Valerios' head, but she saw no other signs of injury. Using light slaps across his cheeks, she tried to rouse him. When that didn't work, she struck harder. Sure enough, Valerios snapped awake and lashed out in defense. Rayna side-stepped his attack, causing him to fall into the dirt.

"Come, get up," she said, lacing her arm under his. "We need to move."

To her relief, Captain Falkon gathered his men together. To her surprise, he chastised them in her favor.

"Why didn't you fools help Rayna while she battled the Shadax? You're supposed to be the king's most decorated soldiers and yet you all lack the courage to be bestowed that honor."

The men bowed their heads and slumped their shoulders like beaten dogs. Having their morale stripped away in the face of great danger wouldn't be helpful. With Valerios on her arm, Rayna stepped up to intervene.

"It's alright. I feared too."

"The difference is you still acted," Falkon countered. "These lot stood there pissing themselves."

"There's time for reflection later," Rayna told him. "We have to move."

Falkon nodded agreement, then motioned for two of his guards to help Valerios. As they took his weight from Rayna's shoulders, she held fast to his hand.

"You're not allowed to die," she told him.

"Nor you," he replied.

They pressed forward on swift feet. Escaping the forest floor would keep any more Shadax from lurching out from the trees. To gain the distance they needed, it meant scaling the Graven Peaks in the dark of night.

Heights did not agree with Rayna. The further her boots lifted off the ground, the more she felt a loss of control. An overwhelming sense of fear gripped her as she stood at the base of the peaks.

Rayna had not intended to climb until the morrow. They all needed a night of full rest to traverse the slippery slopes. In that time, she had hoped to make peace with her fear of heights. Or, at the very least, she would've smoked enough ashwa to dull her senses.

The dark dragon awaited them at the top, but death could easily come from a slip over the edge of the peaks. Unfortunately, if they stayed down below for too much longer, it would also bring peril. The faster they climbed out of the forest, the less reach Shadax held. They were damned in either direction. Taking the high ground would only give them a moment's reprieve. For Rayna, it would prove to be a challenge for the entire climb.

As they made their way up the rounding slopes, a new obstacle presented itself. The higher they climbed, the colder it became. Snow dotted the ground where they stepped and as they moved steadily upwards, it grew in size.

Rayna found her feet pressing deep into pockets of snow that reached the knees. It caused an involuntary shiver. Without being able to see, her footing brought more panic to her already troubled thoughts.

To try and temper her unyielding fear, she leaned against the mountain wall. Inching slowly forwards she tried to calm her breathing, only to let a whimper escape instead. To her surprise, Captain Falkon reached out to her then.

Rayna hesitated before taking his hand, allowing him to lead her out of the snowbank. Falkon gripped her arm and helped her find stable footing.

"It narrows here," he told her. "We should make a human chain to ensure no one slips off."

Rayna looked ahead and found his words to be true. The embankment they traversed became much thinner as they drew closer to the top. She nodded agreement and reached back to take Valerios' hand. Instead, she found one of the soldiers there.

"Where's Valerios?" she asked.

"He slowed pace and fell to the back," the man responded.

Rayna tried to crane her head to search for him, but could not find him in the pack. Ahead of her, Captain Falkon urged movement with a tugging on her arm. She proceeded forward with concern weighing on her mind. Perhaps Valerios sustained an injury from the Shadax far worse than she originally thought.

They marched on with each hand linked to the person behind them. Falkon's grip remained tight, most likely from fear of falling himself. If he slipped off the side, Rayna wasn't certain she could hold him… or that she'd even want to.

He leaned back and tried to speak with her, even as a sudden wind ripped through them. Its howl made it difficult to hear his words. When she understood what he was saying, it made her pause.

"Thank you."

Captain Falkon did not seem to fancy her from the first. Rayna, in turn, did not respect him. But far up in the Shadowed Highlands, he seemed to be shedding his monarch skin to reveal the true man underneath.

"Before with the Shadax, I thought it was my time to leave this world," he continued. "But then you came crashing in out of nowhere. You saved this retched hide and I thank you."

Rayna watched his face closely as he spoke. The snow covered his shoulders, and the cold pinked up his cheeks. But beneath the wind torn warrior, she saw sincerity. It was much obliged.

"Aye, we're on the same side, Captain Falkon. I couldn't just leave you to die."

"You burned bright like a goddess."

To this, she laughed. "Just think of me as one of your soldiers."

"Hardly."

"Besides, your father wouldn't be too pleased if we

returned without you."

"My father would not lose any sleep over my demise."

Falkon grew melancholy at the thought. It was unfortunate that a father did not see the worth of his own son. Even a mewling cur like Falkon deserved his father's love.

Rayna had no words of comfort to give him. Her own father doted on her out of guilt for what he had become. Soon after, Darius the Dreaded stepped in as her father. Her upbringing could be traced back to mercenaries and thieves. But she had their love and for that she was grateful.

At first look, Falkon appeared to have everything. He held a powerful position in a house that ruled most of Atharia. But he could not capture the respect and admiration he so longed for. Perhaps that's why he lashed out the way he did.

A tugging at her back stole Rayna's attention. As she turned, she saw one man tumble over the side. Her breath caught in her chest as she realized it was Valerios who fell. The panic built further as the entire line started to drag down with him.

# 23
# Fire & Ice

Once again Valerios stole the dragonslayer's attention. This time, he captured everyone's interest as he tumbled from the side of the cliff. The soldiers stiffened in unison to catch his fall. Each man held the other as they dug in their heels on the slippery slopes.

Falkon heard this part of the peaks claimed many who dared climb it. He was not ready to join the ranks of the dead below. As the weight of Valerios' fall was felt down the line, Falkon released Rayna's hand.

She pitched backward and tumbled into the soldier behind her. As she knocked him off balance the rest of the line started to wobble. Falkon could hear shouts ring out over the harsh winds. He wanted to order them into silence. Their cries carried north to the top of the peak where chunks of snow began to break off. They tumbled down at a rapid pace narrowly missing the group of them.

As another chunk of snow broke off it came straight for Rayna. Falkon lurched forward and grasped her around the waist to pull her back. She was much stronger than he anticipated. As she held onto the line of soldiers it caused Falkon to take the brunt of the impact from the dense snow.

It struck him in the head knocking his helmet loose. He fell backwards taking Rayna with him. The sudden shift in weight traveled down the line inadvertently helping the men to pull Valerios back up to safety.

Everyone took a breath as one crisis was averted. But the snow above continued to fall with fury. Its descent threatened to sweep all of them off the side if they didn't move from its path.

Falkon took Rayna's hand once more and urged her to journey onward. She followed close behind him trying to steady her legs on the small ravine. In front of them the path they traveled rounded out of sight. Falkon noted the breaking of light through the darkness. If they could just round that bend a reprieve awaited them.

He scrambled faster than he should've and slipped hitting his shoulder against the side of the cliff face. The pain radiated through Falkon's muscle more than the impact should've. When he pulled away, he noted a jagged bit of the rock face had plunged into his arm.

Rayna saw it too as she moved past him. She kept tight to his hand and pressed ahead.

"Slow and steady!"

Following close behind her, Falkon had to pull his hand away to cup the blood dripping down his arm. Behind him the men pushed against each other. They moved with too much haste desperate to get off the ledge.

As they reached Falkon, the front of the line slowed up. But the men in the middle were walking blind within the torrent of snow and wind.

They gathered too close and bumped together. More snow rushed down from the mountain top and carried away one of the soldiers who stood near the open side.

As he tumbled over Falkon could hear Valerios yell out from the back. It took him a few tries to understand what Valerios was saying.

"Chaos Fire!"

The unstable substance from the pyromancer had been whisked over the side with the man who held it. By the time Falkon realized that, it was too late.

A wall of fire rose up from the bottom of the chasm. The heat alone caused Falkon to gasp for air. He shielded his face and crawled blind along the ledge trying to secure himself into a crevice for safety.

The fire itself wasn't the only peril. As the Chaos Fire burst it created a great rumbling that shook the sides of the mountain. This caused larger chunks of snow to tumble down.

More of his men got swept over the side while others trampled each other to find safety. It didn't matter where they ran. The snow cascaded over the side like a frozen waterfall. Falkon regained his bearings and called out among the anarchy.

"Shields up!"

The soldiers closest to him followed orders and raised their shields overhead. One of the bannermen hefted a shield from a fallen soldier and held it over himself and Captain Falkon.

Falkon couldn't find Rayna or Valerios through the avalanche of snow crashing down over them. Soon, he couldn't see anything as they were all engulfed.

# 24

# Dragon Breath

Rayna found her way out from under the wall of snow just in time. She watched as it covered Captain Falkon and his men in a frozen grave. The thought of losing Valerios made her heart twinge with ache. She hesitated for a moment to asses whether she could dig them free.

With heavy chunks of snow continuing to fall from above she realized there was nothing she could do. Better to continue the journey and finish what they started, so they didn't die in vain. Rayna made a silent offering to gods she rarely spoke to and then continued on.

Her breath labored as she forced herself higher up the mountain. The thin air coupled with the cold made each inhalation feel like a thousand daggers on her lungs. Wind numbed her lips and burned her cheeks but she pressed on.

When she found surer footing, perhaps Bhrytbyrn could be unleashed to cut a swath into the pile of snow covering the men. With hands shaking from the cold she pulled the sword free. Setting her sight upon the blade she readied herself to enact the fire but something else took the attention of her dragoneye. It was the dragon itself.

Rayna only saw the scaled tail slip out of sight but she knew it was the beast she came to slay. All her thoughts became consumed with killing the dragon. She wasted no time going after it.

Scrambling up the slope she pulled herself over the lip of the mountain. Once on top it felt like a different world than what lay below. The sting of the cold air vanished. Little snow stood on the top of the peak. What remained showed tracks throughout. The pattern of the dragon stood out. Massive claws and a singular tail dragged through the snow. Dragon's breath kept its nesting area warm. This meant the size of it would be massive.

Rayna could feel the anticipation mounting. She was so close to fulfilling a lifelong goal. Edging towards the tracks she felt heat upon her skin. Off instinct, she threw herself into a tuck and rolled out of the blast zone. An enormous flame shot out behind her singing the heavy furs she wore.

Rayna shrugged off her coat letting it fall into the

dilapidated snow. She needed freedom of movement and the leathers were too restricting. Bhrytbyrn in hand she stood her ground eyeing down the mighty dragon across from her. It was indeed a massive beast with knots of bone raised upon its tail and a dangerous fury in its eyes. But something was terribly wrong. The dense scales upon its body shone a bright red not dark. This wasn't the dragon she sought but another.

The variance caused Rayna to hesitate the attack. She became overwhelmed with questions as to the true nature of this quest. Had King Favian been mistaken or did he intentionally lead her astray? Her pause gave the red dragon an opening of its own. But instead of devouring Rayna, it opened its mouth and spoke.

"What's wrong girl? You've faced dragons before."

Rayna staggered backwards almost losing her grip upon Bhrytbyrn. Having the winged beast engage her in conversation felt like a trick of the mind.

"None of them have ever spoken before," she replied. "What magic spell am I under?"

"The same one you've always been under, fool girl," the dragon told her. "My brothers and sisters never got the chance to speak with you slaughtering them in their sleep."

"That's a lie!"

Rayna stepped forward, Bhrytbyrn now held high overhead. The dragon huffed. Plumes of smoke rose from its nostrils. Its warning caused Rayna to lower her sword.

"You're not the brave warrior you pretend to be, Rayna the Dragonslayer. If given a fair fight, my kind would've ripped you to shreds long ago."

"I'm standing here now, dragon. Fair enough for you?"

"You can call me Saarath. And I'm not going to fight you. I'm going to make a pact with you."

"I don't deal with dragons. My father made that mistake long ago and its been my living curse ever since."

She pointed up to her dragoneye alive under the new sunlight breaking over the Graven Peaks. Here in the presence of Saarath, the eye ebbed with a pressure that ached. Each pulse made Rayna want to pluck it out of her own head.

"A dragon didn't curse your family, fool girl." Saarath hissed. "Dark magic has led you astray."

The words spoken by Saarath burned on Rayna's ears. Lies did not become a dragon. But they did use cunning to outwit their opponents. However, the implication that dark magic was involved in swaying Rayna to her cause brought back memories of a time long ago.

Magic was on the air the day of Rayna's first kill. So enthralled was she by felling a dragon that she let the circumstances of it alone. Only years later did the fortuitous encounter with a strange old woman weigh on her mind. She blocked it out, leading with her sword instead of her heart.

Her dragoneye encouraged her to fight as it did now. Excited by the presence of the dragon, the eye pulsed within its socket until Rayna's head throbbed. Voices in her mind compelled her to ignore Saarath's words and strike before it was too late.

Eager to quell the whispering, Rayna obliged the dragoneye's desires. She set her sight upon Bhrytbyrn and lit it up to relieve the pressure on her eye.

Saarath saw it as an act of aggression. She growled in anger and snapped her massive jaws. Rayna angled her body to side-step the dragon's bite. Coming up on the side of the great beast, she instinctively slashed out at Saarath's neck.

The dragon proved quicker than Rayna anticipated. She only managed to catch the scales with the tip of her sword. Saarath shifted her weight and swiped the ground with her massive tail. It tripped Rayna up and knocked her off balance.

Then Saarath flapped open her wings. If she took to the sky, Rayna would lose track of her. But the dragon didn't intend to fly. She used her wings to fan the air and bring up a storm of dust and snow. It blinded Rayna enough to make her shield her face. When she drew her hand away from her eyes, Saarath spit flame at her.

Rayna threw herself out of the line of fire and landed

atop a bevvy of broken weapons. Concealed beneath the dirt and snow, they held the sigil of King Favian's elite guards. The men who sought the dragon before met their end atop this very cliff. Rayna did not intend to share their fate.

Using a bent shield as a distraction, she lobbed it towards the dragon's face. Saarath turned her head to avoid taking the shield to her eye, and when she did, Rayna attacked.

With a running jump, she dove towards the dragon once more. This time, she angled Bhrytbyrn downwards in a stabbing motion. The flaming blade caught Saarath between her scales, just above where the heart lay. She howled in pain and then shook Rayna free. The fall from the dragon's body was long, and it knocked the wind out of her.

Rayna struggled to get to her feet. The thin air and the arduous battle drained her energy. She shifted over onto all fours and, as she did, a strange object caught her eye. In fact, it called out to her dragoneye as though it was a long sought loved one. Rayna crawled towards the object and as she drew closer, she realized it was a dragon's egg.

Deep within the cave atop the mountain, Saarath nursed a baby. It was perhaps the last baby dragon in all of Atharia. As Rayna slithered closer, the egg moved. She staggered back and readied her sword. Pieces of the shell broke off as small, scaly hands pushed out. Then a larger hole opened up and a newborn baby dragon's head emerged. Its eyes sought the world for the first time and when they opened it found Rayna.

Looking past the red scales into its small face, she could not bring herself to strike. Even as the dragoneye screamed for slaying, Rayna lowered her sword. Behind her, she heard Saarath cry out.

"Stay away from my child, murderer!"

Rayna turned and found the great dragon lumbering forward. The wound she inflicted was grave, but still Saarath tried to defend her young.

"I'm no murderer. Your kind destroyed my family. This is vengeance, and it is my right. Today I was meant to complete my quest and defeat the legendary dark dragon or die trying. Instead, I found you."

Even as she said the words, she no longer believed them. Rayna couldn't help but see herself in the baby dragon. Having her mother torn away from her by an act of malice, she would be forced to learn the ways of the world alone.

"As I said before, you're a puppet on strings guided by dark magic. We were never your enemy," Saarath muttered. "At least now the mighty dragonslayer can claim one more for her tally."

Rayna was incensed by the dragon's words, but mostly because they rang true. She felt violated and dirty at the prospect of knowing her words and actions were not her own. All along she felt at war with the curse of the dragon. But if the dragon's had not cursed her, then who did?

The sword shook in her hand weighted by a sudden guilt. The wound to Saarath's proved too great. Rayna's next course of action surprised even herself, but she knew it had to be done.

"What pact did you mean to offer me, dragon?"

Saarath lowered her head to the ground and made her plea. "It's too late for that. My wound is grave."

Rayna felt her compassion dueling with her need for vengeance. Somehow, even with the insistence from the dragoneye to strike, her compassion won out.

"Please, let me help you."

"What's this? The dragonslayer has a change of heart?"

"If what you say is true, then I have been played for a fool," Rayna explained. "There must be something I can do to make amends."

"Protect my child," Saarath pleaded. "In doing so, it will lead you to the truth."

As Saarath's last breath slipped from her, the mewling of the baby dragon caught Rayna's attention. Glancing over her shoulder, she saw it struggling to free itself from the remainder of the shell. The sight of a baby in need of its mother tore at Rayna's heart. Rushing back to its side, she helped it free and then stepped back.

The pull of the dragoneye proved too strong. It began making demands for more killing. Cutting her way through all the dragons on Atharia, she only ran across adults. Never did Rayna strike down a child and she couldn't bring herself to do so now, no matter how much her wicked eye demanded it.

She cut a swatch of cloth from her leathers and wrapped it around her eye. With the dragoneye now docile, she could think more clearly. Instinct guided her to scoop up the little dragon in her arms. It squawked and struggled against her as it looked out at the fallen body of its mother.

"I swear, no harm will befall you."

Rayna did not know where the words came from. She only knew that she meant to keep her promise. At her words, the small dragon shifted his attention from its mother's fallen body to Rayna. He chirped at her as though he understood the vow she had just made to him. Looking down at the helpless creature in her arms, Rayna knew she would keep the vow no matter what. Once again, dragons had shifted her course in life.

# 25
# Duty of a Deadman

Valerios encountered three perilous close calls within a brief span of time. He knew setting off on this journey would be dangerous, but facing down death three times over shook him.

As the snow tumbled down from overhead, threatening to bury them alive, Valerios thought it was the end. Somehow, facing that grim fate, he still held his wits.

At the last possible second, he called for defense. The men followed the command down the line, holding their massive shields overhead.

"Angle!" Valerios called again.

Each man then tilted their shields. When the snow struck, it would be steered over the cliffside instead of directly on top of them. It took a lot of effort to hold the heavy shields high while the mass of snow crashed down. But these men had been trained to withstand the worst.

After his battle with the Shadax, Valerios felt weak. His legs already gave way once, pitching him over the side and causing this horrible predicament. He wasn't about to allow himself to falter again.

Even with legs shaking and arms growing numb, Valerios held position. The rest of the men kept the line as well. More snow fell, blotting out what little sunlight shone upon them. As it grew dark, Valerios said a prayer for his beautiful love, Kemi. Should he fall this day, he hoped The God of Wind would take his words across the sea to her ears.

Lost in his incantation, Valerios didn't realize the snow stopped falling until one of the soldiers roused him. The shields successfully guided the icy debris away from them. Although they were surrounded by snow, they remained mobile. Up at the front of the line, Valerios could hear Captain Falkon calling out orders.

It gave him joy to hear his friend still lived. Even though they had harsh words back at the castle, Falkon remained as a brother to Valerios. He only hoped that Rayna made it safely through the pass before the snow came crashing down.

Time was against them as they tried to push through to more stable ground. They only walked a few paces before debris and chunks of snow fell again. Above them, sounds of a ferocious battle sounded. Valerios could hear the bellowing of a mighty beast. It appeared they awoke the dragon.

His thoughts went to Rayna, who traveled at the head of the pack the last time he saw her. She must've made it to the top and dared to face the dragon alone. Her guts as dragonslayer were admirable, but he feared they would get her killed this day.

Concern for Rayna's well-being gave Valerios new vigor. He hurried past the soldiers moving too cautiously on the crest of the mountain. But as he made it to the front of the line, he found a wall of snow stood in their path.

Falkon had a group of soldiers digging with shields and bare hands to open the pass. When Valerios arrived, he didn't waste anytime with words. Instead, he dropped to his knees and began helping the soldiers. When Falkon saw him join, it compelled him to act as well.

The more men who hacked at the wall of snow, the faster it fell. Soon, they were rewarded with the gleaming of sunlight as it broke through the snowbank. Falkon and Valerios pushed ahead, forcing their tired legs to move up the mountain.

As they made it to the top, the men halted at the sight of the massive beast. It held the length of a warship with twice the mass. Any other time Valerios would be awed seeing such a creature. Of all the stories he'd heard and read on dragons, nothing compared to being in the presence of one. But it was the dragonslayer who mattered more, and she was nowhere in sight.

At his side, Falkon trembled as though fever overtook him. Valerios had to steady his friend as they slowly moved around to the front of the beast. It did not seem to be moving, though that didn't mean it wasn't lying in wait. The way Rayna explained it, dragons were as intelligent as fearsome.

Valerios wanted to call out to her, but doing so would draw the dragon's attention. He continued to move slowly and silently until he passed its prone body. Behind him, Falkon caught his foot on a dented shield buried in the snow and tripped. He fell into Valerios, knocking them both to the ground in a clattering of chainmail and armor.

The noise echoed over the sky loud enough to wake the dead. Valerios scrambled to his feet, sword drawn, ready to face the wrath of the dragon. But its large head remained motionless resting upon a mound of dirt.

"You needn't worry, it's dead."

The sound of Rayna's voice made Valerios' heart flutter. She lived and had bested the dragon by herself! An impressive feat he wouldn't have believed if not seeing it with his own eyes. When he located her at the mouth of a nearby cave, another surprise came his way. She held a baby dragon in her hands.

"By the gods," he muttered.

Falkon was not as impressed. Fear or fervor drove his actions, and he lunged towards the baby dragon. Valerios caught him by the arm and pulled him back.

"What're you doing?"

"That thing is coming with me."

As Valerios tried to reason with Falkon, he saw Rayna draw her blade. Now that the dragon was slain, and her job was complete, she would not cater to Falkon's demands any longer. But her reasoning as to why surprised Valerios.

"The child stays with me," she said. "I made a vow."

Falkon gave a laugh edged with the same madness his father held. He struggled free of Valerios' grip and drew his own sword; the tip pointed towards Rayna.

"She's touched in the head."

"No, I'm seeing clearly for the first time," Rayna disagreed.

Valerios stood between the two of them, trying to broker peace. Over near the edge of the cliff, the soldiers appeared. When they reached the three of them, Falkon would give orders to kill Rayna, which the soldiers would blindly follow. Valerios had to get them both back on terms before that happened. He started with Rayna, who seemed more sensible.

"What do you mean, you made a pact with a dragon? I thought they were your sworn enemy."

"Something isn't right here, Valerios," she told him. "Look there, the dragon skin is red, not the black scales of my sworn enemy your king led me to believe would be waiting."

"What difference does it make?" Falkon yelled. "A dragon is a dragon and they must be killed!"

Rayna angled her body so the baby dragon was out of the line of sight. Then she held her great broadsword up in a defensive position, her attention on Captain Falkon.

"You'll not be killing anything."

Valerios sheathed his own sword and raised his hands in a show of peace. Rayna glanced at him, but her attention remained fixed on Falkon, who grew edgier by the minute.

His eyes kept darting to the side as though a presence there guided him. But when Valerios looked over, he saw nothing. Ironic that Falkon would accuse Rayna of being off in the head when he seemed to be the one touched.

"Rayna, please don't do this," Valerios pleaded.

"I have to."

She tucked the baby dragon closer to her breast. If Valerios hadn't been impressed with her before, he certainly was now. The reasons she held for not wanting to give up the small dragon were her own. He admired her conviction even if it seemed out of place for one known as a dragonslayer. Falkon drew other conclusions while listening to their discussion.

"She means to take the dragon and sell it to the highest bidder."

Valerios turned his attentions to Falkon to calm him. All the remaining soldiers had made it up the mountain and were fast approaching. Valerios was running out of time to solve the matter without bloodshed, and now Falkon pressed him with orders.

"The dragon is dead. We no longer have any use for the slayer. Do your duty and get rid of her like I told you to."

At Captain Falkon's words, Rayna readied herself to face Valerios. As she angled her sword his way, Valerios held his in defense. Looking over the noble warrior woman before him, ready to face death to protect a once sworn enemy, he made a decision. For the first time in the many years since Falkon saved him from certain death, Valerios defied his friend's orders and lowered his sword.

"No, I shall not kill her."

Falkon's eyes registered disappointment, then flashed like a gemstone in the same enigmatic hue of perse King Favian's held. The magic madness had infected Falkon as well. Valerios should've known by the way his good friend had been whispering to an invisible presence for the last few days. But he'd been preoccupied with thoughts of Kemi and facing a damned dragon.

Now, as the tip of Falkon's sword ripped through his stomach, he regretted his misjudgment. The monster he should've been concerned about was the one he called friend.

# 26
# Dragon Forged

Rayna watched in horror as Captain Falkon gutted Valerios with his sword. She was too far away to intervene in time. Fresh blood patterned the patches of snow as Valerios' body fell to the ground. Her gaze remained fixed on him as he writhed in pain and then lay still. His cold, dead eyes looked back at her with shock. Valerios trusted his friend would never betray him and he died for it. Rayna didn't trust anyone.

For a moment, Falkon seemed surprised by what he'd done. He stared down at the body of Valerios and looked at his sword hand as though he'd been detached from the action of killing. Then, as though a hidden entity spoke new orders to him on the air, he turned towards Rayna.

Dispatching Captain Falkon would give her great pleasure, especially after watching him murder Valerios.

But the troop of soldiers coming to join the fight would be a challenge.

One arm burdened with the baby dragon, Rayna couldn't call upon her dragoneye to light the fire of Bhrytbyrn. Setting the youngling down to fight would prove perilous as well. The tricky Captain Falkon would keep her distracted long enough to snatch the baby, or worse. So, Rayna would fight one-armed against many.

~

At first, watching his childhood chum fall dead gave Falkon great remorse. But as Xara explained how Valerios was a threat that needed to be eliminated, things became clearer. How foolish he was to stand between Falkon and the dragonslayer. That he would choose the woman over his commander and comrade of many years proved what Xara said was true.

*"He's a traitor and he must be stopped. Kill him!"*

Her words spurred Falkon to take the needed action he may have otherwise balked from. When the cold steel ripped into Valerios' flesh it felt as satisfying as laying with a lover. Now the dragonslayer is all that stood in Falkon's way.

She cradled the baby dragon in her arms in such a manner that calling her slayer no longer seemed appropriate. In fact, her tenderness towards the child lost her all merit of worth in Falkon's eyes. She was no slayer, just a one-eyed woman about to join Valerios in death.

As his soldiers began to circle, they gasped at the sight of Valerios dead on the ground. His blood had mingled with the dirt and snow like a tapestry. Lifeless eyes stared up at Falkon and dared to question why he'd run him through.

The soldiers would also wonder. Valerios was well-liked among the men. Revenge would be sought on the one who dispatched their brother in such a heinous manner. So, Captain Falkon gave them their target.

"Kill that one," he said, pointing his sword towards Rayna. "She butchered Valerios, as he was unarmed."

The men drew their swords and started towards her. Falkon stayed back and watched the impending attack unfold. Soon they would slay the slayer.

*"And the dragon child will be ours," Xara whispered.*

"Yes," Falkon agreed. "The dragon child will be ours."

~

As Rayna expected, the soldiers would heed their captain's order. But Falkon upped the stakes by claiming Rayna killed Valerios. Now vengeance drove the men, and they would not be deterred by anything other than a blade.

Contrary to rumors about her abilities, Rayna wasn't a sellsword. She did not accept money to murder men or women. Hers had been a noble cause to rid the land of the dreaded dragons. Now that story went up in smoke, just like her home years before. And with it, her entire moral code shifted.

Most times, when confronted by men who wished to test their skills or take her against her will, Rayna chose to render them unconscious. Now, as the group of Falkon's soldiers charged her, she knew nothing but death would dispel them. For if she didn't stop their advances, she would fall and the baby dragon with her.

The first of the men came rushing in with no plan of attack, just blind rage to drive him. Rayna pivoted away from his blade and slashed him across the stomach, just under his breastplate. He tumbled to his knees, then fell face first on the ground. One man down, several to go.

The others grew wiser and came at her together. Three of them approached her this time. The bannerman was a part of this group and he used the long staff that hoisted the king's colors as a weapon. Its length proved troublesome as it kept Rayna at a distance.

She could not get close enough to strike at the man, so she used his own weapon against him. Next time he struck out at her, she forced the staff away with her sword. It swung out of the man's control and hit the other two soldiers as they moved forwards. The three of them tumbled to the ground, giving Rayna a chance to secure new positioning.

Holding the baby snug in her arms, she ran back

towards the first fallen soldier. There upon his belt sat the Chaos Fire she sought. She had to drop her sword to grab the jar, leaving her unarmed for the moment. That is when Captain Falkon engaged the fight.

~

How did the bitch best his guards? One lone woman against the best soldiers in the world, and she still managed to topple them. To think nothing but fools stood in his ranks angered Falkon to the point of action. He would leave the dragon bitch laying himself and the world would know of his triumph.

Standing on the outskirts of the fight, Falkon waited for the right opportunity to strike. That moment came when Rayna abandoned her sword. As she bent to retrieve Chaos Fire from the soldier's belt, Falkon tackled her. Both the bottle of black magic and the dragon baby tumbled across the ground. Falkon remained on top of Rayna, where he struck her in the jaw and then began to strangle her.

It felt good wrapping his fingers around her throat. He could feel her breath cut off beneath the weight of his hands. She struggled beneath him as he straddled her, pressing tighter to her throat.

"Die you one-eyed bitch!"

His glee was short-lived as somehow Rayna pried his fingers from her throat. The musculature of her body wasn't just for show. She'd been honed through warfare and training to give her ample strength. That strength started to best Falkon's as she freed herself from his grip.

He reared back and went to strike her again. If he knocked her unconscious, they could bring her back to town and string her up. A death in Sandhal Square for all to witness would see Falkon rise to legendary status.

But as he punched down towards her jaw, Rayna blocked it with her forearm. She wrapped his arm in hers and then thrust her forehead up into Falkon's nose. The blow knocked him dizzy, and he staggered backwards. Rayna helped him the rest of the way off her with a swift kick to his stomach.

Falkon fell high upon his shoulders and the momentum rolled him over onto his stomach. When his vision cleared, he saw Rayna standing over him with the Chaos Fire in hand.

~

Captain Falkon fought like a cutthroat, trying to pry loose coins from an unwitting patron. Rayna almost blacked out from the strangulation hold he held upon her throat. But somewhere she found the strength to force herself free.

Now with the advantage returned to her favor, she needed to move fast. The soldiers were back on their feet and paces away. The dragon baby cried out. Chaos Fire in hand, Rayna warned King Favian's guards to stand back. Then she looked to Falkon to call off his dogs.

"You know as well as I that Valerios fell at your blade," she said. "Let me walk away and I'll let you keep that secret."

He slowly rose to his feet and dusted the dirt from his clothing. Rayna saw a sparked color change race over his eyes as though marked in magic. It appeared Captain Falkon hadn't been calling out his own orders for a long while. She could almost smell the magic in the air. Someone else pulled the strings, and they did not care about honor or valor. Only death would do.

"Foolish girl, who would believe you?"

Falkon gave a laugh, then motioned for his men to advance once more. Rayna expected as much. A truce of any sort would've been a miracle on that mountain. So, she acted swiftly, hoping that the plan she worked out in her head would come to fruition without fault.

As the soldiers advanced, she retreated just far enough to stand out of the blast zone. Then she lobbed the Chaos Fire over their heads and into the face of the dragon's lair. As the liquid fire struck, chunks of rock broke free and came crashing into Falkon and his men.

Rayna was rocked backwards by the blast. Falling hard upon her rear, she then scrambled towards the baby dragon and shielded its body with her own. The foundations of the dragon's lair came crumbling down until nothing remained. When Rayna looked back, she saw that Falkon and his men were covered in debris.

Gently, she scooped the dragon child into her arms. After retrieving Bhrytbyrn she stopped to honor Valerios one last time. He'd been one of the best men she'd ever known and died without just cause. For that, she felt guilty.

If she ever made her way across the sea to the jeweled isle of Ischon, she would seek his Kemi and tell her tales of Valerios' bravery. For now, no time was left to mourn. Rayna's focus became the well-fare of the dragon child. That meant she needed to put enough distance between them and Saltwood Stronghold as possible.

Once King Favian learned of his son's demise, he would want answers. Rayna only hoped that they would think her dead beneath the rubble alongside the others. Then she could disappear with the dragon child without the threat of soldiers at her back.

# 27
# Glory of the Kill

Falkon heard voices all around him as he lay unconscious beneath the rubble. One of them sounded like Valerios crying out. As Falkon shifted awake, the cries from his good friend remained in his memory. Though no words crossed his lips when the sword ran him through, Falkon imagined Valerios shouting from the grave. He spoke of betrayal and a shattered kinship. Then another voice spoke, this one clearer on Falkon's ears.

*"You mourn your friend."*

It was Xara, the only one who stood by Falkon's side without judgment. She told him the truth on matters he could not always see. Blinded by emotion, his thoughts fell to anguish.

"I am shattered," he told her. "I killed my closest ally. Let me remain here, buried beneath rocks and snow, as it is a fitting end to my story."

*"You are not to blame, good captain,"* Xara replied. *"Rayna betrayed you all. She swayed Valerios with her sex and made him turn against you. Then she stole off with the dragon child and left you for dead."*

Once again, Xara spoke true. It was Rayna's doing. Valerios fell because of the dragonslayer. She needed to atone for such actions. Falkon shifted his body beneath the rocks and began the arduous task of wriggling free.

He managed to get his hands out, allowing him to grip deep into the dirt and drag himself the rest of the way free. The first thing he saw when he broke loose was Valerios. He remained on the ground where he fell, a new dusting of snow covering him like a sheet.

Falkon staggered over with tears in his eyes. He kneeled down and touched Valerios on the forehead. His skin felt like ice and his eyes had glassed over. No longer did Falkon see the burning light of brilliance staring back at him. His flame was extinguished forever.

"The warrior woman will pay for this," Falkon vowed. "She betrayed us all and she will pay with her life."

When he tried to shut Valerios' eyelids, he found them frozen stiff. Instead, Falkon cut a swatch from his leather coat and lay it over his friend's face. He wasn't a man of prayer, but he knew Valerios would've wanted last rites. So Falkon stumbled through prayers to the Source Gods as best he could.

The gods of fire, earth, and wind weren't as well known to him as the Goddess of Water. Spending so much time at sea with his father's battalion let him come to know such a god intimately. But even the Goddess of Water could not help him now. His task ahead could only be fulfilled by himself.

Falkon didn't bother searching for survivors beneath the rocks. The day waned, and he needed to find his way off the Graven Peaks before night fell.

Scrounging up any supplies he could find, he trekked down. Then a thought occurred to him and he circled back. The mighty red dragon remained still in death where Rayna had left it. But that tale would not be told. She did not deserve the credit of slaying this dragon.

If he let word travel back into the towns that the dragonslayer fell another beast, it would only enhance her reputation. Falkon wouldn't allow the bitch such a triumph. Her stories of slaying were about to be erased and replaced with a bounty on her head.

Instead, the glory of the kill would be his. It took much effort, but he climbed the dragon's body and hacked off one of its teeth. The massive incisor was the length of his sword and twice as heavy. Falkon slipped it into a sheath at his back and then began the long march home.

The trek back to Saltwood Stronghold left Falkon with time to plot his revenge on Rayna. Dragonslayer no more, she would be labeled a traitor to the throne and hunted down like a pheasant.

In his journey home, Falkon also thought about Valerios. His trusted advisor and friend was now forever lost atop the Graven Peaks. Without a proper burial at sea as was customary for their kind, Valerios' spirit would walk the Shadowed Highlands for eternity. Such a disturbing end for one they called "The Valiant."

Falkon measured himself fortunate that Xara remained at his side. In his isolation, he may have wandered off the path back to Sandhal, never to return home. But Xara kept him focused on the task at hand. They needed to track down Rayna and get that baby dragon back. Falkon wasn't sure as to the reasoning of keeping the dragon, but he knew not to question Xara. She was wise in her ways.

With Xara's help to guide him, Falkon made it to Pelanor Pass. There he flagged down a farmer's cart, headed into town. On Xara's advice, Falkon played himself as a beggar rather than the Captain of the Guards, and it helped to garner a ride from the stranger.

In the back of the cart he found bushels of fruit, which he indulged in when the farmer wasn't looking. The sweetness of apples and pears gave Falkon new vigor. By the time they made it back into town, he felt at full strength again.

Bruised but not beaten, Falkon leaped from the cart as it entered Sandhal Square and he started a run up to the

Saltwood Stronghold. The last time he entered his father's throne room in haste, he was chastised for his filthy appearance. This time, the wounds of war would tell a different tale.

As Falkon pushed through the heavy doors and entered the great hall, all eyes fell on him. The gentry and chamber maids gave audible gasps and whispered as he passed. Falkon ignored them all. His sights were set on his father as he strode towards the throne room. When Favian saw his son's triumphant return, he would finally laud him with the praise he deserved.

Having his father accept him was an image Falkon played out in his mind many times. Now as he approached the king on his throne, his anticipation for its fruition made him stand a little prouder. His father didn't waste any time knocking that pride out of him.

"How is it you've returned and no others?"

Falkon measured his response, noting no joy rested in his father's eyes at his son's safe return. Then he spoke plainly and without remorse.

"All dead."

Favian shifted on his throne at the disturbing news. A shaky hand ran over his grizzled beard as he pondered the ramifications of Falkon's words.

"Valerios?" the king asked.

His concern was evident in the way his lip quivered as he spoke Valerios' name. It made Falkon finally understand his place. He was a mongrel dog under the king's boots while Valerios had been a son to him.

Falkon thought about telling his father that he'd been the one to kill Valerios. Watching the shock and pain fill his eyes would warm Falkon better than any fires. But at Xara's urging, Falkon kept his original story as explanation.

"The dragon woman turned on us. She killed Valerios and then ran away, leaving me to best the mighty beast."

Falkon moved to retrieve the massive dragon tooth from its sheath, but Favian wasn't interested in seeing it. He no longer cared about the threat of the great dragon or even Rayna's betrayal. Favian's only concern was the loss of Valerios.

"Gods, what have I done?" Favian muttered.

"What do you mean, father? I conquered the dragon as you requested. Now we must track down that lying bitch and retrieve what she stole from us."

Favian pounded his hand on the armrest of his throne. The singular movement drained him of energy and he slumped his shoulders. But his thoughts remained diverged on a path of sorrow rather than vengeance.

"The only thing stolen from the kingdom on this day is precious life. What am I to tell Emperor Kivu Kazo?"

"Who cares about that old man?" Falkon argued. "Tell him I'll marry his precious daughter if it means that much."

"He doesn't want you!" Favian shouted, rising from his throne on shaky legs. "The emperor demands a man of substance to marry Kemi. That is the pact that we made. You weren't even an afterthought for his second daughter, K'lani."

*"You know what you have to do,"* Xara whispered.

Falkon saw her now in the safe space of the throne room. She slithered over the back of the massive throne, caressing it like a lover. Then she beckoned for Falkon to join her in his rightful place.

"You're wrong, father. I have more substance than that dead man laying bloodless upon the Graven Peaks. And I have eternally more substance than the bag of bones that stands before me."

"How dare you!"

"How dare I? How dare you, father! I've given everything to you and still you chastise my very existence. Well, now I'm done giving. It's my turn to take."

As he spoke, Falkon retrieved the dragon tooth from its sheath. It took all the strength in him to heft it, but once he got it under control, it made a fine weapon.

While Favian looked in awe upon the massive tooth, he noticed too late that Falkon thrust it towards him. Son stabbed his own father through the heart, marking a changing of titles there for all eyes to see.

None dared approach Falkon to stop him. They knew

he would not be stopped. Even Favian finally acknowledged his son's determination. It took death for him to recognize what Falkon was really capable of. But Falkon no longer cared about his father's praise. As the former king reached out to touch his cheek in a final show of affection, Falkon pressed the dragon tooth deeper. It pierced through Favian's back and struck the throne, almost tipping it over.

"Die, old man," Falkon whispered.

He waited and watched as the light in Favian's eyes dimmed, and death took him. Only then did he step back and address the people.

"Hear me now as your new king," he began. "There is no time for weeping or weakness. My father lost sight of what has kept our kingdom strong for many years. That is swift and mighty justice. There is a betrayer in our lands that shall not go unpunished. As the new king of Atharia, I proclaim a bounty be placed on the head of the warrior woman known as Rayna. Let the hunter become the hunted!"

# 28
# Debt of the Dragon

Caring for a baby dragon wasn't the same as rearing a human child. Truth be told, Rayna had spent little time with human infants as well. She didn't know what to feed a youngling out on the road. When that child preferred the taste of flesh, it made things more complicated.

Rayna had been on the run since fighting her way down from the Graven Peaks. She was tired and Saarath's words weighed heavy on her mind. Perhaps it was hearing a dragon speak for the first time that stuck with her. But Rayna knew it was the words Saarath spoke that burned on her mind.

*Dark magic has led you astray*

She did not have time to absorb the words and their meaning before war waged with Falkon. Now they mingled with her grief over Valerios. When Rayna set out towards the Graven Peaks, she never expected such an outcome, especially carrying a baby dragon on her back.

It mewled and huffed, trying to wriggle free from the satchel. Rayna felt its tiny clawed hands press into the flesh of her shoulder. She tried to calm it as best she could, but the child missed its mother.

"Calm down, child," Rayna whispered. "I'll find us some food."

As she spoke, the dragon settled. It cooed like a bird and nuzzled its tiny head against the back of Rayna's neck. She spoke, and it responded as though it knew her. Perhaps the child didn't miss its mother afterall. It had mistaken Rayna for its caregiver the moment they locked eyes. In essence, that's what she was now.

They trekked through barren fields longer than Rayna cared to. Being out in the open for too long often invited trouble. No rivers or streams presented themselves. She couldn't even find a burrow for shelter. Her muscles were tight and sore from the battle with King Favian's men and the odious Captain Falkon. Bruising circled her neck where he tried to strangle her. If the gods were just, he would suffer a long, drawn out death beneath the pile of rocks for what he'd done to Valerios.

Exhaustion was setting in the longer she walked. Still new to the world, the dragon had fallen asleep at her back. She could feel its hot breath tickling the hair on the nape of her neck. Somehow, that comforted her as she walked alone.

Before nightfall, she would need to find them food and shelter. She didn't know how far west she'd run to determine where the nearest town would be. Going east would've brought her deeper into the Shadowed Highlands, where the magics owned most of the land. They would've taken one look at the baby dragon and tried to capture it as their own.

In fact, upon seeing the small dragon, most fools would think of fetching a profit and confront her. Then Rayna would have no choice but to fight them off. Better to keep the child hidden. Since she was a dead woman now, the anonymity would help her hide.

Her legs ached from walking for such a long stretch, but the pain did not compare to the disturbance from her dragoneye. Ever since she lay eyes on the dragon child, her eye had throbbed like never before. Even now, Rayna could feel it pulsing beneath the leather patch as though it sought to escape. The pressure was giving her a headache, with no relief to come.

Then, out in the distance, she saw a farmhouse standing on acres of land. She forced herself to increase the pace towards the homestead. As she got closer, Rayna saw the farm remained in good standing. A working farmhouse meant there would be ample supplies.

She could find food for both her and the dragon child, then tuck away in the hayloft for the night. But she would have to do it quietly as the farm was attached to a small dwelling, and the owners shuffled about inside.

Rayna tucked a hood up over her head and slowly crept through a field of wheat towards the barn. Staying low and out of sight, she found her way up to the stables where the horses settled. At the same time, the dragon baby shifted awake at her back. Once it saw the horses, it chirped as though horse meat would soon be its dinner. The horses took it as a threat. They whinnied and struck their hooves against the walls.

The commotion caught the attention of the farmer. Rayna saw movement heading towards the front door and she ducked out of sight. Staying covered and trying to quiet the baby dragon, she didn't get a good look at the man. The sound of his heavy boots told her he held considerable size. Most farmers who toiled land all day were burly and strong. This is someone Rayna didn't have the energy to contend with at the moment.

Fortunately, after a few passes through the stable, the farmer decided no predator lurked about. He gave a harsh whistle to quiet his steeds and then returned to his home. Once she felt certain he was gone, Rayna made her way towards the grain loft, hoping to find food.

Her first pass through found only dry barley and wheat. In a pinch, she could mix it with water for sustenance. But the dragon wouldn't be able to stomach it. Pushing further inside, she was rewarded in her search with crates of fruit and barrels filled with nuts. A bountiful harvest the farmer probably intended to sell at the local markets. Rayna would relieve him of some supply in the meantime.

She also found jugs filled with fresh milk. That meant cows would be lurking close by. She would have to keep the dragon child away from them or else it would act up again. For now, she settled in to eat and feed the child. She slivered off pieces of fruit with her knife, to which the youngling refused. Only when she pushed a saucer of milk beneath its snout did it finally indulge.

"You're like a scaly red cat," she laughed.

It wasn't much of a bounty, and Rayna knew she would need to find them both meat soon, but it would sustain them for now. With her belly full, she leaned back against a pile of hay and shut her eyes. The dragon child scuffled about on the floor, still trying to find its legs. Rayna reached out and tucked the baby against her breast. It shifted and flapped its little wings, but then found peace at her side.

As she slept, Rayna was plagued with visions of death. First, her family burned alive in her home. Then, Valerios' gray body called out to her. He spoke a soundless warning she could not make out. When she tried to escape, he grasped her hand. The icy touch of his skin on her own shot Rayna awake. She then found herself staring down the spikes of a pitchfork pointed towards her face.

"What're you doing in my barn?" the farmer asked.

Surprisingly, her first thoughts went to protecting the dragon child. And in that moment, she found a lie to spin. She only hoped the farmer would believe her.

"Please, I have a child."

Rayna motioned to the dragon tucked against her bosom. It's body covered by her furs it could pass for human if one didn't look too closely. The farmer hesitated as he looked over at the babe in her arms. Rayna could see beneath his gruff exterior lay a soft heart. She aimed to pierce it with words of a poet rather than her sword.

"We've been on the road many days," she continued. "I saw your barn and only sought shelter for the night. A thousand pardons for trespassing, good sir."

As she suspected, the farmer was a burly man. He had thick forearms and shoulders that tucked up against his ears. Black, thinning hair hung down to his back. His fingers were gnarled at the joints, making it difficult to control the pitchfork. Even though he held size and strength, age had taken its toll. In that age, he had wisdom as well.

"You shouldn't have broken into my barn," he told her.

Rayna's hand fell to the hilt of Bhrytbyrn, tucked away in the hay near her hip. She readied herself for a fight that didn't come. The farmer tucked his pitchfork away and reached a hand out to her.

"You should've just knocked on my door," he continued. "I would've welcomed you."

Rayna hesitated to accept his hand. "You would?"

"Of course. Only a barbarian would've turned away a woman and her child in need. Now let's get you inside where it's warm."

Rayna gave a crook of a smile and then accepted his hand. She kept the dragon baby tucked out of sight as she carried it. As they walked towards his home, the farmer explained how he'd been widowed only last winter and lost his son the year before.

"My son was meant to inherit my lands," he explained. "Every morning we'd be out working in the fields together before he grew ill. He was a good lad and strong as an ox… like you. I've never seen a woman with the build you have."

"I was a blacksmith's apprentice further south near Valeuki," she lied.

"Don't see many women blacksmiths. From the looks of you, I bet you'd be good at tilling land."

"You seem to be doing fine on your own."

"Looks can be deceiving." He flexed his hands several times, trying to get the ache out. "Truth is, I have to hire help on most days just to keep up with the harvest. That cuts into my profits quite a bit. I'm uncertain how much longer I'll be able to keep my lands. But if you stayed on and helped in exchange for room and board, I could see this place thrive again."

By that time, they'd made it up to the house. Before going inside, Rayna knew what must be done. The farmer, Josep by name, painted a grand picture in his mind. He wanted to welcome Rayna into his home, and eventually his bed, to replace the family he'd lost over the years. Many cracks lay within that picture, the first being that the child in question wasn't human.

Josep seemed a kind enough man, perhaps just a little sad and lonely. Rayna would refute his request of her with as much empathy as she could muster. But if he did not listen, she lamented the child would need to make a proper appearance.

"I thank you for the kind offer, Josep, but I am sorry to say I must turn you down."

"But why, Kathryn?"

She'd used her mother's name as an alias before, but hearing Josep speak it with such disappointment in his tone stung her heart. They stood at the threshold of his home, the door halfway open so the warmth from a stoked fire caressed her face.

Rayna must've been a fool to turn away a stable home and companionship, but that type of life wasn't meant for her. She was a warrior duty-bound to make things right for past deeds. Not only did she seek justice for her family, but now she owed a debt to all the dead dragons she had slain under false pretenses.

"My destiny lies on another path and I must continue my travels towards it."

"I suppose I can understand that. Though I wish you would reconsider."

"I will help you with your chores in the morning as payment for your hospitality. But I cannot stay."

Josep gave her a nod, and then they clasped hands in agreement. It was the best Rayna could do under the circumstances. She needed the warmth of a bed for sleep, and supplies for the road, so she would pay her way with hard work. If all went as planned, it would be a nice barter. It remained to be seen if the baby dragon would behave itself.

# 29
# Price of the Dragon

The farmer, Josep, gave Rayna a place to sleep for the night. In the morning, they shared a hearty meal and friendly conversation. Most of what Rayna contributed were stories spun of lies. Josep had many questions about the baby's father and how Rayna lost her eye. She told him just enough to keep him from suspecting otherwise.

Anytime he asked to see the child, she spoke of not wanting to disturb the babe while it slept. Then she claimed the emotions of such hardships were too heavy and that she didn't want to talk any further. So, Josep opened up about his own grief as a way to bond with her.

Rayna listened quietly while keeping the dragon baby fed and out of sight. For the most part, it was quiet but now and then it let a sing-song loose from its throat that she had to mask with a cough. Josep wondered if she were coming down with an ailment and recommended she stay on a few more days to rest. She thanked him for his kindness but knew it was time to press on. Before she left the lands, Rayna did her part to help around the farm.

It was honest, hard work toiling the land under the hot sun. Working in such a manner brought her a strange sense of peace she'd not known before. Perhaps, when her duties no longer pulled at her like the calling of her dragoneye she could settle down on farmland of her own. Now was not that time.

With the work completed, Rayna set out on her way. Josep gave her one of his horses and loaded its saddlebags with supplies. She was fortunate to find a good man in a world gone mad.

As she traveled, Rayna's thoughts turned to another good man. She only knew Valerios for a short time but he held all the qualities of a true warrior. Rayna couldn't claim to be anywhere near as noble and pure of heart as he. Anything she did was measured by the return it would give her. Valerios put others before himself. Even on the Graven Peaks he tried to broker peace for all amid battle. That selfless act cost him his life. Had he chosen sides he might still live.

Rayna chose sides as well. The baby dragon tucked away at her back had changed her perspective. Now she put another's welfare before her own.

Because of this new dynamic, Rayna had grown even more cautious. So, when a pack of men shuffled out onto the pathway and blocked her route she knew it meant trouble.

They held the look of mercenaries. Hired men meant to complete dirty deeds for pay. What she didn't know is whether they found her by accident or skill.

Such a large grouping told her this was a chance meeting. Mercenaries usually traveled solo or in tight formation when on a job to not bring attention to themselves. At a quick glance Rayna counted ten men in front of her. Still others closed in at her flank to cut off any retreat.

Josep provided her with fresh skins to wear. She had draped them over her armor and weapons to appear as nothing more than a lowly traveler. The sight of a lone woman burdened with supplies may have caught the attention of such scoundrels. Easy prey to rob and rape.

Rayna focused her attention on the man who stepped out in front of the others. He stood tall enough to meet the eye of her horse. A long mane of dirty blonde hair traveled the length of his back. He had a square jaw and green eyes clouded in mischief.

"Let me pass, sir." Rayna spoke with a softness and kept her eyes down. "I have no quarrel with you."

The man reached up and pulled the coverings away from her face. Rayna had to steel herself from fracturing his fingers as he touched her. As he looked at her, a spark of recognition flashed in his eyes and he gave her a crooked grin.

"I have no quarrel with you either. But your pretty little head is worth a lot of coin so no, I cannot let you pass."

While they conversed, Rayna studied her surroundings. They stopped her in an open grove with no trees or tall bushes to cover an escape. The pack of them arrived on foot, their horses or wagons set up further out to not attract suspicion.

Now they drew swords from sheaths and knocked arrows to bows. She would not get out of the predicament without a fight. The words she spoke next were only meant to delay the inevitable as she readied her own weapon.

"You have me mistaken with someone else. I'm just a farm girl on my way to market."

The man looked her over from head to foot. At first, his stare coveted her features, and he made his want known with a lick of his lips. Then his gaze fell upon the patch covering her eye and he broadened his crooked grin.

"Coraise, fetch me the one-eyed warrior woman, they told me," he began. "Her body chiseled from granite; her hair the color of wheat under the morning sun."

To stress his speech, Coraise pulled a scroll from his belt and unrolled it for Rayna to see. Her likeness was drawn on parchment with the word BOUNTY scrolled at the top. By order of the new king of Atharia, Falkon Fourspire, she was to be taken dead or alive.

"There is a larger sum due to us if we bring you in alive," Coraise said, tucking away the scroll. "So, be a dear and step off that horse nice and slow."

The bastard Falkon had lived. And all the while Rayna spent time as a farmhand he was building an assault against her. Coraise Kennethgorian was known to her by reputation alone. A skilled tracker and swordsman who sold his skills to the highest bidder. Rayna wasn't concerned with his hunt for her or the fact he had her boxed in now. The disturbing part of the parchment, the one these mercenaries must not have paid heed to, was at the bottom.

It read: *to all parties who seek the slayer - the creature she carries must be returned to the king unharmed in order to claim the bounty.*

King Falkon wanted Rayna's head on a pike and the dragon child as his slave. The mercenaries who surrounded her now wanted the massive bounty Falkon promised. They would do anything necessary to claim it. Rayna wasn't about to make it easy for them.

She reared back and kicked Coraise right in his smug face. His reflexes were sharp, and he avoided the flat of her foot. Only her toes grazed his cheek, but it was enough to move him from her path. The group of men behind him would prove to be more of a challenge.

Rayna spurred the horse on its sides to initiate a gallop and charged towards the lot of them. She barreled through the first two who stood in her way, but the few at the back were prepared for her charge. In tandem, they raised long staffs and struck out at both Rayna and her horse. She took a few rough blows, but stayed in the saddle. The horse didn't fare as well.

A stiff shot to its front legs brought the beast down and Rayna with it. As she fell, her instinct to protect the dragon child took over, and she angled her body to avoid falling atop it. Down on the ground, she was easy prey for the pack of mercenaries. They would beat her soundly until they could more easily transport her back to Sandhal.

Once King Falkon had her in his grasp, the beatings would truly begin. And the dragon child would become an abused pet, or worse. Rayna shifted to her haunches as the mercenary pack came for her. With a swift hand, she drew Bhrytbyrn and lashed out at them. One man took a slice to his fighting arm and fell back. But there were too many of them closing in to fend off with wild swings.

She needed to light up the sword in fire. Each time she tried to remove the patch from her dragoneye, the men closed in and she had to defend herself. The dragon baby was throwing a fit at her back. Its cries sounded scared, which amplified Rayna's protective nature.

"Back away dogs, lest you wish to taste death today!" she shouted. "Yes, I am the warrior woman you seek. The one who has slain mighty dragons with ease. Imagine then what I could do to the lot of you men."

She spoke a good defense, but it wouldn't scare off this pack. They only grew smarter in their approach. The knock of an arrow upon bow string gave her concern. She could not easily dodge both ground and air attacks from so many.

To her surprise, the arrows didn't come for her. Instead, they found their target in the necks, stomachs, and sometimes the groins of her attackers. Someone in the distance was picking off the mercenaries one-by-one.

Rayna used the distraction to her advantage and pressed forward with her own attack. She hacked open one man's guts, then chopped off another's hand. Fighting through her assailants, she came face-to-face with the leader.

Coraise had drawn his own greatsword, the blade an impressive eleven inches in length, and matched her blow for blow. Rayna struggled to keep him at bay and also protect her back from oncoming attack. Then, Coraise resorted to underhanded tactics and lobbed a mound of dirt in her face.

Her good eye fell blind to the trickery, and she lashed out her sword with reckless abandon. She missed her target as he ducked low and cut her across the stomach. His blade ripped through her modest leathers and caught flesh.

Rayna felt the warmth of her own blood spill out from the fresh wound and it doubled her over. Coraise grabbed her by the collar of her coat and dragged her back. Rayna wriggled out of it in time, but wound up exposing the dragon baby latched to her.

"By the four gods, is that a dragon I see?"

Coraise's words were filled with awe and underlined with greed. Rayna turned towards the direction of his voice, trying to keep the baby dragon shielded from attack. She still could not see well from the dirt in her right eye, so she exposed the left. Once the dragoneye felt freedom, it roared within its socket; the iris pulsed with wanted destruction. Rayna obeyed the eye and let it set fire to blade.

With Bhrytbyrn lit up in her hands, she drove back her attackers using sweeping arcs. The men looked equally terrified and mesmerized by the woman with the dragoneye spewing flame. Each time they advanced, Rayna countered. The stalemate continued as more joined the fight.

She counted five men encircling her. Then a sixth joined the fray, but he did not side with the mercenaries. Instead, he came shoulder-to-shoulder with Rayna against the attackers.

Uncertain of his intent, she circled back to keep him within striking distance. At a glance she saw he was well muscled with shaggy dark hair and a long beard that ended in a V-shape at his chest.

"I stand with you," he called out, not taking his eyes off the mercenaries.

"Why? You don't know me."

"One lone woman against a pack of cutthroats… it's an easy call to make."

Whether he was being chivalrous or foolish, Rayna let him help her. The mercenaries were too many to take alone while trying to protect the precious cargo with her. She only hoped this stranger beside her knew how to handle himself.

The hand-carved bow at his back told her he'd been the one lobbing the arrows before. In his grip, he held a massive double-edged battle axe. It had a short, customized handle which lent more power to each swing.

Rayna watched in appreciation as the axe cleaved a man's head clean from his shoulders. Not to be outdone, she used her broadsword to cast the same stroke on a man who dared step near her.

The leader continued to keep his eyes locked on Rayna. Now that she revealed her special gifts, and the dragon at her back, he wanted both in the worst way. A man's wants rarely concerned her, but Rayna would gladly let him taste of her sword.

To her side, the bearded man fell another opponent. This time, the blade of his axe landed square in the other's chest. It cut through the rib cage and sternum so deeply withdrawing it took effort.

By the time he got the axe free, another mercenary was rushing in. Rayna offered her sword to dispatch the common enemy. She swung low and hacked the man's legs clean from the bone. As she stepped in to help the bearded man, Rayna realized the baby dragon would be directly in his path. To her surprise, he said nothing on the matter.

She angled back out in front towards the leader, Coraise. With Bhrytbyrn still alive in flame, she began swinging it overhead. The fire licked out as though it meant to scoop up the enemy and drag them down to the Goddess of Earth's lair.

Coraise Kennethgorgian gave one last attempt to move towards Rayna and wound up tasting flame on his bare arm. Some of his long hair sizzled as well. Patting the burn out, he turned to the remaining men in his unit and called a retreat. They took off down the road, but not before Coraise gave Rayna one last covetous look. She knew that wouldn't be the last she'd see of him.

As the mercenary pack ran out of sight, the bearded man at her side started a little victory dance. Arms overhead, he scuffled his feet and howled in joy.

"Stop that," Rayna told him. "You're drawing

unwanted attention."

"My dear, if the sounds of such a battle didn't draw wandering eyes, then my excitement at living will fall on deaf ears."

"The unwanted attention is mine," she explained. "I have a tremendous ache in my eye and you're making it worse with your jubilation."

"Not only that, but you're bleeding heavily."

He pointed to her wounded side. It stained the ground with her blood. Rayna cupped a hand over the wound while still trying to hold the weight of Bhrytbyrn in a shaky grip.

"Who are you?" she demanded.

"I am 'Defiant' Demaris de Paz," the man replied with a little bow. "Most just refer to me as Paz."

"They call you 'defiant' and you lead with that?"

"It's an earned moniker. I don't play well with others," he admitted. "Unless, of course, they look like you, gorgeous."

Rayna studied him. He had an appealing look but also one of a sellsword, or worse. She continued to hold Bhrytbyrn aloft while she questioned him.

"You're a bounty hunter, then?"

"Best in the world. And you're the famous dragonslayer?"

"Best in the world."

"A dragonslayer by trade, yet you're keeping watch

over a dragon baby? Sounds more like a dragon defender."

"It's complicated."

Rayna winced from the increasing pain at her side. Paz stepped towards her and she backed away, keeping Bhrytbyrn between them. The sword of fire didn't seem to bother him.

"Let me help you," he said.

"Why would I let a bounty hunter at my back when the new king decreed my head for all the coin in the land?"

"I'm not interested in the bounty on you."

"I don't believe you."

"My days as a bounty hunter ended years ago. The troop I ran with sought to collect bounties, no matter the cost," he explained. "One night we sought a woman and her daughters wanted for practicing witchcraft. The townsfolk who hired us put together a handsome reward if we dealt with the threat. When we finally tracked the women down in an old hut on the outskirts of Corinth, things got out of hand.

"The men I ran with back then forced themselves on the sisters. It didn't sit well with my moral code, so I stopped them. It turned bloody. After that, I left the life and thus earned the moniker of being 'defiant.'"

"A bounty hunter with a moral code? That's a first."

"Surely, you can understand how one encounter might shift a person's path. Unless you intend on eating that baby dragon."

At his assumption, the dragon child snapped its jaws, which made Paz jump back. Such a big man growing startled at even the smallest dragon showed how much power they held. Whether or not Rayna believed his story, she didn't have the strength to dispel it. Wound weary and exhausted from blood loss, she opted to stand down.

"My friend doesn't like your inference, Paz," she told him. "But I'll give you a pass since you helped me dispatch those mercenaries."

Rayna tamped out Bhrytbyrn and sheathed it. Then she slipped back on her leather patch. As the dragoneye fell to darkness again, she felt the ache in her head begin to fade. But as the pain in her head dissipated, the wound at her side made her dizzy. She almost stumbled over her own feet and Paz had to keep her upright.

"I can stitch up your wound."

"I'll do it myself."

"You're a stubborn woman. Anyone ever tell you that?"

"All the time. Just point me towards my horse and I'll be on my way."

"I'm afraid your horse limped away when its bearings returned."

Rayna searched the grounds and, sure enough, there was no sign of the horse anywhere. All the supplies

Josep loaded her up with had gone with it. The disappointment was enough to drag her down, but Paz remained steadfast to her arm. Finally, she gave in to his insistence.

"Alright, you can help me."

Paz gave a chuckle. "You honor me, dragon defender."

"My name is Rayna."

"Well met, Rayna."

"Well met, Paz."

He clasped her hand in a proper greeting but lingered too long before releasing it. She searched his gray eyes and could not read his intent, though felt a strange yearning herself even in her weakened state.

Paz insisted he sew up her wound before they traveled much farther. Rayna was losing too much blood from the gash to keep her feet steady for long. They managed to find a thicker brush and a small grouping of trees further down the road. The heavy thicket would keep them concealed from prying eyes. With the bounty on her head, and Paz's own sorted past, they were targets for every cutthroat looking to make some extra coin.

Paz had a small bag of supplies that included equipment for wound care. At a glance, Rayna saw herbs and fruits mingling with assorted weapons inside his pack. He knew how to travel light, carrying only the essentials with him.

As he stitched her up, Rayna checked over the small

dragon for any wounds of his own. Several times she felt Paz's eyes go to the dragon and then look away before Rayna caught him. So, she pulled the child into her lap and let Paz get a good look.

"I killed its mother," she admitted.

"But you couldn't bring yourself to kill the baby?"

"No."

"See, you have a moral code as well."

"It's more than that. I owe a debt for my past deeds. Caring for this dragon child is just the start."

"What's the debt?"

"It's a long story I do not have the want or energy to tell just now."

They both fell silent as Paz finished patching her wound. His large hands had a gentle touch against her skin. Each time he grazed her flesh with his fingers, Rayna felt a tingle of a thrill.

Paz stitched the wound and left a pulsate over it for faster healing. Then his hands traveled to another patch of skin. He sought the scar tissue of a burn left by dragon's fire. His fingers traced the scarring until Rayna pushed his hand away.

"That old wound is a bad one. How did you survive that?"

"Just lucky, I guess."

They sat in an awkward silence. Only the dragon baby made any noise as it fussed in Rayna's arms. It was hungry and probably a little scared from the altercation. She needed to get back out on the road and find fresh supplies.

"Thank you for tending my wound," she told Paz. "You can go now."

She extended her arm in thanks, but he wouldn't take it. He didn't intend to leave just then. Her invitation for his help had inadvertently saddled her with a new traveling companion.

"Nonsense. I can't leave before dinner."

Paz pulled neatly wrapped packs of parchment from his bag. He set them down across a well-worn blanket and opened each of them to reveal various spiced meats. Smelling the food caused the little dragon to scramble out of Rayna's grip. She caught him just before he ravaged the entire spread of meat. Paz gave a laugh and then offered Rayna some of the deer jerky. She took it from his hand and let the dragon child feast.

"Hungry little guy," Paz said, then he offered another sliver of meat. "What about you?"

Rayna wasn't in a position to deny food. She took the sliver and ate it slowly, savoring every bite as though it were her last. To her surprise, it held just the right amount of spice to give it flavor but not overload it. And despite the leathery texture, it had also been cooked to perfection.

Paz must've learned the art of curing meats to keep

him sustained on the road. It was a craft Rayna always meant to learn herself but never found the time for. Her free time was always spent drinking and fucking instead.

"So, what's the little guy's name?"

The question caught her off guard. She chewed slower to give her more time to respond. But even mulling over the question didn't give her any new insight.

"It's mother didn't tell me the name before she perished."

"Then you should name him."

"Why would I do that?"

"Just a thought. It would be better than calling him dragon."

Paz had a point. Even Rayna's sword held a name. She supposed giving one to the dragon child was her duty while it remained in her care. Looking down at the dragon as it curled up in her lap, a name came to her.

"Ryu."

"Ryu the red dragon. It suits him," Paz said. "Rayna and Ryu, I like it."

Rayna liked it as well. Now that the dragon child had a proper name, things grew very real for her. Since leaving the Graven Peaks, she had been on the run with nary a chance to catch her breath. One situation after another presented her with distraction. Now, with a slight moment of peace, Rayna could reflect on the new burden she carried. One heavy yolk had been replaced by another just as important. But where she went from here, she did not know.

Fortune had placed this man Paz in her path. Like Rayna, he was well traveled, and he knew these areas of lands where she did not. He offered to lead them to a place of safety out by the Watersnake Winding River.

To this, Rayna accepted. She needed a proper washing. And as she looked down at little Ryu's face covered in meat juices, he needed a cleansing as well. They packed up and went on the move under the cloak of darkness. Rayna survived another day. She didn't know how many were left ahead of her, but she intended to protect Ryu until her last one.

# 30

# Dragon Keeper

Paz kept his word and led them safely to the river. Rayna felt a crispness on the air coming off the water as they approached. The first rays of the sun touched down over the river and glinted like specks of gold.

Rayna fell to her knees at the edge to drink of the coolness. She splashed the water over her face and arms, then pooled it in her hands to offer Ryu a drink. He lapped it up with his small tongue, and she dipped her hands back in for more.

Paz kneeled beside them and began filling water skins. He watched as Ryu continued to drink from Rayna's hands.

"He trusts you."

"You sound surprised."

"Dragons aren't known to interact with any but their

own kind," Paz explained. "But since Ryu believes you're his mother, it makes sense."

His reasoning took Rayna by surprise, and she reacted with a defensive tone.

"I am *not* his mother."

"Of course not," Paz replied. "But he thinks you are. So, he trusts you."

"If Ryu knew the truth of matters, he would devour me."

"He'd need to be a little bigger for that," Paz chuckled. "What is the truth?"

Rayna left Ryu to chase a grasshopper through the weeds while she told Paz her woeful story. Hearing the mother Saarath speak before left Rayna with concern. Should Ryu also understand the common tongue, she did not want him to hear the tale she was about to tell.

"I killed so many of their kind out of a need for vengeance," she explained. "But I'm starting to believe that black magic has been involved the entire time."

"Why do you think that?

"A dragon told me so. I'm inclined to believe her."

"You speak to dragons as well, then?"

Rayna shrugged. "Something like that."

"You really are incredible. I'm glad I stepped in to help you before," Paz admitted. "Though nothing I do seems to wash away the innocent blood from my hands."

"Nonsense. Blood can be cleaned away if you scrub

hard enough."

Rayna washed her hands within the river water to showcase her point. She spent extra time on the creases of her knuckles and under her nails until no trace of blood remained.

"It's the conscience that stays stained," she said.

"Now you sound like a philosopher."

"Just picked up a few things from someone I spent time with. He had wit and charm with a gallant heart besides."

"Speaking of blood, we should re-dress your wound."

"I'm fine."

Rayna stared out over the river as thoughts of Valerios consumed her. The sun had moved higher in the sky, leaving the water dark and concealing the depths below. It matched the world in which they walked through. Elements of death hid in every crevice, waiting to claim the lives of the unsuspecting. Such thoughts made her wary of Ryu wandering too far away.

"The man you speak of. What happened to him?" Paz asked, as though reading her thoughts.

"He was betrayed and slain by the man who now claims to be king of Atharia."

She felt a raw mix of grief and anger well up behind her eyes. No tears would flow. She wouldn't allow such emotion to be shown in front of anyone, let alone a man she hardly knew. Instead, Rayna hopped up to her feet and searched the tall grass for Ryu.

Paz stood and came to her side. She didn't regard him even as he spoke. Her focus remained on finding the baby dragon.

"I'm sorry for the loss," Paz told her softly. "I hope in time I could be someone you consider a trusted friend. Though I'm not anywhere near as smart as this man you speak of."

"Be smart enough to silence your tongue and help me find Ryu."

"From what I saw, he did not yet have the strength to walk yet, so he couldn't have gotten far."

Paz spoke the truth. Ryu was developing fast, but he still could not carry the full weight of his body on his small legs. His movement came from little hops propelled by his wings. Having him out of her sight for even a moment made Rayna's heart beat faster. She studied the thick of the grass and watched for signs of him. Out towards the mid-line, much further than she anticipated he could travel, she saw the blades of grass swaying.

"There," she pointed towards the spot and then called to her small companion. "Ryu, come."

Instinct told her to call out, though she wasn't expecting him to listen. However, upon hearing her voice, Ryu stopped and chirped a response.

"Amazing," Paz said. "Call to him again."

In all her research, Rayna knew dragons to be a stubborn lot who followed their own path. Answering to a human's order was unheard of. But she called to Ryu again and was surprised by the response.

"Here to me, Ryu."

They watched as the blades of grass began moving again. The little dragon came towards them at a much faster speed than Rayna expected. He breached the tall grass and presented himself on sturdy legs. His tiny wings spread out to help keep his balance. And he moved with certainty.

"I was wrong," Paz said. "He can walk."

Rayna bent to greet Ryu. He shuffled forward with a singsong in his voice as though he were happy to see her. The sight of him walking on his own, coupled with her thoughts on Valerios, pulled the tears from her eyes.

She could no longer hold back the emotion, nor did she care to. Scooping Ryu into her arms, she let the little dragon nuzzle against her bosom and felt a bond like no other she'd ever known before. If Falkon wanted Ryu, he would have to pry Rayna's cold, dead hands from him first.

# 31
# A King's Desire

The warrior woman remained elusive to capture or killing. More than once, bounty seekers tried to con the king with falsehoods. They brought in appendages and even severed heads that resembled Rayna to try and collect the reward. Falkon had them all cast into the dungeons.

When Coraise Kennethgorian, leader of the Righteous Wardens, stood before him empty-handed, Falkon considered killing him there in the throne room. But Coraise brought with him valuable information and for that, his life would be spared.

Unlike the others, Coraise actually crossed paths with the dragonslayer. When asked, he described her in perfect detail down to the jeweled dragoneye embedded in her face and the magic fire from her sword.

"I wounded her," Coraise explained.

"But you did not kill her."

"Another joined the fight. Built, bearded, and well-trained in tactical fighting."

Falkon's fingers gripped the arm of the throne so hard he could feel his nails dig into the wood. Coraise description of Rayna's companion sounded much like his beloved Valerios. Could it be that his friend still lived and chose to fight at the enemy's side?

*"Valerios is dead. Another holds her favor now."*

Xara's words were at once a comfort and a painful reminder. Valerios was indeed dead by Falkon's own sword. He watched as his friend struggled to draw breaths until he no longer breathed at all. Xara also reminded him how easily Rayna swayed men to her cause. Her lean, muscular body must provide her with such epic bedroom skills that men went mad without her.

Even now, as Coraise recalled his dealings with Rayna, his voice held a fire in it that spoke of wanting more. The thought of laying with that bitch made Falkon want to retch. He preferred the soft, sensuous touch of his Xara.

She sat at the foot of his throne, trailing her fingers up and down his thigh. As Coraise concluded his tale, Falkon dismissed him with a wave. The mercenary leader held fast as though he were going to ask a question but decided against it. A wise move, considering how close he'd come to losing his head for failing to catch the dragonslayer.

Falkon patted Xara's hand, then leaned back in his

throne with an audible sigh. Exhaustion ran over him like a fever. He worried the toils of running a kingdom would wear him down to the bone as it had his father.

If not for his precious Xara, a plague of demons may set themselves within Falkon's mind. Still, he couldn't just sit back and let Rayna wander Atharia freely after what she'd cost him.

"Perhaps I should seek this dragonslayer myself," he said.

Xara slithered up from the floor until she seated herself in his lap. Her hand caressed his chest, then his cheek. He drew her in for a kiss, to which she balked.

"What is it, my love?" he asked with concern.

"You cannot seek to warm my bed when you speak of leaving."

Falkon gathered her close against him. "I will never leave you again."

"Do not forget, your place is on the throne now. We need you as ruler to instill change where your father failed."

"Who is this *we* you speak of?" Falkon asked, confused.

The touch of another's hand upon his shoulder startled him. When he turned to chastise the servant girl for interrupting, he saw a beautiful woman with tawny skin. Her features resembled Xara's though with hair the color of midnight and eyes dark as coal. She smiled when Falkon saw her and the touch of her hands soothed his weary mind. Xara introduced the beauty as her sister, Xiomara.

"I did not know you had a sister."

"She has been waiting for this day to honor the true ruler of Atharia."

"Honor me, she shall."

Falkon pulled Xiomara towards him and tasted of her full lips. She returned his affections with an approach much more aggressive than Xara's. The two of them were opposites in every way. Thoughts of enjoying the sisters at the same time aroused Falkon. He turned to Xara and began kissing the nape of her neck while his hands continued to explore Xiomara's firm body.

Things grew heated, but he did not care who watched. He could feel the eyes of the servants and the sentries staring at him with judgment. But Falkon was king, and the throne belonged to him. If he wanted to indulge his desires right there in the throne room, so be it. Who would stop him?

He slipped out of his heavy robes and began undoing his belt when a wave of heat overtook him. It felt like steam that billowed from a blacksmith's hut had filled the room. Within seconds, the massive fireplace lit upon its own and the heavy doors to the throne room burst open.

Entering without concern for the guards in her path was a woman of unmatched splendor. She had height to her and carried it well on a lean frame.

A pale complexion contrasted the dark essence of long, black hair and piercing eyes. She wore elaborate jewelry accents on a flowing purpura gown with a heavy cloak to match. Her full lips were gem-like, giving her a look of ethereal beauty. Dressed with pomp and power, the woman carried herself in the same manner. That unnerved Falkon.

As she strode towards the young king, he waved off his guards and let her approach. This enchantress pulled all his attention away from the sisters. Her eyes alone held a power in them that Falkon coveted. He needed to know who this woman was. Should he not like what he hear, she would spend her days in the dungeon for such disrespect. There he would have his way with her again and again until her beauty faded and her bones grew brittle.

She stopped halfway to the throne and studied him. A chill ran over his body as he wondered if she were reading his thoughts. A smile crossed her thin lips, and she motioned to his manhood.

"Do you need a moment to pull yourself together before we converse?"

Falkon cursed as the swell of his pants betrayed him. He shifted his breeches and adjusted himself until his arousal faded. The embarrassment of the situation helped with that.

"No need to feel ashamed, wise king. My daughters have that effect on men," the woman said. "Unless, of course, it's me you covet, in which case I'm flattered."

"Daughters?"

Falkon looked at both Xara and Xiomara who remained seated on his throne like pixies in a dream. Their luscious bodies still called to him, but he turned away. His interest now lay in finding answers about this mysterious woman who breached his castle without so much as a warning.

"Who are you?"

"My name is Nadiuska," she replied. "I am your future queen."

# 32
# Dragon Alliance

They followed Watersnake Winding River as far south as it led them. All the while, Rayna thought about the supplies she gathered from the farm gone missing with her runaway horse. Ryu fidgeted in the papoose at her back. He'd grown hungry again and the small grubs along the river bed did not satisfy him.

"We need to find horses," she told Paz.

He took up the rear to guard their flank from any surprise attack. But more than once, Rayna caught his eyes on her backside rather than the perimeter. The next time she looked back, she found him staring at Ryu. When he noticed her solitary eye watching him, Paz quickly adjusted his gaze.

"It's better to travel by foot for now," he replied. "There will be less attention on us."

"Aye, but horses will get us to our destination much swifter and we won't be out in the open vulnerable to attack."

"You make a fair point. It would be helpful if you told me where that destination lays."

Rayna stopped to ponder and take a pull from her waterskin. She'd been on the run since the events atop the Graven Peaks. All that mattered was to keep moving as far away from Sandhal and the monsters that ruled from Saltwood Stronghold. Now, when questioned, Rayna realized she didn't have a destination in mind.

Paz helped her remove Ryu from her back and she let him stretch his wings. Setting him down, she felt the weight of him had become much heftier than before.

"He's growing fast," Paz said, as though sensing her concern.

Rayna gave Ryu a drink from her skin. He lapped up the water as it dribble down into his mouth and didn't stop until half the skin emptied. Rayna gave him a tender pat on the head and he squeaked out what almost sounded like a "thank you." A revelation came to her then that was heart-wrenching, but true.

"I can't take care of him," she said.

"What do you mean? You seem to be doing a fine job."

"As you say, he's growing swiftly. He needs care that I cannot give him. All I know about dragons is how to kill them. I don't even know what to feed him."

Paz set his hands upon her shoulders and squared her to him so she would keep his gaze. His tanned face was worn, but he held wisdom behind his eyes and in his words.

"A good hunter would've learned everything about their intended target," he said. "Even if your initial intent was to slay them, the research you did on dragons gave you the knowledge you need now to care for one. All you have to do is search your mind and it will come to you."

Rayna smiled. "A bit of truth in there."

"I'm just telling you what you already know," Paz said with his own smile. "Now come, let's seek food. I'm hungry as a wolf."

He started forward on the path again, and she caught his arm to pull him back to her. Confusion creased his brow until Rayna glanced a kiss off his cheek. Then a large smile crossed his lips, baring teeth that held a surprising point to them Rayna had not seen before.

"What was that for?" he asked.

"A thank you for your help," she replied. "I'm not the best with words, so a kiss will have to do."

"I'm a man of action myself. A kiss will do just fine."

Paz slid his burly arm around Rayna's waist and pulled her body to his. The warmth of him ran higher than she expected, but she welcomed his touch, nonetheless. His other hand cupped the back of her head and he set his lips to hers.

She stiffened at first as a familiar instinct of distrust gave her pause. But as his tongue mingled with her own, she relaxed into the kiss. Only when she heard the squeak of Ryu call out did Rayna pull away.

The tiny dragon stood at their feet, looking up with curious eyes. Paz gave a chuckle and then backed away with arms up in defense. Rayna was at once sorry he stepped away.

"I don't think he approves of me touching you," Paz said, looking down at Ryu.

"He may not, but I do."

Rayna scooped Ryu up in one arm and then extended her other hand to Paz. They interlocked fingers, and Rayna felt the roughness of his palm against hers. A fighter's hand for certain. She knew that much when he stood by her side to fight off Coraise and his men. Rayna wondered what else he could do with those hands.

"Do you believe there's one special person out there for everyone?" he asked.

"I believe the world is full of depraved mongrels and the moment you let your guard down, they'll tear out your heart and your throat."

"So, you don't believe then?"

She gave pause to reminisce before answering. "I loved someone once."

"What happened?"

"He betrayed me, so I killed him." She searched his eyes. "You're not going to betray me, are you?"

"Of course not."

They briefly kissed again, making Ryu squirm in her hands. She slipped him back inside his satchel and placed it upon her back. He poked his head out and gave an annoyed chirp. Rayna had to smooth a finger over his nose to settle him down.

"He's cranky," she told Paz.

"I think we could all use some proper sleep," he replied. "There's a town I know just a few miles west of here. They'll have lodging and supplies."

Rayna balked at the idea. "I cannot be seen in towns with the bounty on my head."

"Turk is welcoming to all," he said. "No one will bother you there. But just the same, it's best to cover up."

Without another destination in mind, it seemed like a sensible plan. They could rest and gear up while deciding the next best course of action. Rayna was good at revenge, but lying low would continue to be a challenge. The list of those she owed a debt of death to seemed to grow by the day. But they would be spared for the time being.

# 33
# Bringers of Chaos

Nadiuska watched Falkon Fourspire try to intimidate her. He failed. In his mind, he acquired the throne of Atharia on his own. He'd become rightful king of all the land, and anyone in his presence should bow before him.

The truth told a different tale. Nadiuska set the plans in motion many years before. An argument could even be made that all the events leading to Falkon gaining the crown began centuries ago.

Nadiuska was a younger woman then. A powerful witch with the world at her fingertips. Now, it took almost all her strength just to venture out to Saltwood Stronghold. She didn't intend to let Falkon interfere with her plans the way his father had.

In her many years of life, she learned it took more than strength and steel to rule. Cunning played a significant role in mastering one's opponent. That is something the dragonslayer never understood, and it is why Rayna would not stay hidden for much longer.

"My good woman, you are a luscious beauty to be sure, but if my father arranged our union before his death, I do not know of it," Falkon began. "Besides which, I am king now and I shall choose my own queen."

He trailed his fingers under Xara's chin, trying his best to infer his decision was final. To Nadiuska, he looked like a small boy playing dress up in his father's royal furs. It was unfortunate her grip on King Favian did not hold. Now she had his arrogant son to deal with. But there were no other choices and Xara already held great sway over him.

Her Daughters of Chaos had done a fine job manipulating the rulers of Atharia. Nadiuska would take over from then on. A quick flip of her wrist undid the jeweled clasp on her cloak. It fell to the ground at her feet and she stood before the king in a thin shift of a dress.

The garment clung to her curves with precision, revealing just enough of her body to entice him. Men often held the same weakness of lust. Though Falkon's interests sometimes seemed muddied.

Often, Xara reported back on how Falkon's focus lay more with his advisor Valerios. They held a strange, special bond and one that proved to interfere with

Nadiuska's plans. Thus, Valerios the Valiant needed to be removed.

With no more distractions, King Falkon would now be her puppet. She ran her hands over her half-naked body as though they were his. Her invitation did not go unanswered. Intrigued, Falkon descended from the throne and approached. When he reached her, Nadiuska set her hand upon his chest and halted him.

"My daughters are yours to enjoy, but you need a woman of stature on the throne beside you."

At that, she lifted her hand and let him touch her. His groping was a small price to pay to get what she truly longed for. It was their shared mission that would finally seal the deal between them.

"I know your plight," she whispered. "The warrior woman evades your capture."

Falkon stepped back and stared into her green eyes. As her gaze fell upon him, he grew helpless under her command.

"I want the bitch's head," he muttered.

"And I do as well," Nadiuska admitted. "Even as we speak, my Night Howlers are closing in on the dragonslayer."

"Night Howlers?"

"A group of changelings in my employ," she explained. "They are the fiercest hunters in all the land."

"Why do you seek the slayer?" Falkon asked.

Nadiuska took his hand in hers and set it between her rising breasts. The heat of her body flooded into Falkon's own, causing him to gasp. She held him there until his knees shook.

"Because ours is a bond unified in blood that shall only be broken in death."

The words Nadiuska spoke delighted King Falkon, but they were not meant for him. She allowed him to kiss her then to truly leverage his power as king. Her words were true enough, but the bond she spoke of was not with Falkon Fourspire.

She sought the dragonslayer for more than she let on. Ties that bound Nadiuska to Rayna were forged many years before. Though the slayer did not yet realize their connection, she had still weakened it. Over time, it would sever completely if they could not find Rayna.

Nadiuska intended to make her pay for that. But more than anything else, she coveted the creature that Rayna carried with her. The power of the dragon belonged to Nadiuska and she would achieve it by any means possible.

# 34
# Hunger Inside

The only route to the town of Turk was through a forest with trees so tall they blocked out the rest of the day's sun. According to Paz, The Mammoth Woods were so massive travelers had become lost inside never to return.

With their combined tracking skills, Rayna felt confident they would make their way through. But by the time they reached the opposite end, night would have blanketed the earth. Nightfall made staying out of sight easier, but it brought new challenges as well.

All manner of creature came out when the sun went down. Sharp-toothed mongrels seeking food and other deviants who would slit your throat for a single copper.

Little Ryu had succumbed to sleep and rested comfortably on Rayna's back. She feared he may be growing weaker without enough to feed on. Paz marched on ahead of them, looking for ways to remedy their growing hunger.

He kept his body low with arms taut, holding his bow out in front. An arrow was knocked and at the ready, awaiting a deer or rabbit to amble by. So far, they had no luck.

Rayna only ever hunted dragons, and she never tasted of their meat. Her meals usually came free from grateful tavern owners or the patrons who wanted to bed her. Having a bounty on her head made her unwelcome in the towns that once praised her.

Up ahead she saw Paz halt his steps and crane his neck. He was listening for something. Rayna steadied her breathing and slowed her own step to listen as well. In the distance, a wail sounded out. The howl barely hit her ear, yet Rayna still knew it as the distinct call of a wolf.

While she listened, another cried out from further in the woods. Still another answered that call, this one closer to them. A pack roamed the woods, and they searched for prey.

Rayna motioned for Paz to keep moving. When she turned back around, she found him focusing his bow in her direction. She went for her sword, but too late. His arrow launched from its knocking point and traveled swiftly on the air.

Paz shot with such precision, Rayna didn't have time to move. As it turned out, she had no need to. The arrow barely caressed her cheek as it flew past her and into the intended target.

Head on a swivel, Rayna followed the arrow and watched it land between the eyes of a stag. The large animal fell to the forest floor without a sound. Paz started towards the beast with a smile on his face.

"Dinner," he said, passing Rayna.

She caught his arm, turned him to her, and slapped his smug face.

"Don't do that again," she told him.

He seemed startled, but didn't retaliate. Instead, he simply nodded and returned his bow to his back. Then he went to collect the deer. Showcasing impressive strength, he hefted the stag up over his shoulders and walked back onto the path out of the woods.

They moved through the rest of Mammoth Woods without words. Rayna felt bad for striking him, but in the moment it felt right. He had to learn that none drew a weapon on her without receiving retaliation.

The sun waned yet still bore its harsh rays upon them. Rayna's covers did well to hide her features from bounty seekers, but also blocked the direct sunlight.

Ahead of her, Paz took the brunt of the heat across his back. She watched his muscles flex as he shifted the carcass on his shoulders. An impressive sight to watch him carry the weight of the stag right up to the entry of Turk.

Even more impressive was the town itself. They built it into the crest of the Majestic Mountains, so no attack could come from their flank. According to Paz, the town was filled with working-class folk. All manner of trade was accepted at the various stands. Bartering rather than coppers or coins kept Turk running.

"We'll find the skinner and have him shave us some deer meat," Paz said. "Then we can barter the rest of the carcass for a night's lodging."

They shuffled towards the opposite edge of town where the skinner's tent stood. Rayna made a point of covering her mouth and nose with a thin cloth so as not to draw unwanted attention. She kept her head low so none would see the patch over her eye and grow suspicious.

Nearing the skinner's tent, an aroma of smoked meats filled the air. The aroma woke the sleeping dragon, and he started to mewl. Rayna slid the pack around into her arms and rocked him like a baby until he settled.

"You better go in yourself," she said. "Ryu will go on a rampage if he gets too close to the meat in there."

Paz nodded. "I'll be quick."

He slipped inside the tent, leaving Rayna to observe the town of Turk in full display. The sun was setting, meaning the last few hours of trade were taking place. She watched groups circle the different merchants. Each person yelled out their needs and what they would give for it. Some knew how to haggle down the cost where others just accepted what they got.

Rayna smiled at the sight of it. The way things ran in Turk made more sense than groveling for gold at the foot of some ruler. In this town, everybody's needs were filled. Unlike in Sandhal, where former war heroes like Cyrus were left begging for scraps.

When things calmed down for her, Rayna imagined she could settle in a place like Turk. It held a charm to it like Theopilous, but the lot that lived in Turk seemed less inclined to slit your throat while you slept.

To her chagrin, Rayna noted a group of guards walking through town. At first, she thought they were employed by the town of Turk to keep the peace during mass barters the likes she viewed now. But as they came closer, Rayna recognized the sigil on their armor.

These were men of a royal house sent to scour the lands for Rayna and her dragon companion. The dual flying fish emblazoned on their crest made matters worse. These men were Saltwood Soldiers.

Rayna hunched herself over and tried to blend into the crowd. Shuffling through the people caused one of them to bump Ryu awake. He began a fit of chirps that drew too much attention. Rayna tried her best to calm him, but the group of townsfolk all yelling out their trades made him uneasy.

The Saltwood Soldiers noticed the commotion and

started towards her. Rayna could not afford an altercation to break out. Slipping through the people, she hurried back over to the skinner's tent. As she stuck her head inside, Paz was making his way out and they knocked foreheads. She winced and backed up to run her hand over what would likely be a bruise in the morning.

"Gods, your head is hard!"

"Yours isn't a feather pillow either," Paz replied.

He stepped out carrying satchels filled with meat. The skinner had stripped and separated the edible parts of the stag from the bones. The remnants he kept as payment to fashion into fur quilts and weaponry.

"They don't waste their scraps here," Paz told her.

"We have a problem," she replied, motioning over her shoulder at the guards.

Paz watched their approach and pulled Rayna closer to him. His eyes told her to remain silent as his words spun a tale worthy of the finest bards.

"There you are, wife." He kissed her on the cheek and then waved to the guards. "Thank you for finding my woman. She tends to wander off."

"That's your wife?" one asked.

"Indeed."

Paz spoke with pride in his proclamation, but the guards had other ideas. Rayna's efforts to look haggard apparently fooled them. They gagged and mocked Paz's choice of mates. Their mockery did not concern her, only that they continued on their way.

"We need to get out of sight," she whispered. "Did you ask the skinner where we could find lodging?"

"Yes, he's lent us his own cabin for the night."

"Why would he do that?"

"I paid him handsomely."

For a town that ran on trade, she knew that meant Paz gave up something precious to him. Looking him over, she noticed his bow and quiver were gone. She halted him and went back inside the skinner's hut.

"I cannot let you barter your bow for a single night of sleep," she said.

Paz caught her arm and pulled her back out of the tent. When she tried to jerk away, he held fast to her.

"It's done, Rayna."

"Undo it."

"We need a proper rest and a good meal. That's worth the cost of a worn out bow and some arrows."

She shook her head. "You're a fool."

"There's a warm bath waiting," he said to entice her.

Rayna recognized he would not budge on his decision. Far be it for her to continue fighting him on it, especially when a hot bath was in the mix. Besides, something told her the Saltwood Soldiers would make another pass through town and she didn't want to wind up in their path again. She motioned for Paz to lead the way.

Inside the skinner's cabin, it smelled of oils used for tanning leathers. Rayna also sensed the lingering odor of heavy spices. But it was the fermentation of yeast that truly caught her attention.

They settled their belongings on the floor and she let Ryu loose before she sought the source of the smell. As suspected, a jug of ale sat in one of the cupboards. She retrieved it with a smile, then pried off the top with her teeth.

"I don't think he meant for us to drink his ale," Paz said.

"Then he shouldn't have left it here."

Rayna let the strong, bitter taste slick her throat. She drank so long and fast that a great deal of it spilled down her chin onto her breasts.

Paz reached out and took the jug from her. "You're making a mess."

"So, I'll wash up."

She began undoing the threads of her tunic, but halted as she saw Paz watching her.

"You said there was a bath, right?" she asked.

He nodded, then turned his head and took a swig from the ale jug. Rayna huffed a small laugh, then scooped up Ryu and made her way to clean up while Paz prepared them a meal.

The bath was housed separately just off the kitchen and tucked behind a makeshift wall. Rayna held no modesty, but the way Paz cast his gaze upon her it made her feel as though he were an animal stalking its prey. Thoughts of what he may do if she allowed him to catch her were arousing.

She cleaned Ryu first, then let herself sink into the warmth of the bath. As the water touched the wound at her side, she winced. The poultice and stitching Paz applied held up even through their long journey. But the wound remained tender to the touch, which gave her concern.

"Paz, I need your aid," she called.

"In the bath?"

Rayna huffed in exasperation. "Can you assess my wound or not?"

"Of course."

He poked his head around the corner and almost fell backwards at the sight of her naked body. The bath she'd drawn had been laced with soaps to give the water a milky film. After scrubbing her dragon clean, little of the soap remained. But she stayed focused on the task and beckoned Paz forwards.

"The angle of the cut makes it hard for me to see," she told him.

Paz kneeled at the side of the bath and looked at the wound. With a shaky hand, he ran his fingers over the stitching and pressed on the surrounding skin.

"It will take time to heal fully," he told her, "But it is

coming along nicely."

She caught his hand before he withdrew it. "I'm sorry about slapping you before."

"I suppose I had that coming," he replied. "I'm sorry I kissed you before."

"No, don't apologize for that."

As though she'd given him permission, Paz leaned in and kissed her again. While their lips lingered together, Rayna pulled his hand deeper into the bath water. She moved his fingers across her stomach and down past her navel. Slowly, she guided him inside of her. Paz let her show him the way to her pleasure, then took over himself. His large, rough hands proved surprisingly gentle even when he increased his stroke.

The water spilled out over the floor as Rayna writhed from his touch. Then Paz reached deep into the tub and pulled her from it. Holding her wet, naked body in his arms, he carried her back into the main part of the cabin. Just then, Ryu ran across his path, almost causing Paz to stumble. He caught his balance but had to set Rayna onto her own feet.

She pushed Paz out of the way and directed him towards the bed that cornered the room. As he undressed, she filled a plate of meats for Ryu and left the dish for him. With the little dragon distracted, Rayna and Paz were free to come together.

Once joined, he ravaged her with a fierceness that she

likened to a beast. He grunted and bit her high on the shoulder as he took her from behind. Rayna found climax many times until her body was left shaking in the wake of it. Their dinner would go uneaten as the rest of the night was spent coupling until they both fell to exhaustion.

The next morning, Rayna felt fully rested and relaxed. She stretched her naked body over the soft furs and then reached across for Paz. When her hand found his bedside empty, she immediately sensed danger.

Jerking up to a sitting position, she scanned the cabin. Paz was nowhere in sight, and neither was Ryu. Heart pounding in her chest, Rayna jumped from bed and scoured the cabin for her dragon. She didn't want to believe it but the pieces all fit together.

In her foolish lust, she'd let her guard down, and Paz took advantage of it. He lured her to bed only to betray her in the morning by snatching Ryu.

It was bad enough that she let him touch her intimately, but the thought of his dirty hands on her dragon made Rayna flush with anger. She dressed in haste and secured her weapons. Leaving Bhrytbyrn for her would be Paz's last mistake.

# 35
# Dogs of War

Her foolish heart fought with her mind. It tried to give reason to Paz's early morning departure. Perhaps he'd slipped out to collect provisions for their continuing journey. But after seeking information from the skinner, Rayna learned the truth.

The man lay on the floor of his tent with an arrow in his chest. His skin was cold to the touch indicating he'd been dead for a long while. What's more, the stag Paz brought to him had not been skinned and stripped of meat. It remained on the carving table just the way Paz had carried it inside. He must've filled the satchels with scraps found from other carvings. Everything Paz told her was a lie.

She cursed herself for such blindness to his ways. All

the signs had been there if she had been paying better attention. If she kept her wits about her, then perhaps she would've seen through his deception.

The one thing Paz hadn't told falsehoods about was leaving his bow and arrows inside the skinner hut. Rayna didn't know why he would've abandoned his weapons but she would use them to her advantage. The only thing she could do now was search for Paz and hope that Ryu had not fallen to harm.

The fool man was dealing with the world's greatest dragon hunter. Her entire life had been spent tracking dragons. If she could find creatures as elusive as those, finding a mortal man would be easy. Also, she could track her beloved Ryu the same as any dragon before. Only this time, it would be a rescue rather than a hunt.

With Bhrytbyrn in hand and the bow at her back Rayna started after Paz. He did a good job of covering his tracks but Rayna still held a few tricks of her own. She picked up his trail heading back into The Mammoth Woods. He intended to let the thick brush hide his direction. Rayna moved slowly through the trees knowing Paz would not have taken the same route they'd used before.

Eyes sharp and ears keen for any foreign sound she made her way deeper inside. Every other step she noted snapped twigs or shuffled leaves indicating someone had passed through. In her heart she knew it was a false trail to lead her astray. So, she chose her direction with care.

Rayna never spent much time on the Source Gods. If they existed, she held no concern over their opinion of her. But the angst in her heart from losing Ryu had her reaching out to them for help. She asked that the God of Wind might bring Paz's scent across her path. A whisper to the Goddess of Earth came next in the hopes She may present a new discovery among the trees. No answer came. This infuriated Rayna.

"What good is prayer if you do not answer?" She shook her hand at the everlasting sky. "Answer me!"

As she cursed the Source Gods a strange sound traveled through the woods across an echo. Perhaps the God of Wind answered her after all. She stopped her shouting long enough to determine the sound as a high-pitched howl. The same wolf pack she heard before must've made The Mammoth Woods their home. Now that Rayna strayed off the path they were closing in on her.

She had no time for a fight with wolves. Even if she survived, they would no doubt get in enough good strikes that could hinder her movement or even leave her bleeding out. So, Rayna fell upon the one action she rarely employed when faced with danger: she ran.

Instinct pulled her south away from the howls of the wolves. It also seemed the logical route for Paz to have taken. With a baby dragon in arms he would've needed to move swiftly lest the wolves see it as a snack. But as Rayna hurried through the tall trees, she stumbled on prints not made by man but of beast. Somehow the wolves got ahead of her.

She led with the point of Bhrytbyrn through a dense patch of shrubbery only to find that she'd been right. A massive wolf crossed her path.

At first sight, she knew this was no ordinary beast. It held no trepidation in the presence of a human. Moving with long limbs supporting a massive frame of thick, gray fur, it lumbered towards her. The abnormally large head turned to look directly at Rayna with eyes that glowed liked a burned sun.

This creature was summoned from the darkest of depths, of this she was certain. No line of wolf she'd ever run across held such size and intent as the one she faced off with now. Then two more wolves joined the stand-off, one at either edge of the forest.

They were of similar stature, with tan fur and glowing eyes that fixated on Rayna. She looked the three of them over and a shudder fell across her back. An entire pack of wolves of this size with such intelligence in their features were not of this world, but one thought lost long before.

"Magic," she muttered.

Rayna wondered if it were a case of man laying with beast to create such an atrocity. Legends held that in years past, the creatures that walked the land held all the source magic while men and women coveted their power. That type of unholy union could've spawned such creatures.

Faced with magic beings in the past, Rayna would spark up Bhrytbyrn to even the odds. But she could not risk setting fire to the woods and being trapped within. Instead, she tried reasoning with the wolf pack.

"Let me pass, wolf," she said to the leader, hoping it understood the language. "My quarrel is not with you."

The wolf snapped its jaws in response, then moved closer. Matching their leader's movement, the other two started down from their posts as well. Rayna steadied herself for a fight double gripping her sword.

She could not run now. If she dared rush back from where she came, the three wolves would tear her down and maul her. No, the only thing to do was stand her ground. She stepped one foot back to secure a sturdy base and prepared herself to swing her blade on the first wolf that moved towards her.

Before the blow could land, a fourth wolf joined the fight. A dark shag of fur shot past Rayna like a whistling arrow and tackled the gray wolf in front of her. The two wolves went at each other with vicious claw swipes and gnashed teeth.

With their leader under attack, the tan wolves disregarded Rayna and came to his aide. Rayna didn't understand why the wolves fought with each other, but she would capitalize on the distraction. First, she would even the odds for the dark wolf who had come to her aid.

Rushing past the wolves entangled together, Rayna landed a swift kick into the ribs of a tanned one. It yelp and skidded across the ground. Seeing its brother attacked, the other tan wolf broke off from the fight and came for Rayna. This one received a cut across its flank as it leaped towards her.

With the odds evened up, she let the leader and the dark wolf continue to battle while she slipped away. Pushing through the trees, she rushed out into an open field and did not stop running until she could no longer hear their howls.

# 36
# Death of Dragons

As a gift for their impending wedding, and as a token of his love for her, Nadiuska asked Falkon to retrieve the blood of the dragon Saarath. Any questions he had as to why were silenced by spells. Even though Nadiuska's powers waned, being close to her daughters again made her much stronger. But it had taken almost everything she had to travel down from her sanctuary. That is why she needed the blood of the dragon. Her body ached for the power it possessed.

While King Falkon gathered his best men to send them back to the Graven Peaks, Nadiuska explored her new home. It had been a long time since she walked freely in the world of man. With the rule of the king to lean on, none dared question her actions.

Even as she strolled through the great halls within

Saltwood Stronghold, the people there did her bidding. The throne and crown were symbols of power that should not be crossed. But without Nadiuska there to enforce Falkon's rule, he would never be taken seriously. Likewise, without his title of king, the townspeople would march on the castle to root out the witches as they'd done years before.

The only hitch in her plan was that the feeble King Favian had been replaced by an eager King Falkon. His needs were almost always sexual in nature. Nadiuska let her Daughters of Chaos fulfill those needs and Falkon seemed satisfied. But soon he came for the mother witch herself.

She moved from chamber to chamber until she stood within the very place where Favian hosted the dragonslayer. Rayna's scent remained on the chairs and the sleeping chiton. The bedding, though freshly washed, still maintained the musk of sex. Rayna lay here with Falkon's adviser, Valerios. Nadiuska remembered it all in great detail.

Looking out across the bed picturing their love-making in her mind, she felt Falkon's hand at her breast. He slipped in from behind her and pulled her to him.

"My men are on their way to collect the dead dragon's remains," he whispered, his breath upon her ear. "While they're gone, it seems a fitting time to consummate our union."

Nadiuska plucked his hand away. "In due time, my king. But should we not hold ceremony first?"

"Damn tradition, I want you now!"

Falkon pulled her back to him and began kissing her neck. A disdain built in her gut. It was becoming a chore dealing with this fool king and his lustful whims. But she needed to bide her time until her full strength returned to her. So, she did his bidding, but on her terms.

"Very well," she said, pushing him back towards the bed.

He fell upon the bedding and then reached out for Nadiuska to join him. A few motions of her hands left a simple spell in play. To Falkon, it appeared as though Nadiuska slipped from her gown and came to him. In reality, she let him experience pleasure without ever touching him.

While Falkon rolled around on the bed by himself, Nadiuska continued to feel Rayna's presence. Everything Rayna saw, she saw. The girl did not feel at home in the castle. Her heart was wild and would not be satisfied without true purpose. Nadiuska had given her that purpose only to have it shunned at the most inopportune moment.

All the time Rayna spent in the Saltwood Stronghold, her intentions remained fixed on finding the dragon who burned her home. Even as she lay with Valerios, her thoughts still lingered on that time from her past. But now Nadiuska sensed something had changed in the girl. Rayna no longer sought the death of the dragons. What's more, their connection had become clouded since she refused to kill the little one.

Nadiuska cursed the misfortune of circumstances and unwittingly broke her connection with Falkon. He sat up on the bed with a mix of strained arousal and confusion on his face.

"What's happened, my love?"

She couldn't help but grin at how fast he'd fallen for her. The magic coursing through her blood was still strong enough to puppet the weak minds of those she needed to control. Except for Rayna. The once great dragonslayer grew too strong-willed and Nadiuska feared she lost any sway over the girl. Turning her attentions back to Falkon, she gave a wounded response.

"Did I not please you, my king?"

Seeing the feigned hurt on her face made Falkon eager to console her. He jumped from the bed and embraced her with affection.

"Of course you did. I've never felt such passion before!"

She locked eyes with him, ensuring her control remained strong. The flicker of indigo laced through his iris' told the tale. Falkon would do her bidding now, not the other way around. She rewarded him with a smile and a small kiss.

"I am glad to hear it," she said. "Perhaps now you are fit for ceremony."

He clasped her hands. "Immediately! I want the entire land to know I've taken a woman as magnificent as you for my bride."

"Excellent. Now go make the arrangements."

She sent him on his way to fetch the minister and procure the necessary scriptures that would solidify them as king and queen. All Nadiuska cared about was getting that crown upon her head. Once she held the throne, Falkon would no longer be of use to her. For now, she let him think he maintained control.

With Falkon tending to the duties she set him on, Nadiuska made her way back to the throne room. There she found one of Saarath's teeth. It had been mounted on the wall above the throne to showcase the weapon Falkon used to become King of Atharia.

The solitary tooth meant so much more to Nadiuska. She reached up and trailed her fingers across the coldness of the bone. Her body shuddered with the remembrance of great power running through her body.

The power of dragon's blood gave her more abilities than any other magical creature she'd sacrificed. She wanted to feel the warmth of that energy surging through her once more. So long she'd waited and now only one thing stood in her way. Such irony that the weapon she built to kill the dragons for had become her detriment.

While she looked over Saarath's massive tooth, The Daughters of Chaos joined her in the throne room. She kissed them both and gave Xara an extra embrace for fulfilling such a difficult mission.

"The way you put up with that foul Falkon will not be forgotten," Nadiuska told her.

"It was vile, mother, but I did it all for you."

Nadiuska took both her daughters' hands, and they walked to the throne up on the dais. Many long nights did they plan on this moment, and it was coming closer to fruition.

"We are so close to complete power, my daughters," Nadiuska told them. "Soon, none shall stand in our way."

Reveling in the moment, a new problem presented itself. The Night Howlers called out to her. A wave of her hand brought them to her as though they were there in the throne room, not miles away. Even in her vision, they appeared disheveled and bruised. Thick clumps of blood were matted in their fur and at least one walked with a limp.

What Nadiuska did not see was Rayna or the little dragon in their possession. Her anger at their failure lit up the room in a flash of fire that shook the stone walls. The large dragon's tooth tumbled from its perch and cracked in half as it struck the floor.

The howlers whimpered at the sight of the fire and bowed their heads down with tails tucked back. Such a pitiful disgrace from her most loyal pets. With a snap of her fingers, Nadiuska pulled back the fire, then motioned to her dogs.

"Rise."

On her command, the Howlers rose on their paws and then each shifted to their human forms. Arec stood in front, as always. His silver hair and grizzled features showed a man-beast well past his prime. But he held wisdom behind his gray eyes and he always served Nadiuska well when she needed him the most. This time, his failure did not go unnoticed.

The twins stood on either side of him, literally licking their wounds. A large gash caused Drue to fidget back and forth on his human legs. His sister Davinica held one arm across bruised ribs and bowed her head in shame. They all knew what they had done.

"I see by your lack of tribute for me that you have failed."

On her words, all three of them dropped to their knees and began to whimper again. The sight of them in human form begging like animals was degrading for everyone. Nadiuska didn't have time to scold her dogs. Their punishment would come later. For now, too many moving parts were already active and yet the most important one remained missing.

"Shadow Strike interfered," Arec told her.

"Shadow Strike?"

Nadiuska had not been surprised in many moons. What Arec told her now left her reeling. She motioned for the Night Howlers to rise and insisted Arec explain.

"How did he find you?"

"He was always the best of us when it came to tracking," Arec admitted. "At first, we believed he sought to rejoin our pack. But when we had the girl surrounded, he came to her aid instead."

Strange bedfellows. The day a Howler and a Slayer worked together for common cause was not one Nadiuska expected to see. But in her thousand years upon Atharia, she saw many unexpected unions. The one she made with Falkon Fourspire, and his father before him, was one of convenience. Perhaps Rayna and Shadow paired for the same reasons.

"And the dragon?" she asked.

"Nowhere in sight."

This last bit of news troubled her more than Shadow's further betrayal to their cause. It took Nadiuska time and energy to track the baby dragon. Finding it again without the resources she once held would be impossible.

With each passing year, her sight dimmed and tracking Rayna's whereabouts became more difficult. As the girl aged into a young woman, she became less inclined to follow Nadiuska's whisperings and the witch herself grew too weak to impart them.

Time was of the essence, and they needed to get back on task. That meant Nadiuska would have to use the remnants of her strength to seek the girl. Failure would not be tolerated, not when she was so close to getting everything she desired for so long.

"It was foolish for you to reach out to me empty-handed," she said, scolding her dogs. "Now I'm going to have to track the girl myself."

The once powerful witch would commence her own search, as she'd done many times before. Sitting on high in her sanctuary brought much interference to her waning powers. She could only hold on to bits and pieces of Rayna's whereabouts then. Now, stepping foot on Atharia, she felt the power of those that came before her dwelling in the very core of the ground. It beckoned for her to taste of it.

Slithering up the dais, she lowered herself into the king's throne. Gripping the arms of it she reveled in its magnificence. The longer she sat upon the throne, the more excited she felt at the prospect of ruling over Atharia. No true power ran through the twisted wood, only a symbolic significance. But she knew what that symbolism meant to those with nerve enough to enforce it.

Once Falkon's men returned with the blood of the dragon, she would be back at full power. Then symbol and strength would combine and the land would belong to her alone.

For now, she shut her eyes and leaned back. Drawing deep within herself, she sought what little energy remained there. She felt used up, withered and depleted, but Nadiuska knew that something extra must be stored deep down.

Even just a thimble full of dark magic would let her eyes see what Rayna saw. The arc of the land would come to her in bold colors and shapes and she could pinpoint where the dragonslayer had run off to.

Trying to dredge up the full force of her magic with very little remaining hurt like a knife twisting in her guts. Still, Nadiuska pressed on with her task. Slowly she saw pictures in her mind's eye and she knew where to seek the slayer.

"Head back out to the eastern crest of Mammoth Woods and you'll pick up her scent," she told Arec. "If Shadow Strike gets in your way again... kill him."

Arec nodded, then motioned to his companions, and they squatted down to the ground. There, a mix of magical genetics and enhanced spellbinding found the three transform back into their wolf-like forms.

Nadiuska motioned for the three to leave. Fleet of foot, they scampered out of sight. Nadiuska broke her connection with them and slumped down on the throne with exhaustion. She needed her pets to seek the slayer and the dragon she cared for. Only then could the witch rest easy.

# 37
# Black Wolf

The ache in her heart felt heavier than any cuts or bruises gained in battle. Rayna would swap a thousand lashes to the back for the pain that lay on her now. She moved on swift legs as if she could outrun the guilt of losing Ryu. It only brought her more angst as she struggled to find any sign of where he may be. The anger bubbling up from Paz's betrayal is the only thing that kept the sense of loss at bay.

Since escaping the wolf pack, and slipping from The Mammoth Woods, she wandered without aim. Paz's trail fell cold, and it made Rayna wonder whether he still lived. He may have fallen prey to the wolf pack; his lifeless body dragged back to their den for supper. What then of Ryu?

She thought about turning back, but a sudden pulsing

in her dragoneye stopped her. It hadn't ached in such a way for quite some time. Coupled with the angst she felt over Ryu, the pain grew unbearable enough for her to remove the patch.

Squinting under the mid-day sun, Rayna tried to assess her surroundings and make a new plan. A strange whispering in her mind told her to mark logistics and points-of-interest. She recognized nothing.

The erratic nature of her travels sent Rayna far past the point of familiarity. She only knew they'd traveled northwest for a long stretch of road. The town of Turk lay at the base of the Majestic Mountains, which is as close to that part of the world as Rayna wanted to trek. To the east lay Saltwood Stronghold and King Falkon's bounty on her head would've poisoned most towns in that direction. Knowing this, Paz may have circled back to leverage the bounty in his favor.

Now she knew why he helped before when Coraise Kennethgorian and his men outnumbered her. Paz wasn't being noble. He simply didn't want to face Coraise himself should Rayna fall. Tricks and cunning were what "Defiant" Demaris de Paz used to get what he wanted. It was a well-played ruse, but the games would end now.

Rayna took a minute to catch her breath and formulate a plan in her mind. Turning back meant she would have to brave The Mammoth Woods again. In her haste to get away from the wolves, she had come out the wrong side. There was no other way back onto the road towards Sandhal besides going through the woods.

As she tried to map out a plan, she felt the pulse in her eye grow stronger. She tried to focus on the tall trees of the woods and the pull became too great to ignore.

Rayna began a slow run back towards the woods when a dark figure caught her attention. Standing on a hillside a few yards away was the black wolf. The waning sun framed his body, and he stood poised and ready for attack.

With Bhrytbyrn still in her grip, Rayna lifted the large blade and pointed it towards the wolf. It was a measured salute to thank him for saving her, yet it also stood as a warning. Should the dark one choose to finish where the other pack started, he would have a fight on his hands.

He stared at Rayna a moment longer, and something in his eyes gave her pause. His eyes did not share the same magical coloring as the other wolves. Even from a distance, Rayna could see glowing eyes like two flames in the night. Then all at once the glow faded to be replaced by eyes that held a familiarity to their gaze.

Rayna lowered her sword and began a slow, measured tread towards the wolf. He saw her coming, which sparked a low howl to warn her off. She did not heed his warning and pressed on, waiting for his charge. Instead, he turned tail and ran in the opposite direction.

"Come back!" she shouted, wondering if it understood the common tongue.

Tucking Bhrytbyrn away in its sheath, Rayna started after the wolf. He already held a lead on her and moving on four legs gave him the advantage of speed. So, Rayna took another approach and pulled the bow from her back.

She slid her eye patch back on to increase her visual acuity. Taking a wide stance, she knocked an arrow against the bowstring and set her aim. The wolf was further out than any target she ever fired at before. Swords and hand-to-hand combat were Rayna's preferred method of fighting. But her time in Kartha gave her an appreciation for projectile weapons as well.

Steadying her breath, she followed the wolf's path and then released the arrow. The black wolf had become a speck in the distance, but Rayna's aim was true. She heard a yelp and watched from afar as the dark spot tumbled to the ground.

Returning the bow to her back, Rayna hurried towards her fallen prey. The arrow was meant to cripple the wolf and keep him from running away. She had no intention of killing him until she somehow gathered answers.

That mindset changed as she came into the clearing where the black wolf had fallen and found Paz there instead. He lay on the ground whimpering with the shaft of an arrow sticking out of his leg.

# 38
# Blood of the Dragon

After her Howlers left, Nadiuska re-targeted the lock on Rayna's whereabouts. With the eyepatch gone, she could see everything that Rayna saw. She looked on as the girl watched Shadow Strike out on the hillside. It pleased the witch to see Rayna pull the bow. Perhaps Shadow wouldn't be a problem for much longer. But before she could enjoy watching the kill shot, the damned leather patch returned to Rayna's eye and their connection broke.

If Nadiuska could not see, she could not track her. Thus, the problem she had been facing for so many years since the last dragon was slain. Rayna started wearing the patch often to avoid the questions from tavern dwellers and other travelers. As if the opinions of sheep mattered to such a fine warrior.

Because of her shame, she hid the eye and it let her slip off Nadiuska's map. A simple piece of leather had become a great detriment to the witch's existence. Now it shunned her again.

Frustrated, she stepped from the throne and began a fit of rage. She swiped at chalices and plates that dressed the long table for dinner. Sparks flitted from her fingertips as she ached to unleash power that she no longer held. Her daughters came to her then, trying to console her, but she dismissed them.

"It's not your fault, girls," she told them. "I just need to be alone."

"I fear that your solitude will be interrupted, mother," Xara said. "King Falkon returns."

"Returns? Don't tell me that weak little man actually went back up the Graven Peaks?"

Xara shook her head. "No, he's been hiding out at the docks awaiting the return of his guardsmen."

"We believe he intends to delight you with fabricated stories of retrieving the dragon's blood himself," Xiomara added.

Nadiuska scoffed. "Let him do his little dance, then take him from my sight and reward his supposed efforts. I should like to savor my sustenance in peace."

As expected, Falkon burst through the doors in triumph, proclaiming victory for deeds only his guardsmen had handled. Nadiuska and her girls waited for him in the throne room like chaste maidens. He sampled all three with a kiss, then turned back to offer his gifts.

"Behold, my wedding present to you, dear Nadiuska."

At the snap of his fingers, the guards hurried forth and set crudely wrapped packages at her feet. Towards the back of the main hall, she noticed four of the men carrying a body covered in a shroud. The sentimental fool had requested his men bring back the body of his counsel for proper burial.

The sight of Valerios the Valient's corpse made Nadiuska smile. Once she was back at full strength, she could puppet his remains to plague King Falkon with guilt and drive him mad. For that, she would need her dragon's blood.

"It proved impossible to bring the entire dragon back down from the peaks," Falkon explained. "But we carried as much of it as we could... for you."

A few of the men grunted as Falkon used the word *we* to suggest he had a hand in the procurement of the dragon's remains. Nadiuska noted which men spoke up. She would use their disdain for the new king later.

Stooping to inspect the packages, she smelled the sweet, intoxicating scent that could only be found in magical blood. Each one was a piece of an outstanding puzzle that none could see but her. All things considered, it really was a grand gesture for a wedding gift. But Falkon wasn't finished yet.

He pulled a long chain from the pouch at his waist,

then fitted something upon it. When he presented it to her, Nadiuska's eyes lit up. Another tooth pulled from the mouth of the mighty Saarath. This one was much smaller than the other that adorned the wall. It made Nadiuska wonder about the authenticity of the find. She said nothing as Falkon set the necklace upon her.

He stepped back to admire the sight, then demanded applause from the gentry. All present put their hands together and showered Nadiuska with appreciation. Though not genuine admiration, she did not care. Respect that was taken through fear suited her just fine.

"I don't pretend to understand why you wanted such a strange thing as a wedding gift," Falkon said. "But I hope you like it."

It was now that Nadiuska would spin a lie and solidify herself as Falkon's queen.

"The death of the dragon represents the most glorious of days," she began, "for that is when you ascended to greatness. Falkon Fourspire shall forever be recognized as the protector of Sandhal and all of Atharia for stopping the creature's descent from its perch and decimating the land."

The fool had done nothing other than cower behind the true dragonslayer. But he played a good little puppet and for that he would be spared of indignity.

Once again, the gathered crowd feigned support for their new king with cheers and applause. For a boy seeking approval from everyone who crossed his path, Falkon ate up the false affection like a sweet dessert.

Nadiuska continued to layer on the adulation. She kissed him on the cheek and both daughters did the same. Then the girls did as she bid them and brought Falkon to his chambers, leaving Nadiuska to bask in blood.

# 39
# Wolf Skins

Rayna stood over Paz with sword at the ready. He lay naked but for the arrow jutting from his upper thigh. The shot crippled him and kept him from rising. Knowing this, he held up his hands in defeat, trying to keep Rayna from lopping off his head.

"What sorcery is this?" she asked through gritted teeth.

Paz winced out a reply. "Allow me to pluck this damned arrow from my leg and I will explain all."

Rayna took hold of the arrow shaft as if she were about to withdraw it from his flesh. Instead, she drove the arrow deeper into his leg and watched with pleasure as he screamed in pain.

"Where the fuck is my dragon?" she demanded.

"He's safe."

"So you did take him!"

This admittance earned Paz more pain as Rayna now drove her boot down on his wound. He dared to take a swipe at her leg, which cost him a hard kick to the face. The force of the blow bloodied his lip and nearly knocked him unconscious. Rayna leaned down and slapped him across the cheek to bring him around. She didn't have the time or patience to wait for answers any longer.

"You swayed me with sex and then took Ryu from me in the night. Now I want him back!"

"As memory recalls, you initiated our love-making. I just found an opportunity and took it."

In his naked state, Paz was vulnerable in areas that would prove precious to him. Rayna pointed the tip of her sword upon his manhood with just enough pressure to curb his arrogance.

"I also see an opportunity," she told him. "If I cut off your human balls, does it castrate the wolf as well?"

"You wouldn't want to do that after all the pleasure I gave you."

She increased the pressure, which drew a small speck of blood from his shaft and caused him to yelp.

"I will gladly start hacking off bits of you if you don't give me some straight answers. Starting with what type of accursed beast are you?"

His face grew solemn. "I am indeed just that. Cursed, same as you."

"Except I do not sprout fur and fangs." She spat on the ground. "I cannot believe I lay with you."

"But you did, and I saved you, Rayna. Don't forget that," he argued. "I saved you twice now. Once with the mercenaries and again when my pack had you surrounded."

"Your pack?"

"The Night Howlers," Paz told her. "They were set on your trail by a powerful witch to bring the baby dragon back to her."

"And you thought to get the credit for yourself? Tell me, what is this witch promising you... a return to human form? Or do you prefer wolf?"

"My curse does not come from her. I was born with it." he explained. "But many years back, Nadiuska found my people and enslaved them to do her bidding. The story I told you before, about the woman and her daughters accused of witchcraft, that was Nadiuska."

"You said they were slain."

"A lie. My pack wasn't sent to collect a bounty on them, rather they found us. The witch captured us and used our skills for her bidding year after year. But what I told you about defecting was the truth. I did not want a life of servitude under such a woman."

"Why not just slay the witches and be done with it? Surely a wolf pack as formidable as those I just ran across could handle such a task."

Paz shook his head. "Nadiuska was too powerful in those days. Only when her power waned did I have a chance to break free and I took that chance without a second thought. The others had grown accustomed to their roles of subservience and opted to stay. So, now I've become their enemy as well."

"None of that explains why you took my dragon or where he is!" Rayna shouted. "I believe you sought me for the same reasons as your pack. You wanted Ryu for yourself to get back in the good graces of this powerful witch you wronged. So, you sought me, swayed me with lies, and when my guard was down, you took Ryu from me. Now I'm done asking. Tell me where he is or I'll start cutting."

Paz nodded. "Alright, but please pull the arrow from my leg. I'm losing much blood."

He reached towards the arrow, and at the last second darted his hand into the dirt. With a flip of his wrist, he tossed a mound of it into Rayna's face. Specks of dirt, grass, and small rocks struck her and effectively blinded her one good eye. It was enough of a distraction to allow Paz to escape from under her sword.

Snapping the shaft of the arrow in half, he started running as best he could. Struggling to regain her vision, Rayna slipped off her eyepatch and watched through blurred eyes as the man shifted into wolf once more. It both frightened and enthralled her to see.

His flesh was replaced with dark fur; his limbs formed into paws. Then he hit the ground running at a furious pace. Even with a limp in his rear leg, Paz moved fast in wolf form. Rayna hurried after him, intent on not letting her chance to find Ryu slip away again.

# 40

# Power of the Dragon

While The Daughters of Chaos kept Falkon distracted, Nadiuska began the ritual which would return her to full power. She instructed the guards to move the bits of dragon to a secluded location out on the grounds. They did the bidding of their future queen without question and then left her as she requested.

The spot she chose sat among the gardens, giving her ample space to perform her ceremony but still shielded her from prying eyes. It took a delicate hand free of distraction to pull the power from the dragon's blood.

Nadiuska absolutely relished the ritual of her seance. She sat upon the grass with each piece of the dragon Saarath encircling her. One-by-one she picked up a section and inhaled deeply. Saarath had been one of the last ancient dragons to roam the land. She'd done a good job of hiding herself from both Nadiuska and her dragonslayer. Having the child is when she slipped up and exposed herself. To secure the baby's future, Saarath doomed them both.

The power that lay within her remains lit up all of Nadiuska's senses, both fundamental and magical. Saarath's blood would sustain her for some time to come.

Day fell quickly into night, and the gardens were lit by torches. Nadiuska placed a lone candle upon a smooth, flat stone and began the ritual. Reaching deep within the folds of her cloak, she retrieved an arcane staff marked with amethyst runes. Imbued with an ancient, crystallized energy, the powerful staff served as a key only Nadiuska could wield.

Using a slow, cross-hatch motion, she began her communion with the staff. Somewhere out of reach from the living and beyond the veil of death existed a darkness. Many weak minds before Nadiuska's time, and some after, tried to pierce the veil. Those that succeeded were driven mad by the truth they found there.

Only Nadiuska alone unlocked the shadowy secrets. The depths of this darkness, unfathomable to the human mind, had not been called forth in many moons...until now.

Clutching her ancient and powerful staff to her bosom, Nadiuska forged a shadowy, ceremonial dais before her.

Atop it stood a crystal chalice and within sat the blood of the dragon pulled from Saarath's remains. The sorceress rose from the shadows that rolled in all around her and dared to call forth from the void. Peering into the gloom of the profound darkness, she drank from the chalice.

Immense eldritch power rushed over her entire being. Arcane energy from the dragon's blood imbued itself to Nadiuska until she seized upon the ground.

Shivers racked her body and sweat pulled from her brow as the blood took effect. The shivers brought horrors both terrifying and awe-inspiring to the deep recesses of her mind. As the ache of transformation faded from her body, she could see clearly once more. Her purpose was known... her power unfathomable.

# 41
# Quest of the Dragon

When Rayna caught up with Paz, she saw him scurrying from an underbrush holding a satchel between his teeth. From the size of the bundle he carried, she knew instinctively it was Ryu. The dirty dog stuffed the little dragon into a sack so he would be easier to carry in wolf form. He would pay for such disrespect.

Teeth gritted in anger and legs propelled by vengeance, Rayna increased her speed to gain ground on Paz. He saw her coming and tried to run faster, but the arrow to the leg hampered his gait. Soon, Rayna closed the distance to where she could reach out and grab the bastard's tail. Instead, she made a move based on ruthless aggression and dove on top of him.

Latching herself to his waist, she felt the thick sinew of muscle flex up beneath his dark fur. As a man, he held great strength already, but in wolf form it was even more impressive. Rayna had to dig her heels into the dirt to stop Paz from dragging her forwards. Still, he struggled against her grip and refused to go down.

Remembering the cheap tactics of dirt-throwing he used before, Rayna opted for her own. She reached out and swept the healthy hindquarter, leaving Paz with only the wounded leg to balance on at the rear. He stumbled, then fell nose first into the ground. Both Rayna and baby Ryu tumbled across the ground at the same time.

Scrambling to her feet, Rayna went for the satchel with her dragon inside. She got a hand on the thick canvas sack only to have her wrist pulled back. Paz had returned to human form once more, and he intended to fight her for Ryu.

Rather than try to pull away, Rayna stepped into his grip and turned Paz's arm behind his back. Her time training with the Foresaken Force gave her many skills to use in close quarter combat. The more Paz struggled to get free of her grip, the more Rayna increased the pressure on the joints of his wrist. Then, she struck at his wounded leg, causing him to fall to his knees.

"Give up before I break your arm!"

Her warning was met with a back elbow to her face. The impact caught her high on the cheekbone and forced her to release him. She staggered back while Paz kept coming towards her in attack.

To Rayna's chagrin, she found that Bhrytbyrn had been

dislodging from her belt during the struggle. It lay in the dirt paces away, but Paz got to it first. He could not bring flame to the blade, but that didn't mean he couldn't still wield it. With only the dragon dagger left to defend herself with Rayna had to be cunning in her defense.

She took the dagger from the small of her back and held it out in front of her face. Paz double-gripped Bhrytbyrn and attacked Rayna with her own sword. She dodged his clumsy swings easier than expected. Either he intentionally did not strike to kill or else he wasn't used to the weight of the blade. Given his weapon of choice was a massive double-axe, she knew he could handle Bhrytbyrn just as well as she could.

"If you don't start getting serious with your attacks, I will kill you," she warned.

"I will not hurt you, Rayna," Paz told her. "But I can't let you take that dragon."

"The only way you're going to stop me is to kill me."

Rayna lunged for him only to have Paz sidestep her thrust. Instead of cutting her down with the sword, he ducked low and clamped his teeth onto her exposed thigh. It felt like a thousand small knives ripping into her delicate flesh.

Paz had used his wolf's teeth to latch onto her leg, and she could not shake him free. The rest of him remained in human form, making it almost impossible for Rayna to fight him off. The more she struggled, the worse the pain grew.

Using the handle of her dagger, she struck a blow to the top of his head, which finally caused him to release her. Rayna dared to look at her wound, which bled down across her boots in a torrent. Now they both walked in a limp only Paz seemed to be getting used to his.

Once Rayna knocked him loose from her leg, he turned towards the satchel instead. Baby Ryu had found a way to free himself, and he was on the move. Seeing the tiny dragon again reinforced Rayna's need to protect him. Blood still pouring from her leg, she forced herself to chase after Paz.

Ryu seemed to be headed towards the edge of a cliff, which made Rayna panic. He still lacked the strength to fly on his tiny wings. If he didn't realize the cliff broke off into a steep fall, he would be lost.

She called to him in hopes the sound of her voice would make him stop. But something else held Ryu's attention, and he continued to head towards the cliff without fear. Seconds before he slipped off the side, Paz caught him by the tail and pulled him back. Rayna was relieved he didn't fall, but now the wolf had him.

"Let him go, you damn dirty dog!" she yelled, still too far away to get her hands on him.

Paz made a gesture as though he were going to throw

Ryu over the cliff. Then he gave a wry smile as he teased her.

"Be careful with your wording, dragonslayer."

He pulled Ryu back away from the cliff and as he did, the ground shook beneath them. A great bellowing came from below as something over the side stirred awake. Paz dared to peer over and see what caused the disturbance. He didn't have to wait long for his answer.

Bursting up from the valley below came a massive creature. The wings showed first, rustling the trees and disturbing the ground with each flap. Then Rayna saw its head rise over the crest and it terrified her.

Row upon row of ash colored scales framed its face while coal dark eyes looked over the scene. Higher it rose until the full length of the dark dragon could be seen. Black as midnight, it stared down at the speck of the man which held one of its own in his grasp. An angry roar came from its belly and up into its throat.

"Paz, drop the dragon!" Rayna warned.

He stared back at her with a look of terror on his face.

"Drop Ryu!" she called again.

Paz turned back towards the giant black dragon and gently set Ryu upon the ground as though he were an offering to the Source Gods. Seeing one of his own kind made Ryu chirp with both delight and confusion.

The dark dragon looked first to Ryu, then back towards Paz. Rayna knew what horror was about to take place and she did not want to see it happen. Paz had wronged her, but to be burned alive was an extreme punishment. The dark dragon thought otherwise.

It reared back its head and Rayna watched the spark of fire light up within the lining of its throat. Paz must've seen it too, because he started to run. Transforming himself back into wolf form, he did his best to escape such a gruesome fate.

When the flame shot from the dragon's mouth, Rayna winced from the heat of it. The blast carried out over a mile, tearing through anything that stood in its way, including Paz. She heard a yelp from the wolf, then the screams of the man, until he finally fell silent.

One burst of flame is all that was needed to take down Paz. Now the dragon turned its head towards Rayna. Still hanging in the air on its big, leathery wings, it growled at her to elicit the same fear that Paz felt.

Instead of running away, Rayna ran forwards. Her damaged leg ached with every step as the puncture wounds pulled open even larger. She did not let it deter her. Nor did she stop running when the dragon turned its massive head to follow her route. Only when she scooped up little Ryu in her arms did Rayna stop.

She turned to face the dark dragon then holding Ryu tight to her and knowing the dragon wouldn't char its own kin. The dragon let out an angry cry which frightened Ryu. He huddled against Rayna for protection, and she intended to give it to him.

Seeing this, the dragon set itself down upon the field just inches from Rayna. She'd been hunting the dark dragon for so long she began to believe he was a myth. But here he stood, as large as a mountain peak right before her.

His presence washed away all the guilt she'd been wrestling with since facing Saarath. Now Rayna's vengeance returned to her tenfold. Her dragoneye encouraged her to advance an attack but having Ryu in her arms made Rayna pause.

The great dragon chuffed, bringing small wisps of smoke out through his nostrils. Head on a swivel, Rayna found no way out of her current predicament. The only end to this stand-off would be when one of them fell in death. Then the dragon decided otherwise as he opened his mouth and spoke.

"Hand me the tiny dragon and I'll spare your pitiful life."

His voice boomed across the skies like a thunderclap. Rayna gripped Ryu tightly in one hand with Bhrytbyrn in the other. She squared her base and raised the tip of the sword towards the enormous dragon.

"No."

Laughter from the dragon shook the valley. Rayna watched as his large eyes coveted the babe at her breast. She didn't know his intentions for Ryu, but no one, not

even another dragon, was going to take him from her
again.

"You dare defy me?" he asked. "I will eat you alive and
use that tiny sword to pick my teeth."

"Defy you? I've been waiting my entire life to find and
slay you."

The dragon crooked its head. "I do not know you,
human girl."

"But I know you, dark one," she replied. "Now is the
time you pay for destroying my family."

Even as she spoke with such valor, she felt the weight
of great fear facing down her long sought enemy. But
something in her words brought the dragon pause.
Rayna could see his eyes suddenly flash in recognition of
her. So much the better to have him know why she
intended on killing him.

"You're the dragonslayer," he began, "I am called
Nazalon and I am not the target of your vengeance."

"A massive dark dragon put a curse on my family,
saddling me with this stigma," Rayna said, pointing
towards her eye. "That same dragon burned my home
with both parents inside. Now, here I've finally found
him."

"You seek the seance dragon, otherworldly and
ominous, with a coloring of palatinate so dark it's often
mistaken for black scales," Nazalon explained.

As Nazalon told the tale, Rayna felt her eye pulse

stronger. It urged her to slay the dragon, but her thoughts betrayed her. The memories that she held from her youth waged war with the words the dragon spoke.

"You're the second dragon to tell me such tales. I see now she meant to sway from my true crusade. Why would I believe your lies?"

Nazalon motioned towards Ryu with his snout. "Clearly a part of you already does."

"That won't protect you."

"Very well, I'll give you another reason your account of things doesn't add up. Dragons do not have the power to levy curses but witches do. Witches have sought the great magic that flows through our blood for thousands of years, not just on this land, but across many seas. They've been our greatest enemy… until you came along. An instrument of their making sent to slaughter us all. The seance dragon is not a dragon at all. Your dark dragon's true form is that of the witch Nadiuska. A sorceress who changes her shape at will. The very same witch who cursed your family and burned your home to the ground. The vengeance you seek has been built on a lie."

At the mention of the witch's name everything fell into place. Rayna's entire life's purpose had been built on a falsehood. The same wolf who enslaved Paz and his wolf pack had done the same to Rayna only she wasn't wise to it.

In her heart, she knew that killing dragons no longer proved satisfying. Something shifted in her atop the Graven Peaks when she cast her eyes on little Ryu. Acting as his protector over the past few days awakened a new purpose in her now. Nazalon did not agree with it.

"What makes you think you can care for this baby dragon when you're so consumed with revenge?"

To answer his question, Rayna sheathed her sword, took a deep breath, and then stepped forwards. Nazalon spread his massive wings out as though he expected an attack. Ryu cooed at the sight of it, and Rayna also grew impressed.

Never in her time as a dragon hunter had she fought such a specimen. Had she run into Nazalon when the anger consumed her and vengeance is all she sought, it may have been her final battle. As she stood in front of him, now she wondered if she may still meet her end. All she could do to deter that from happening was speak her truth.

"Revenge no longer controls my actions," she said. "My only concern is for the safety of Ryu. I made a vow to his mother and I intend to keep it."

She hefted Ryu in the air, then set him at her feet. It left her standing exposed without the shield of the tiny dragon to keep Nazalon at bay. If he opted to set forth his dragon flame, she would be burned alive the same as Paz. But Ryu had ideas of his own.

Rather than go towards Nazalon and return to the care of his own kind, Ryu turned around and latched himself to Rayna's leg. Seeing the way his small claws clung to the leather bindings of her boot brought tears to her eyes. It affected Nazalon as well.

"The youngling favors you," he said, his voice soft now yet still booming across the sky as he spoke. "And I have no doubt of your conviction to protect him, but you are not equipped to do so. You must take him to the Isle of Dragons. There, he will be safe from the evils that dwell on this land."

*Isle of Dragons.* The reveal struck Rayna like a boulder to the head. How could such a place have gone unknown to her in all her years of dragon hunting?

"If such a place exists, why are you not there now? Safe from the poachers of Atharia?"

"It exists, kept secret and hidden from those who would do us harm...like you. But it should be known that I am not welcome on the Isle of Dragons," he told her, his voice a solemn whisper on the air. "In my younger days, I carried a temper and my reckless behavior brought shame upon me. I was cast out for my deeds and told never to return or else face the wrath of the council."

Rayna blinked her one good eye in surprise. "There's an entire council? How many dragons roam on this hidden isle?"

"At one time, more than you could ever hunt in a thousand years. Now only a few remain." His tone grew serious then as he pointed one gnarled, clawed finger towards Ryu. "If Saarath trusted you with her child, then I shall not stand in the way of that. But you must vow that you will guard him with your life and keep your oath to her."

"I swear it."

"Good. He will be safe from harm on the Isle of Dragons and learn what it means to be a true dragon, not the hidden, sorry wretches we've become here."

"Much time has gone by. Perhaps you could return home as well."

"No. My past deeds are not easily forgotten. You should understand that more than any other human."

Rayna nodded. "Then I will bring Ryu to the island at once."

"See that you do, dragon warrior," Nazalon warned. "For if any harm should fall upon that small dragon, I shall track you down and burn you alive."

"I do not trust having a dragon at my back," Rayna explained. "If you're so concerned I will fail, then why not offer us your protection?"

Her question caused Nazalon to lift and take to the air. His wings stirred a strong wind that whipped her hair across her face. Ryu still clung to her leg so as not to fall over. She scooped him up and awaited Nazalon's response. His words brought her both dread mixed with anger.

"The chaos witch has returned to Atharia. I can sense her. I'll be an easy target for her to track. My presence would only put you both in harm's way. But I will be watching, dragon warrior."

In a single swoop, Nazalon turned and began to fly out of sight. Rayna rushed to the ledge of the cliff and called after him repeatedly to wait.

"How do I find this witch?" she yelled.

Nazalon did not look back but imparted strange words as he left.

"You should sense her as well, warrior. Be careful, she is closer than you think."

Rayna watched the mighty black dragon fly away until he became nothing more than a speck in the sky. Ryu's little wings flapped while she held him as though he wanted to fly too. Once he learned how to use his wings, he would become even more of a handful to keep track of.

"I hope that is not the dragon who sired you," Rayna told him. "He's quite cowardly for a dragon of such size."

Standing so close to the edge of the cliff made Rayna's head spin and her eye ache. She stepped back, running the palm of her hand across the eye to soothe it and then covering it once more. Her fingers lingered there as the conversation with Nazalon began to make sense. No dragon caused her stigma, 'twas a witch who marked her. The chaos witch, Nadiuska, would become Rayna's next target.

# 42
# Dragon Warrior

With Nazalon's threat still ringing in her ears, Rayna wasted no time continuing her journey. Having Ryu back with her brought a great sense of relief. His presence alone gave her a renewed sense of purpose and compelled her to press on, though weary and wounded.

There were still many miles to cross until she reached the Isle of Dragons. Before even beginning her travel, Rayna needed to find the elusive island first. Since Nazalon did not feel compelled to leave her directions, she would have to uncover its location herself.

"Don't worry, little Ryu," she said, hiking the dragon upon her back. "I'm the best tracker in the world. I'll find the Isle of Dragons and get you back home."

Whether Ryu believed her, or even understood her words, couldn't be known. But he gave a reassuring chirp and then clung to her shoulder as she hurried towards a location she swore never to return to.

Beyond the Graven Peaks was Mako, unlisted on any map and unknown by most travelers. Those who knew of Mako feared visiting there for few ever returned.

Those who did claimed to have seen all manner of creatures mingling with the people who lived there. But no story Rayna heard about Mako was ever the same. Much like the stories they spun about her own legacy, it was hard to believe that the tales of Mako were anything more than stories spun by bards to earn a coin.

The one part Rayna did believe was the fact that most who ventured that far into the Shadowed Highlands and made it back with their skins intact ever returned. And who would want to try? Mako had nothing to offer but madness and death. Only one stubborn as Rayna would make the journey back. The only way she knew to seek the strange dragon island would be through the use of magic. And Mako was the only place on Atharia that Rayna knew dealt in magic.

Even the thought of it made Rayna's body shiver with a deep sense of dread. Returning to the Shadowed Highlands would be more dangerous than the first time she traveled there. With King Falkon's bounty still levied on her, it meant every able-bodied hunter sought her head. Even the farmers and town dwellers wanted her dead based on the lies Falkon spun. But Rayna saw little choice in the matter. If she wanted to get Ryu to the Isle of Dragons, the magic dealers were the only answer.

Before setting off on such an arduous trek, it was imperative to plan first. The hunger pangs in her belly battled with the throbbing of her dragoneye. Their combined pain coupled with the fresh bite in her thigh made Rayna light-headed. She would need sustenance and rest before carrying on.

Ryu also needed to eat. The little one probably hadn't eaten a thing since being snatched away in the night. If the dark dragon Nazalon truly cared for his well-being, he would've at least left something for Ryu to snack on.

"We're on our own," Rayna told him. "Just the way I like it."

She walked only a mile or so with Ryu on her back before realizing they weren't alone at all. Rayna made a point of not taking the same route back from which she came. Instead, she ventured further south towards Valeuki. Once there, she could find food and shelter for the night before continuing on in the morning.

She intended to scale the great wall known as The Dragon's Backbone, effectively keeping her away from ground forces seeking her head. Once safely across, she would sweep back around towards the Shadowed Highlands.

All the effort Rayna put into keeping those on her trail guessing did little to dispel hunters with a keen sense of smell. First came a rustling from a nearby bush, followed by a low howl. Rayna pulled Bhrytbyrn free of its scabbard and squared off with the hidden howler in the bushes.

Its gleaming eyes locked onto her own and it seemed to taunt her by lapping its long tongue slowly over spiked teeth. Rayna's body tensed at the realization that she recognized this wolf. Tan in color, it had a twin with it before, which now came at Rayna from the other side while she remained distracted.

The weight of the wolf knocked her off balance, but she managed to regain her footing. Then the third and largest of the trio joined the fray. Its gray fur was a blur on the air as it tackled Rayna to the ground. Ryu, sensing the danger, leaped from her shoulders at the last possible second. While Rayna struggled with the large gray wolf, Ryu darted back and forth across the open field, trying to avoid capture from the others.

Down on the ground with the weight of the gray wolf on top of her, Rayna couldn't maneuver Bhrytbyrn to strike. She'd barely got her arm up in time to block the wolf attack. Now he pressed against her armored forearm and snapped his jaws, trying desperately to rip her face off.

The thing's breath was foul and spittle dripped from its mouth onto Rayna's cheek. Soon, its strength would overpower her and she would be lost. But amid their struggle, she saw its eyes flash to human more than once. That's when she knew these howlers were like Paz; part-human and part-wolf.

Knowing they held human foibles gave her a strange sense of relief and allowed her to muster the strength to survive. With great effort, she got her leg beneath the body of the gray wolf. Thrusting up her knee, she struck where a human male's most sensitive of organs would be.

The wolf yelped from the blow, but Rayna wasn't finished yet. She continued driving her leg upwards to create distance between the two of them. Her intent was to kick the beast overhead, but she found the bite in her thigh brought weakness to her otherwise powerful legs. Instead, she opted to sweep the wolf to the side, where she came on top of it.

A wolf on its back proved as helpless as a babe. Knowing this, the creature transformed itself into its human state. He was older than Rayna expected, with long gray hair and a beard to match. She gave a wry smile as he shifted fully, naked and exposed, while she pinned him down.

"There you are."

Before the man could gain his bearings and throw her from him, Rayna struck. Using a move from the wolf's own attack, she bent down and bit out his throat. Blood gushed up into her mouth as she tore into the flesh with as much force as she could. The man tossed her away, but as she went, she took part of his throat with her.

He struggled to stand, then collapsed to the ground where he shifted back-and-forth from human to wolf several times. Soon, he fell spread out across the dense grass, a great torrent of blood pooling beneath his head.

Seeing their leader in trouble, the other two abandoned their chase of Ryu and charged towards Rayna instead. This time Paz would not dive from the woods to intervene on her behalf. Outnumbered and unarmed, she needed to outwit the wolves or risk becoming their dinner. Then she saw her opening.

One wolf favored a limp which slowed him down. Rayna caught of a piece of him in the battle before. The memory of it made her smile, but only briefly. Moving at full speed across the open field, the female would be on her in minutes.

Rayna made a dash for her sword and slipped on the soft, wet ground. The misstep cost her, as the she-wolf wasted no time in attacking. She did not have the weight of the large, gray leader, but her ferocity made up for it.

All four paws scratched at Rayna's flesh, keeping her on constant defense. Then the wolf came in for her throat. Rayna shifted her arm up and blocked the bite with the scaled vambrace on her forearm.

The impact of the armor on the she-wolf's teeth made her draw back. It gave Rayna enough of an opening to go on the offensive. She pulled the serrated hunting knife from her belt and drove it into the howler's belly. In an instant, the fur peeled back, and the wolf shifted to a young woman. Her eyes were wide with panic and blood dripped from her mouth.

Seeing his companion stabbed in the gut, the male increased his speed towards Rayna. But in his haste, he'd forgotten about the dragon. Small of stature or not, Ryu had grown protective of his caretaker and he would not sit idly by while she was under threat.

Using his tiny wings to propel him, Ryu dove forwards and caught the running wolf on his back leg. The dense body of the little dragon proved enough of an impact to send the wolf into a tumble. Rayna left the dying woman and raced to the aide of Ryu. Along the way, she collected Bhrytbyrn from the ground and lit up the greatsword.

At first, when she slid back her eyepatch, the dragoneye quaked inside its socket. Rayna almost faltered as the eye refused to do its duty. Increasing her focus on the blade, the flames came just as the male wolf regained its footing.

Ryu, seeing the flaming sword, backed away to give Rayna room to work. The wolf gave a pitiful cry and for a moment Rayna thought he might run away. Instead, looking over at his dead companions gave him a rush of adrenaline. He growled and bared his teeth, then launched himself towards Rayna.

Shifting her weight to the uninjured leg, Rayna sidestepped the wolf and countered with her own attack. Bhrytbyrn caught him across the side in a downward arc. The moment the firesword touched the furry beast, it burst into flame. Rayna double-gripped the pommel and readied herself for more, but the howler was in the throes of a death fit.

Like the others, he shifted back-and-forth from human to wolf as the fire spread over his body. His howls cut through the air with a sharpness that echoed his agony. He only made it a few paces more before dropping near the body of the woman.

Rayna's dragoneye rumbled in such a way that she needed to cover it back up at once. She took a quick spin around the open field to ensure no others came from over the hill. Satisfied that she dealt with all her attackers, Rayna tamped out the fire from her sword and then collected Ryu.

"You did well," she said, stroking his nose. "Come now, we must press on."

There were too many enemies on Atharia. All of them wanted Rayna's head and to call Ryu their own. She needed to leave this land behind them and seek the Isle of Dragons.

The path of being the dragonslayer consumed her for most of her formative years. Now that journey lay in the past and the beginning of a new one stood before her.

## END OF VOLUME I

I hope you enjoyed *Rayna the Dragonslayer* as much as I enjoyed writing it. Please leave a review at your favorite online retailer.

Reviews help authors maintain momentum with our writing by letting us know which types of stories are resonating. Plus, writing is a very isolating career and I really enjoy hearing feedback from readers!

## A Time of Dragons continues....

# Special Excerpt
# Rayna the Dragon Warrior
# A Time of Dragons II
Copyright © 2023 Cynthia Vespia

As a slayer of dragons, Rayna counted only upon her skill and speed to win the day. That she was a woman in body seemed less important than that she was as skillful a swordsman as most warriors the world could bring forth.

That mindset changed as a pack of heavily armed mercenaries chased her down. As the number one threat to the King of Atharia, a heavy bounty lay on her head. That fee doubled for any man in the land who could abscond with the precious cargo Rayna traveled with.

The words on the bounty scroll were ambiguous. If any knew that Rayna carried a small dragon with her there would no doubt be more would-be hunters on her trail. Entire towns would empty at her passing just to catch a glimpse of Ryu the red dragon.

Having the notorious group the Righteous Wardens galloping up behind her was trouble enough. Their leader, Coraise Kennethgorian, lusted for more than just the massive bounty or even the small dragon Ryu. Coraise wanted Rayna for himself. She sensed his desires the first time they tangled only then to be rescued by a man who bedded then double-crossed her. Since then, Rayna made it a point of not getting into bed with strange men by choice or by force. Coraise had other ideas.

Rayna managed to steal a swift horse from a small farm on her path to take Ryu towards freedom. It gave Rayna a chance to rest her feet from an arduous journey. But a bit of bad luck brought her right across the path of Coraise and his men.

As Rayna routed her way towards the city of Valeuki, Coraise and the others were heading away from that direction. Rayna almost brought her horse headlong into the pack of them. Too late did she recognize his square jaw and long, dark mane of hair. He was handsome enough but Rayna knew that under his striking features lay a special type of malice reserved for women.

She pulled back on the reins of her horse causing it to rear back and whinny. The commotion caught Coriase's attention and when he saw it was Rayna his face broadened with a disgusting grin. Rayna turned her horse around ready to gallop all the way back to where she'd left a trio of human-wolf hybrids dead on the battlefield if she must. Anything to get as far away from the Righteous Warden as she could.

Find out what happens in
# Rayna the Dragon Warrior

# Appendix

Names:

Rayna (Rain-ah)

Bhrytbyrn (bright-burn)

Nadiuska (Nad-e-ooh-ska)

Nazalon (Naz-ah_lon)

Saarath (Sar-rath)

Damaris de Paz (Dah-mare-is-dee-paz)

Xiamara (Zee-ah-mara)

Xara (Zar-ah)

Valerios (Val-air-e-ous)

Favian (Fay-vee-an)

Falkon (Falcon)

Atharia (Ah-thar-e-ya)

Pelanor Pass (Pel-ay-nor)

Ischon across the Sea (E-shawn)

Emperor Kivu Kazu (Kee-Voo Kah-zoo)

Theopilous (Thee-op-ilous)

Corinth at the Edge of the World (Core-inth)

Conchata (Con-chat-ah)

Valeuki (Val-ooh-kai)

Sythian (Sith-e-an)

Coraise Kennethgorian (Core-ace Kenneth-gore-ian)

# About the Author

"Original Cyn" Cynthia Vespia writes fantasy novels for escapism entertainment including urban fantasy vigilantes and heroic adventure fantasy. Her books have featured a secret group of superhero renegades; the dark side of vigilante justice in Las Vegas; and a duo of demon hunters fighting supernatural beings. Her latest novel is the first in an exciting new adventure series about a dragonslayer who has a change of heart.

Cyn received a "Best Series" nomination for her fantasy trilogy Demon Hunter. Her novel Karma ranked #1 on Amazon in three distinct categories including superhero, action-adventure, and contemporary fantasy. She has been published in anthologies such as Skelos Press and Dark Eclipse.

Her characters are outcasts and anti-heroes with depth

and real vulnerabilities. Each novel plot is designed to give heroes a challenge and villains a purpose. The worlds Cyn creates are a gritty mix of fantasy, magic, and the supernatural while exploring the theme of "success through struggle." She's expanded this theme into personal development books and guides.

Cyn has also written content for Microsoft, UFC, WWE, HBO, Netflix, and more. As a former fitness competitor she still enjoys keep active through training but can also be found getting lost in a good story. Cynthia is available for conventions, interviews and workshops.

Sign up for the newsletter and receive the Time of Dragons prequel Rise of the Dragonslayer for free
https://www.cynthiavespia.com/free-story

Follow on Bookbub:
https://www.bookbub.com/authors/cynthia-vespia

Follow on Facebook:
https://www.facebook.com/originalcynwrites

Follow on Instagram: @originalcynwrites

Follow on Youtube:
https://www.youtube.com/c/OriginalCynContent

# Books by Cynthia Vespia

## SILKES STRIKE FORCE
(superhero urban fantasy)

Karma

Kobra

Kaged

Khaos

## VEGAS VIGILANTES
(dark urban fantasy)

Casino Empire

Lucky Sevens

Vegas Valkyries

Sin City Assassin

## DEMON HUNTERS
(heroic adventure fantasy)

Demon Hunter Saga

Demon Huntress Legends

## OTHER BOOKS

The Crescent

Theater of Pain

Sins and Virtues

## NONFICTION

Be Your Own Superhero

343

www.ingramcontent.com/pod-product-compliance
Lightning Source LLC
Chambersburg PA
CBHW051321190726
48290CB00001B/261